Old Bach Is Come

Steve Schach

Wandering in the Words Press

Copyright © 2013 Stephen R. Schach

All rights reserved. No part of this book may be reproduced, stored in a retrieval system or transmitted in any form or by any means without the prior written consent of the publishers, except by a reviewer who may quote brief passages in a review to be printed in a newspaper, magazine, blog or journal.

Requests for permission should be sent to Wandering in the Words Press: 2131 Burns St, Nashville, Tennessee, 37216
www.wanderinginthewordspress.com

All characters in this book are fictitious, and any resemblance to real persons, living or dead, is coincidental.

PUBLISHED BY WANDERING IN THE WORDS PRESS

ISBN-10: 0989153908
ISBN-13: 978-0-9891539-0-4

First Edition

To Sharon

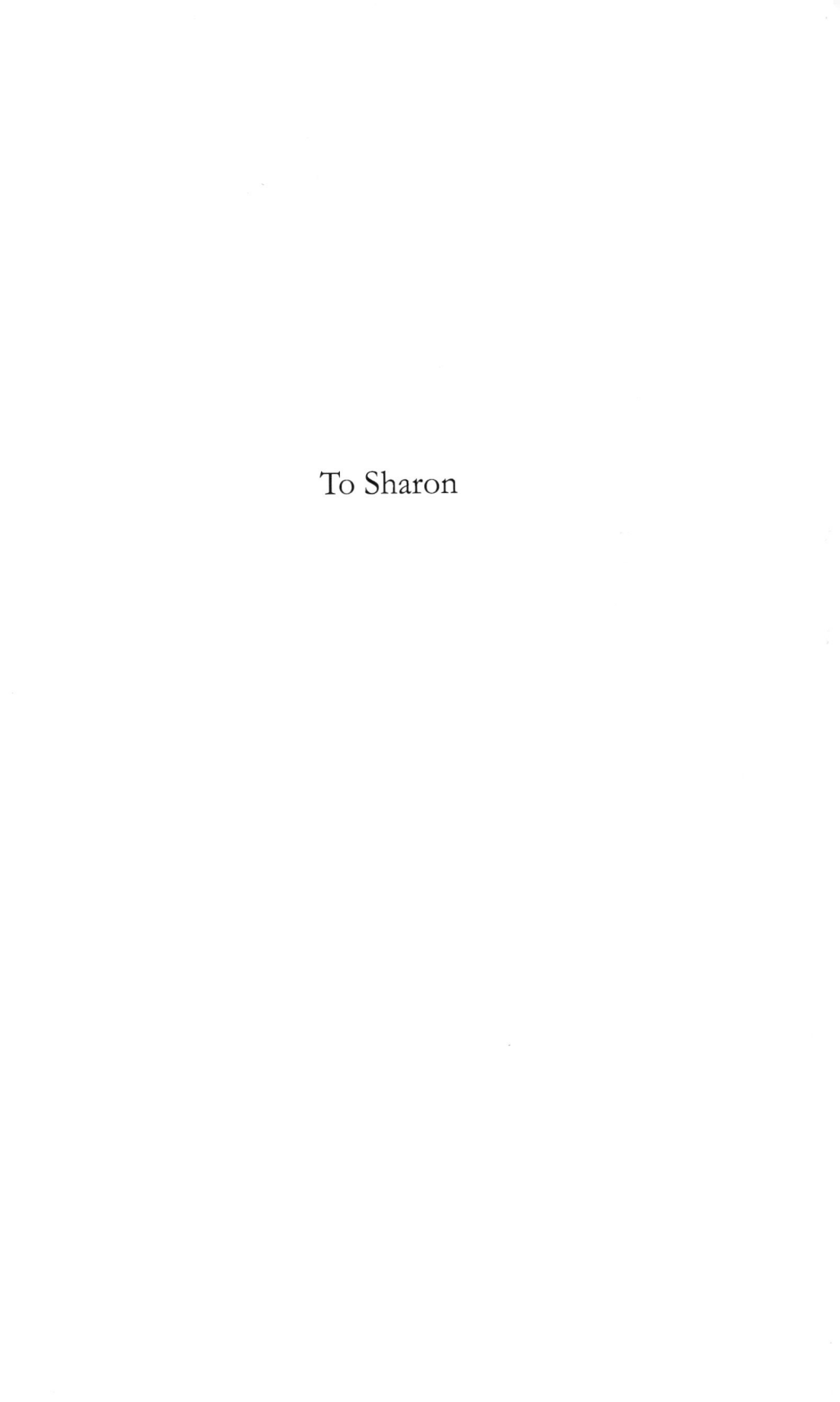

FOREWARD

Frederick the Great, King of Prussia (1712 to 1786), was a patron of the arts, especially music. As an outstanding flautist himself, he enjoyed maintaining a royal orchestra and employed many of the leading composers of his time, including Carl Philipp Emanuel Bach, the second son of Johann Sebastian Bach.

In 1747, King Frederick invited the 62-year-old Johann Sebastian Bach to visit him at his Sanssouci Palace in Potsdam. On the evening of May 7, when the King was about to participate in his regular evening concert, he was handed a list of the strangers who had arrived at his Court that day. On seeing Johann Sebastian's name, Frederick set down his flute, turned to his orchestra, and announced, "*Meine Herren, der alte Bach ist gekommen!*" ("Gentlemen, Old Bach is come!"). He cancelled the concert and sent word that Bach was to come immediately, without changing out of his traveling clothes. When Bach arrived, Frederick invited him to try out the King's large collection of keyboard instruments. Bach then asked the King to give him the subject for a fugue, which Bach improvised extemporaneously on the Silbermann fortepiano with his usual brilliance.

Published accounts of the meeting between Bach and Frederick the Great include an article in the Potsdam newspaper on May 11, 1747, and a description in the first biography of Johann Sebastian Bach, *Johann Sebastian Bach; His Life, Art, and Work*, written in 1802 by Johann Nikolaus Forkel. In addition, Frederick's *Royal Theme* and the resulting Bach three-part fugue (*Ricercar a 3*) are well known. So there is no reason to doubt that Bach visited Sanssouci at the behest of Frederick the Great, King of Prussia. The rest of this story, however, is a work of fiction.

CHAPTER ONE

The mud-caked coach limped through the gathering darkness into Sanssouci Park at sunset, arriving in Potsdam several hours late. Johann Sebastian Bach, bad tempered at the best of times, was in a white-hot fury. The other passenger, Wilhelm Friedemann Bach, his eldest son—and the oldest of 20 children by his two wives—had tried everything he could to calm his father.

"Why was our coach stopped and searched six times?" Johann Sebastian asked. "And why did we have to get out while those unmannerly officials went through every single item in our luggage?"

Wilhelm Friedemann pretended that this was the first occasion that his father had asked the question and started to explain. "In 1740, King Frederick of Prussia conquered and occupied the Austrian province of Silesia. The resulting war lasted six years. The conflict ended 18 months ago, with the signing of the Treaty of Dresden on Christmas Day, 1745." He looked up at his father to make sure he was listening. "Maria Theresa, the Empress of Austria, never forgives and never forgets," he added. "Even though there's peace now, she's still trying to have Frederick assassinated in revenge for annexing Silesia. They say that Prussia is crawling with Austrian secret agents sent by Maria Theresa, and that there are dozens of men infiltrating the country for the purpose of killing the King. King Frederick is a brave man and a truly brilliant general, but he's terrified of being murdered. To protect the King, his Minister of Police, Baron Manfred von

Hochenheimer, has set up a vast spy network. It's so large that King Frederick has been heard to boast that he is always preceded by a hundred spies, whereas French Marshal de Soubise is always followed by a hundred cooks."

Johann Sebastian cocked his head at his son. "So, if he has all these spies," he began, "why have we been stopped six times and why was our luggage searched each time—surely Frederick is in control of the situation?"

As before, Wilhelm Friedemann responded as if this was the first time that the question had been asked. "There are now so many spies that it's becoming harder and harder for them to find enough work to justify their salaries. So they repeatedly stop travelers, search them and report what little they discover to their masters."

For the moment, this reply seemed to satisfy Johann Sebastian. He sat back in the coach, which slowly made its way down the gravel drive to the entrance hall of the Sanssouci Palace. When the vehicle came to a standstill, uniformed footmen opened the door of the coach, lowered the steps, and helped Johann Sebastian and his son clamber out. Other servants unfastened their luggage from the roof of the coach and carried their trunks into the palace.

A majordomo met the Bachs at the door of the entrance and escorted them through the Marble Hall to one of the palace's five guest rooms. Their luggage arrived soon after.

The majordomo turned to Johann Sebastian. "Your Excellency, may we bring you and your son something to eat?"

Johann Sebastian was ravenous; his last meal had been a hurried, sparse breakfast at the inn near Mühlenheide, where they had spent the previous night in a most uncomfortable room. He was about to reply enthusiastically in the affirmative when a liveried footman ran into the chamber.

"Your Excellency," panted the footman, as he bowed to Bach, "His Royal Highness is most anxious to receive you immediately. He stressed that there is no need for you to change your clothes. Please follow me right away."

The footman led Johann Sebastian back through the Marble Hall into the King's music room. The entire orchestra rose when Johann Sebastian entered. Old Bach noticed his son Carl Philipp Emanuel Bach standing stiffly in front of a Silbermann fortepiano and his son Wolfgang Gottlieb Bach standing just as rigidly with an oboe. Yet, he kept his gaze firmly on the figure seated in front of him, the 35-year-old King Frederick the Great.

The King was surprisingly small for a man known as "The Great." A distinctly aquiline nose punctuated his sharp features. Laugh lines radiated from his mouth, as did crow's feet from his hooded, gray-blue eyes. Snuff stained the cuffs of his uniform and littered his unpolished high-topped boots.

Johann Sebastian had been traveling for two days in a coach over rutted roads. His journey, coupled with the previous night's lumpy mattress, did nothing for the arthritis in his back. As he approached the King, Johann Sebastian respectfully bowed as low as his spine would allow.

"Rise, Old Bach," King Frederick said. "Thank you for coming to Potsdam all the way from Leipzig. We welcome you to Sanssouci Palace. We wish you a long and fruitful stay."

CHAPTER TWO

"Is there a reason why we have to meet in the back room of the only tavern in the whole town of Brandenburg an der Havel that serves undrinkable beer?"

The speaker was a muscular young man of medium height with long, unkempt blond hair. Although born and bred in Austria, he took great pains to speak with the Prussian accent that Max Hirsch, his spymaster, had drummed into him during several months of intensive training in Vienna. His clothes, all of which had been made in Prussia, were pre-owned—to put it charitably—and his gray-brown overcoat was especially threadbare. He had made every effort to look like a Potsdam stevedore because that was his cover job.

A vicious scar held his left cheek. This was not a *renommierschmiss* or dueling scar—the practice of academic fencing was restricted to university students from the upper class. This scar had been inflicted a few months before during a knife fight in Potsdam. The scuffle had occurred on a wharf about an eight-hour walk upstream from Brandenburg.

The name inscribed in clerkish handwriting on his forged papers was Paul Müller; Hirsch was known for choosing unexceptional cover names for his secret agents. Paul's role in the plot to assassinate Frederick the Great was to gather information regarding Frederick's movements. Max was well aware that Sanssouci Palace in Potsdam was heavily guarded, both inside and out. One of Max's many different strategies was to try to determine in advance where Frederick would be traveling, in the hope that he would be less protected in transit. The wharves and warehouses of Potsdam—Paul Müller's domain—proved an excellent source of information. Some of it was accurate, but most of it was wildly fanciful.

The man that Paul had addressed—with his complaint about the tavern—looked like a middle-aged schoolmaster. His *nom de guerre* was Franz Braun. Franz, slender and of average height, wore wire-rimmed spectacles with thick lenses made of plain glass. His carefully combed, short black hair matched his toothbrush moustache. He had been a private investigator in Vienna when Hirsch had recruited him. Thanks to his investigative expertise and strong organizational skills, Franz was the leader of Max's group of 12 secret agents.

At 10 o'clock on the first Saturday night of every month, Franz met with the members of his group. They always gathered in the back room of the Taverne zum Schwarzen Adler (Black Eagle Tavern). The tavern was easy to find. The large wooden sign, proudly displaying the black eagle of Prussia, had recently been repainted, and it flapped back and forth in the light breeze.

Paul Müller always arrived first, and he always greeted Franz by grumbling to him about the undrinkable beer.

On cue Franz always replied, "We have to meet in a public place, because 12 men gathering in a private home would surely excite undue suspicion." The tavern keeper was an Austrian sympathizer, who simply ignored the monthly meetings held in his back room. Additionally, Franz always reminded Paul of the good times the two of them enjoyed when the meeting concluded. After the close, Paul and Franz would head into the main room of the tavern where they would drink beer beneath huge oak beams blackened by smoke from the fire that warmed the large space. Inevitably, the Count von und zu Schnellenbach—a Prussian *Junker* (nobleman) who had fallen on hard times, but who was still 100 percent *Junker* in his speech and haughty mannerisms—would join them. The two delighted in drunkenly imitating the Count on their way home, usually with devastating accuracy. Furthermore, Franz invariably made it clear to Paul that he had chosen the Taverne zum Schwarzen Adler because the back room offered two different escape routes. The large window on the left side of the chamber and the exit door on the right each led into a different alleyway, doubling the chances of a successful escape in the event of a police raid. The members of his group could securely bar the stout door leading from the main room of the tavern, giving them time to get away. Finally, Franz would state that he fully realized that a putative stevedore would have to travel on foot from Potsdam to Brandenburg, and that the eight-hour walk would no doubt generate a serious thirst that could be quenched only with the aid of several tankards brimming with Prussian beer and topped with foam. He concluded by apologizing for the quality of the beer, but insisted that the advantages of the venue far outweighed the shortcomings of the lager.

What Franz never mentioned was that the real reason why he had chosen to meet in the back room of the Taverne zum Schwarzen Adler was because there were *three* exits: the aforementioned door and window, plus a trapdoor that led into the cellar of the tavern where barrels of beer were stored. Franz was always ready to dive into the cellar, bolt the trap firmly shut, change into the clothes he had hidden there and then stroll up the stairs leading from the cellar into the main room of the tavern as if he owned the place. He could then saunter confidently out the front door past the waiting policemen.

Over the next 10 minutes, the remaining Austrian secret agents arrived in ones and twos. As soon as everyone was present, Franz barred the door and addressed his spies in a low voice.

"Do any of you know what 'double agent' means?" he asked.

There was silence.

"King Frederick invented the term. He has ordered his Minister of Police, Baron Manfred von Hochenheimer, to give all captured Austrian secret agents a choice: Either face death or become a double agent—that is, work for him while pretending to still be an Austrian secret agent."

"But that's impossible," interrupted a bald-headed man with a prominent reddish nose and big red ears. "No Austrian could possibly choose to become a double agent."

"When faced with impending death," said Franz, "all sorts of people choose all sorts of alternatives. I've seen irrefutable evidence that Frederick's double agent plan is working. In fact, I wouldn't be the least bit surprised if there was at least one double agent in this room right now, which is why this is our last group meeting. From now on, I'll have to communicate with each of you individually. The risk of the whole group being arrested *en masse* is just too great. In the next few days I'll contact each of you and explain how you and I will communicate on an individual basis going forth. In the meantime, you will all leave this room in the usual way. Paul, you will remain here; I need to speak to you."

The Austrian secret agents began to leave, some alone and some in pairs, the way Hirsch had trained them. Those remaining chatted softly until it was their turn to depart. Finally, only Franz and Paul were left. Franz barred the heavy wooden door again.

"There are two things I have to say to you," said Franz. "First, I want to underline the danger of double agents. From now on, you will have nothing whatsoever to do with anyone else in the group because your role has become even more important than before. And that leads to my second point: in Sanssouci Palace—"

A loud pounding interrupted them. "Police! Open up!"

Franz put his index finger to his lips. He threw open the back door and the window, so that when the police broke into the room, they would think the Austrian secret agents had fled that way. Then Franz rushed to the trap, lifted it and jumped down. He gestured for Paul to join him. Within seconds, both men were in the cellar, and Franz lowered the trap from the inside. He could hear the loud blows of the policemen trying to batter down the door, so he timed the loud snick—made by the shutting of the hefty iron bolt—to coincide with the impact of one of the rifle butts slamming into the thick woodwork outside.

Franz quietly indicated to Paul that they should share the clothing he had hidden there, just in case the double agent who had given them away to the police had described what they were wearing that evening. After changing, the two men carefully examined one another to be sure buttons were fastened and shirttails were tucked. Then they waited at the foot of the wooden staircase leading from the cellar to the main room of the tavern.

The police broke through the barred door with a triumphant shout. "They left through the door and the window!"

Paul and Franz walked confidently up the stairs into the main room. Concerned that there might be other police officers waiting outside, Franz walked with the sort of swagger that a milquetoast schoolmaster who had had one or two beers too many on a Saturday night might adopt. In addition, he pulled his hat down almost to the level of his eyebrows, thereby shielding the top half of his face. Paul walked slowly and tottered slightly from side to side, to give the impression that he, too, had overindulged. Both men forced themselves not to look around as they reached the sidewalk. Instead, they tried to keep their heads still and to look with unfocused eyes in the vague direction of the end of the street.

Once they reached the corner, they crossed the road and continued walking, trying to increase their distance from the tavern.

Both men instinctively realized that under no circumstances should they go anywhere near the small upstairs room that Franz rented from a butcher and his wife. The double agent could have followed Franz home one night in order to inform the police where Franz lived. Accordingly, while Paul and Franz continued to walk away from the Taverne zum Schwarzen Adler, they tried to devise a plan for staying out of the hands of the Prussian authorities.

They took refuge beneath the entrance of an imposing, granite-faced bank building some distance from the tavern, and tried to determine if they were being followed.

Paul's first thought was that they should make for his lodgings in Potsdam. But he realized right away that the double agent might possibly know enough about him to inform the police that Paul was a Potsdam dockworker. "Franz, how much do the others know about me?" he asked, wiping away the droplets of sweat on his face. "Do they know that I live in Potsdam?"

"Max Hirsch is a really clever man," Franz said. "He knows that the Prussian police have torture chambers staffed by experts in the infliction of pain, and that every captured Austrian secret agent will eventually talk, no matter what. But, unless you told one of them where you live or where you work, no one knows anything relevant about you. And all I know about you is that you live in Potsdam, and I know the address of the shop where I can leave messages for you. I don't know anything more, just in case I'm caught and tortured.

"We need to get out of here, and quickly," Franz continued. "If we stay, we'll have to be continually on the lookout for police patrols, as well as Frederick's vast network of spies. Let's make for Potsdam right away, before they start to look for us."

Paul peered out of the entryway and checked for pursuers. "The road goes through a dense forest, and then there's quite a bit of farmland," he informed Franz. "If we can, we'll find a barn and take shelter. We'll get up early, before the farmer discovers us, and walk the rest of the way to Potsdam."

They strode in a southeasterly direction through dark side streets—keeping a close lookout for police, soldiers and Prussian spies—until they neared the outskirts of Brandenburg. In Potsdam, where King Frederick frequently stayed, and in Berlin, the capital of Prussia, police officers or soldiers guarded every bridge and every major crossroads. Spies littered the streets. But Brandenburg, a former capital of Prussia, was now just one of many provincial towns on the Havel River. Baron Manfred von Hochenheimer, the Minister of Police, was in charge of a vast army of law-enforcement personnel, but he could not monitor every single town. Accordingly, he concentrated his attention on Berlin and Potsdam, leaving the rest of the state under the control of the relevant local authorities. The Brandenburgers joked that the streets of their sleepy town were rolled up at eight o'clock every night. The Brandenburg police department appeared to take this jest seriously. As a result, night patrols were few and far between, and Franz and Paul were able to reach the road to Potsdam without being stopped and interrogated.

Now without the shelter of the town's buildings and alleyways, the two Austrian agents had to make use of every possible place of concealment, especially hedges and larger trees. Every time they thought they heard a footstep, they stopped and dived for cover. Eventually they decided to leave the highway and walk in the long grass that lined the road. This slowed their progress, and the faint light from the waning crescent moon did nothing to keep them from stumbling through the undergrowth.

***

After midnight, having walked through the darkened bushes for about an hour, they saw a large dead tree on the side of the road. The tree had been struck by lightning and had burned, but it still stood defiantly with its bare black branches pointing to the sky. Suddenly, they heard distant horses approaching from behind them. They ducked into the forest and hid in a stand of pines. A detachment of forty cuirassiers galloped past, their breastplates and backplates gleaming even in the pale moonlight. After the cavalry was out of sight and earshot, Franz turned to Paul. "Were they looking for us?"

"Yes, I think so. They were galloping. What other reason would warrant such haste at this hour of the night? We have to stay off the main road from now on."

They continued into the forest. They had walked for no more than about 500 feet when they came upon a small wooden hut with a rock chimney jutting out of a thatched roof. They tried the door, but it was locked.

"We're in a forest that doesn't belong to anyone, so this can't be a forester's hut," Paul mused. "It doesn't seem to serve any purpose."

"Did Hirsch teach you how to pick locks?"

"Do you have a knife with a small blade?"

Franz reached into his coat pocket and then handed over a stiletto.

Paul picked the lock with practiced ease and then carefully pushed the door open with one hand. "It's a poacher's hut," he said, taking in the contents in the dim light. From the doorway, he could see a mattress with a coarse blanket laying on top, and a wooden table and chair. Bones and the skin of a small animal lay on the floor near the fireplace.

"So now we have to decide," Franz said, moving into the hut. "Do we spend the night here, sleeping in turns while the other stands guard to watch for the poacher, or do we take our chances in the forest? There may be wild boars. We can probably handle them. But there may also be soldiers and police."

"Poachers set traps; they don't carry weapons. Let's stay here."

"Are you sure about that?" Franz asked.

"If a poacher is caught armed, it means a death sentence. No poacher would be that stupid."

"In that case, you sleep, and I'll take first watch. I'll wake you after two hours. And before I forget, give me back my stiletto."

***

Just over an hour later, a sharp pain in his ribs woke Paul from a dreamless sleep. The first thing he saw was the flared muzzle of a blunderbuss firmly pressed into his chest, directly opposite his heart. Next, he saw the flintlock mounted near the beginning of the weapon's barrel. Behind the flintlock, he could see a grizzled head surrounded by filthy locks of unkempt gray hair. Two rheumy eyes—one crusted with what seemed like dried pus—glared hard at him.

"What are you doing in my hut?"

Paul was terrified that the combination of anger and fright might cause the poacher to accidentally fire his blunderbuss.

"Answer me! What are you doing here? How did you get inside? I locked the door."

A successful poacher has an excellent sense of hearing, so naturally the man spun round when he heard Franz tiptoe into the hut behind him. He swung the blunderbuss back and forth in a 180-degree arc, alternately pointing it at each of the Austrian secret agents.

"We mean you no harm," Franz said. "We're traveling from Brandenburg to Berlin. As you can see, we're unarmed. We found ourselves in the forest and needed somewhere to take shelter for the night."

The poacher clearly was not satisfied by this answer. "How did you get in?" He continued to move his weapon from side to side in an attempt to cover both the Austrian secret agents.

"Are you sure you locked it?" Paul asked, raising his hands. "We found the door open when we came here."

"You lie!" screamed the poacher. He pointed the blunderbuss directly at Paul. Franz saw the opportunity and drew the stiletto from his pocket. He flung it into the poacher's back. The grizzled man dropped his weapon, which fell to the floor and went off. The familiar—and stunningly loud—report of the shotgun masked the poacher's death rattle.

"What now?" Paul asked. "Soldiers will soon be combing the woods for us."

"I'm not so sure about that," Franz said. "The poacher seems to have used his weapon for years without being detected, so the trees probably absorb the sound, loud as it is."

"Well, let's hide in the forest and see if anyone comes. Best not to take chances."

"You've given me an idea," said Franz, as he rifled through his pockets. "Do you have anything that would identify you as Austrian? Clothing perhaps? A coin, say?"

"On the contrary, I was instructed by Hirsch to be 100 percent Prussian in my appearance. What about you?"

"The same," responded Franz. "But I think I can solve that." He took a piece of charcoal from the fireplace and used it to write on the wall.

"Long Live Empress Maria Theresa!" he scrawled.

"Are you crazy?" Paul asked. "Why would you do such a stupid thing?"

"I've got a plan. We're going to wait near here and see if anyone comes."

"Why?"

"Quick, go outside and find a tree."

They located a sturdy oak. In the dense foliage, they would be hard to detect in broad daylight, but in the weak glow of the waning crescent moon, they were essentially invisible.

In the crook of the limbs, they waited. Minutes passed, but eventually, as Paul had suspected, they heard rustling in the distance.

They watched as a squad of five infantrymen arrived. The sergeant pushed his way into the hut.

"There's a dead body in here." He paused, assessing the situation. "Austrian assassins," he concluded.

He immediately ordered the soldiers to conduct a diligent search. Finding nothing, they moved noisily into another area of the forest.

"Can we climb down now?" Paul whispered.

"Let's wait a few more minutes," Franz said, trying to find a more comfortable position in the tree. "Then we need to get as far from the hut as we can. I think we'll be able to avoid the soldiers. They're making such a racket down there. I'm sure they'll think that we've moved on. After all, killers almost always flee. So, they'll broaden the hunt. But by the time they can bring in additional searchers, we should be safely in Potsdam.

"It's getting light," he continued. "We'll return to the road and walk to Potsdam like honest citizens. If we're stopped, we'll show them our papers. We're Prussian, we're wearing Prussian clothes, and we're speaking with Prussian accents, so there's no reason to suspect us. Our reason for travel? We're looking for work in Potsdam."

"But Franz, you haven't slept at all. You can't keep going hour after hour."

"It shouldn't take us more than another six hours to reach Potsdam. I'll get some sleep when we reach your lodgings. We'll wait to eat, too. We certainly don't want to get into conversation with possible spies in an inn somewhere."

CHAPTER THREE

They reached the outskirts of the walled city around noon, where they were stopped for the third time, this time on Luisenplatz, the square just outside the wooden Brandenburg Gate. Authorities again examined their papers, and again, the soldiers simply could not conceive that someone dressed in Prussian clothing, speaking German with a Prussian accent, and holding Prussian papers could be anything but a Prussian. And no Prussian could possibly be an Austrian secret agent—that was absolutely unthinkable.

Keeping to alleyways and minor roads, they soon reached Paul's lodgings, the second bedroom of a workingman's cottage in a poor district of Potsdam. There they wolfed down all the food in his room: half a loaf of bread and a lump of cheese. They were too exhausted to go out and buy more food. Instead, they both flopped down on Paul's bed and slept until nearly midnight.

Upon awaking, they realized it was too late to buy any more food, so they sat and talked in whispers and waited until the shops opened the next morning. Toward dawn, Paul's curiosity became insatiable. "What's this plan of yours?" he asked. "And why did you write 'Long Live Empress Maria Theresa!' on the wall of the hut?"

"Deception."

"What do you mean?"

"We've been sent here to kill King Frederick, but he's heavily guarded," Franz said. "Suppose we decide that we'll shoot him on his official birthday, June 17th. There'll be a choral mass early in the morning at Sanssouci Palace, and then he'll travel by coach from there to Berlin. He'll ride down the avenue of Unter den Linden at the head of his troops. The birthday parade will end at the Berliner Stadtschloss, the Winter Palace situated in Lustgarten Park at the eastern end of Unter den Linden.

"More precisely," Franz continued, "he'll start at Viereck[1], the large square at the western end of Unter den Linden, and then he'll ride the full length of Unter den Linden to the Stadtschloss. The best place to kill him is at Viereck, where he leaves his coach and mounts his horse. He'll be more exposed at that location than anywhere else on the route. The problem, of course, is that Baron Manfred von Hochenheimer, the Prussian Minister of Police, is well aware of the possible dangers of exposure. The royal coach stops at Viereck in front of the cheering crowds; the groom opens the door and lowers the steps of the coach. Frederick exits the coach and waves to his people, then walks along the red carpet to his horse. From the time he mounts the horse until the parade starts, Frederick is at his most vulnerable."

Paul nodded, thoroughly intrigued.

"If you consider the difficulty of trying to hit a moving target," Franz continued, "it's easier to shoot Frederick at the point where he gets on his horse and waits. He'll pause before he rides at the head of the parade. He'll be more exposed at that location than anywhere else on the route. The problem, of course, is that Baron Manfred von Hochenheimer, the Prussian Minister of Police, is well aware of the possible danger of assassination at that spot. Von Hochenheimer will therefore ensure that Frederick will be most closely guarded at Viereck, particularly when he's stationary on his horse. There'll be many more troops there than elsewhere on the route, and there'll be hordes of police and a whole clutch of his spies in that area.

"But," he paused for effect, "suppose we send a letter to von Hochenheimer reading as follows:

Respected Baron von Hochenheimer,

We are the two Austrian spies who escaped from the Taverne zum Schwarzen Adler in Brandenburg an der Havel when the police raided the back room. We have been sent to Prussia to kill King

---

[1] In 1814, the name of the square was changed from Viereck to Pariser Platz (Paris Square). The square is right next to the monumental stone Brandenburg Gate in Berlin, built between 1788 and 1791.

Frederick, and we will do it on his birthday by shooting him as he rides into Lustgarten Park at the eastern end of Unter den Linden.

We remain, Sir, your most humble and obedient servants,
Paul Müller and Franz Braun
Austrian Secret Agents and Trained Assassins Extraordinaire

"When he receives that letter," Franz continued, "what do you think von Hochenheimer will do?"

"Assassins certainly don't send letters of any kind to Ministers of Police, let alone letters announcing their murderous intentions in detail," Paul said, finally realizing what Franz had in mind. "Or, more precisely, sane assassins don't do that," he continued. "So, he certainly won't believe a word of the letter. Instead of taking troops away from the Viereck end of Unter den Linden and putting them at the Lustgarten end of Unter den Linden, where we've informed him that the assassination will take place, he's going to realize that the actual assassination is going to take place at the Viereck end. So the effect of the letter will be for von Hochenheimer to increase the guard at the real site of the killing."

"Exactly!" said Franz. "Any communication we send to the authorities will no doubt be treated with the greatest of suspicion, no matter what. However," Franz went on, "just suppose that Prussian police officers find a plan to assassinate Frederick that was *accidentally* left in a hut in a forest outside Brandenburg an der Havel. Austrian secret agents have already killed a poacher in that hut and they've written 'Long Live Empress Maria Theresa!' on the wall, so that hut is clearly associated with Austrian malefactors of the worst kind. And suppose that the plan that the Prussian policemen find there makes it clear that the assassination will take place in Lustgarten Park at the eastern end of Unter den Linden. What do you think that von Hochenheimer will do then?"

"He'll believe that we intend to kill Frederick in Lustgarten Park at the eastern end, just as we said, and move troops from Viereck at the western end of Unter den Linden to the Lustgarten end to protect Frederick." Paul tucked his fist under his chin before continuing. "That will reduce the forces protecting Frederick at Viereck at the western end, which is where we actually intend to kill him. This 'deception' idea of yours is truly great, but one thing. Why would authorities find such a plan in the hut—if we didn't leave one there?"

"We have to go back," Franz sat a little deeper into his chair. "We have to find a way to get that plan into the hut without being arrested. After all, the police now surely inspect the hut on a regular basis to look for Austrian secret agents such as us. But more difficult than that, we have to find a foolproof way to assassinate King Frederick when he steps out of his carriage in Viereck."

***

After buying food for breakfast, they began in earnest to develop the fictional plan to be left in the poacher's hut near Brandenburg an der Havel for Prussian police or secret agents to find. Dressed as *Junker*, the fictional assassins would blend in with the crowd and be able to find a place near the gates of Lustgarten Park to stand and watch the parade, a viewpoint that would offer an open field of fire. Agreeing on all the minute details to include in the fictional plan took the whole day. They wanted the strategy to sound as plausible as possible. Franz wrote out the steps on a piece of paper, which they then hid inside a book before finally going to eat their evening meal at a nearby café. They always selected traditional Prussian food, in this instance *Eisbein mit Sauerkraut*. As they ate their huge pickled ham hocks, they smiled at one another. Both were clearly thinking about their clever, fictional plan, one that they dared not discuss in public for obvious reasons.

Halfway through the meal, Paul set down his cutlery and swabbed at his face with his napkin. "Eat up, Franz," he said. "We have to totally revise our work."

Both men finished their food as rapidly as they could without drawing attention to themselves. They walked back to Paul's room trying not to race.

***

Finally, behind the locked door, Paul wasted no time in pointing out to Franz what needed to be fixed. "There are two serious flaws in our fictional plan. First, the fictional plan is far too similar to the real plan."

"But we haven't even worked out the real plan yet," Franz said.

"The fictional plan involves two well-dressed people shooting at King Frederick with pistols. If von Hochenheimer falls for our fictional plan, every law enforcement officer in Berlin will be on the lookout for two well-dressed people shooting at King Frederick with pistols. And irrespective of the details of the real plan, it's going to involve two well-dressed people shooting at King Frederick with pistols."

Franz sat down on the wooden chair he had occupied earlier that morning.

"Our fictional plan is supposed to make it easier for us to assassinate King Frederick, not hamper us," Paul continued. "So the fictional plan should involve three Austrian secret agents. They should somehow acquire Prussian police uniforms. Those uniforms will enable them to get close to Frederick at the gates of Lustgarten Park. There, they will kill Frederick using hand grenades, acquired from a Prussian Army grenadier company. If they believe that fictional plan, the Prussian police will be on the lookout for three fake Prussian policemen with hand grenades, rather than two fake *Junker* with pistols."

There was a long silence. Then Franz said, "This deception game is a lot harder than I thought. Perhaps we should've drawn up the real plan first, and then designed the fictional plan to facilitate the real one. So what's your second objection?"

"Suppose that the real plan fails, or suppose that the real plan is postponed for some reason. What will von Hochenheimer think?"

"Now you've lost me again," Franz said. "Explain what you mean."

"There are three possibilities," Paul said, perching on the edge of his mattress. "First, the real plan works. In that case, we'll have succeeded in our mission, and we'll race back to Vienna as fast as we can to save our necks.

"The second possibility is that the real plan fails for some reason. Our pistols misfire, perhaps, or we're discovered at Viereck, rather than at Lustgarten Park as specified in the fictional plan. Baron von Hochenheimer is no fool, and he'll quickly realize that we've attempted to deceive him. He'll now know that no reliance whatsoever can be placed on materials found in the poacher's hut in the forest. In fact, he'll know that everything he's learned from our deception is wrong. In other words, by giving him disinformation from a source that later proves to be deceptive, we're actually giving him information."

Franz nodded. He rubbed at his left temple.

"Also," Paul continued, "he'll be on the lookout for more deception on the part of Austrian secret agents, and increasing his suspicions is something we definitely shouldn't do. Finally, the third possibility is that, for some reason or other, we decide to postpone the real attempt. In this case, von Hochenheimer won't know for certain that information from the hut is deceptive, but he'll certainly treat any other acquired Austrian information with a lot more suspicion than we'd like."

"So what do you suggest?" Franz asked, shaking his head.

"Well, instead of letting a plan fall into his hands, we should let him find a description of the plan."

"*Ach*, you've lost me once more," Franz groaned. "What are you saying?"

"Instead of giving a detailed, fictional plan to the Prussians, suppose we let them find a fictional letter—from you and me and the third secret agent—to Max, asking him to *approve* a plan. Here's the sort of thing I mean—listen to this:

Dear Max,

We have come up with a plan to kill King Frederick during his birthday parade. The three of us will acquire Prussian police uniforms. We will kill him with hand grenades as he rides into Lustgarten Park. Does this plan meet with your approval? If so, please send us another 1,000 reichsthaler via this route—we need it for bribes to get the uniforms and the hand grenades.

With our best wishes,
Secret Agent 79, Secret Agent 312, and Secret Agent 85

"But why is your fictional letter, asking Max for approval, better than my fictional plan?" asked Franz.

"Because if the real plan fails, von Hochenheimer will reread the fictional letter and conclude that Max simply didn't approve the plan outlined in the fictional letter. Instead, Max instructed his men to carry out a different plan, namely, the real plan. There'd be no reason for von Hochenheimer to be suspicious of the fictional letter or, more importantly, to suspect any other fictional material that we plant in the hut later on.

"And if the real plan isn't carried out on Frederick's birthday, for whatever reason, again von Hochenheimer will just believe that Max didn't approve the plan outlined in the fictional letter. Again, there'll be no reason for him to suspect deception of any kind, especially regarding the hut. The hut is our conduit for transferring false information to the Prussians, and it's vital that no suspicion of any kind be attached to it."

CHAPTER FOUR

They drew up the real plan. This consisted of their buying pistols and fancy clothing. Passing themselves off as *Junker*, they would stand in Viereck and shoot King Frederick once he had mounted his horse and was stationary in the saddle, waiting to start riding at the head of his birthday parade.

Next, they drew up the fictional plan. This was almost precisely the plan suggested by Paul the previous evening: Three Austrian secret agents would be standing at the gates of Lustgarten Park disguised in Prussian police uniforms and would kill Frederick with hand grenades.

Finally, they used the fictional plan as a basis for the fictional letter. Once they both were happy with the contents of the letter—asking for Max's approval—they burned the fictional plan and hid the real plan in a book. Franz sealed the fictional letter, addressed it on the outside to Max at his actual Vienna address and hid the letter in another book. After a hurried evening meal, they returned to the room to tackle the next problem.

"How do you propose to get the letter onto the table in the hut?" asked Paul. "It was hard enough for us to get safely from Brandenburg to Potsdam. Now one or both of us have to travel from here in Potsdam to the hut and then return. In addition to the dangers on the road, some of which we've already experienced, the hut itself may now be under continuous police surveillance."

Franz's face lit up. "I've just had a new idea. Why don't we pay someone to take the letter to the hut? If they arrest our messenger on his way, the fictional letter would be found, which will be fine—the letter will eventually end up on von Hochenheimer's desk, which is precisely what we want to achieve. If he gets caught inside the hut, that'll be even better. Not only will the Prussian police have the letter, but also the hut will be an even more credible location for future deceptive items. And if our man gets caught on the way back, the torturers in the police cellars will learn that there's a letter waiting on the table in the hut. So our letter ends up on von Hochenheimer's desk, with a perfect provenance, no matter what."

"But if our messenger is arrested, as he almost certainly will be, won't he identify us?" Paul asked.

"We can go to the pawnshop around the corner and buy second-hand spectacles for you to wear, as well as clothing for both of us that we'll use just once—when we deal with our messenger. We can buy water-soluble dye at an apothecary's shop to change the color of our hair for the meeting and then wash it out immediately afterwards. If we can find a realistic-looking false beard for me and a false moustache for you, that'll help, too. Then we'll go to a tavern on the other side of the city and recruit someone there who really needs money."

Paul waited a moment before speaking. "What we're doing is condemning an innocent man to the Prussian torture chambers." He looked closely at Franz. "Doesn't that bother you at all?"

"Clearly, assassinating King Frederick doesn't bother you at all, otherwise you wouldn't be here. And you haven't said a single word of any kind about my killing the poacher. So why are you concerned about our messenger? In any event, the police will soon learn that he knows nothing and will let him go."

"I suppose you're right."

Franz had worried more than once whether Paul could possibly be a double agent. Franz had no grounds of any kind for this concern; on the contrary, Paul seemed to be completely loyal. However, Franz stayed alive by remaining aware of the many dangers that surrounded him, and a primary danger for every Austrian spy in Prussia was the continual presence of von Hochenheimer's double agents. Paul's concern for their messenger's welfare spoke volumes to Franz, though. He quickly realized that no double agent would possibly speak that way. If Paul were a double agent and was worried about what the police might do to their messenger, all he had to do was to tell his Prussian police contact that the messenger was totally innocent, and that would be that.

***

The next morning Franz put on his scholastic-looking clothes and his glasses. Soon his voice, his posture, and his walk changed appropriately. He said goodbye to Paul in a precise, almost didactic way, and left their room.

He took 20 minutes to find a pawnbroker on the other side of the city. The shop was located on the Judengasse, a street that he had not visited before. He pushed open the door, and a bell rang.

"Good day, sir," said a voice from behind a tall bookcase in the middle of the shop. "How can I help you?" A short, middle-aged man with a large, fluffy, gray beard peeked around the piece of furniture. He was dressed in a black suit with a white neckerchief; his skullcap was black, too.

"I'm a schoolmaster," said Franz. "A colleague and I have been invited to a costume party and we want to go dressed as *Junker*. Can you sell me the appropriate clothes?"

"Certainly, sir," said the pawnbroker. "I assume that you'll want to be dressed as a civilian, because it would be illegal for you to dress in a military officer's uniform."

"Of course," replied Franz. "By the way, my colleague is somewhat larger than I am. Do you have such clothes for him, too."

"Yes, indeed, sir," replied the pawnbroker. He disappeared for a minute through a door in the back of his shop, then returned with two complete sets of clothing: jackets, matching knee breeches, waistcoats, shirts, neckerchiefs, stockings and shoes with buckles.

Franz tried on the smaller set in the back room of the shop. The clothes appeared to fit him quite well. The other set seemed to be large enough for the muscular Paul.

"How much are these?" Franz asked.

"Three reichsthaler and fifteen groschen, please."

Rather than bargain, Franz decided to simply pay the sum asked. He handed the pawnbroker four silver reichsthaler coins and was quickly given the correct change. The pawnbroker carefully folded the second-hand clothes and tied them in brown paper with thick string. Franz walked idly around the shop, looking at the various items. He spotted a brace of dueling pistols. "I didn't realize," he said, "that pawnbrokers sold pistols."

"Schoolmaster," replied the pawnbroker, "if one of your schoolboys misbehaves, I suggest that you beat him with a cane. Using a pistol would be most unwise."

Franz heeded the warning. He looked the pawnbroker straight in the eye, thanked him for his advice, took the large parcel and left the shop. He returned to Paul's room and told him what had happened.

Paul tried on his set of pre-worn clothes. The fit was not quite as good. The items had been made for a fat man rather than a muscular man, but the outfit was definitely wearable.

"You're going to have to visit another pawnshop, wearing your *Junker* outfit, to buy a brace of dueling pistols," Franz instructed. "Just don't go near the pawnbroker on the Judengasse."

Remembering his lessons from Max, Paul spent a few minutes adopting the air of an aristocratic *Junker*. Then he, too, headed to the north side of the city, leaving Franz alone in his lodgings. He found a pawnbroker in a narrow street near the city wall, and strode through the open doorway. "I want a brace of dueling pistols," he announced.

The pawnbroker was totally fooled by the clothes, the military gait, the accent and—above all—the air of absolute superiority. He obsequiously showed Paul two wooden boxes, each containing a pair of identical dueling pistols. Unlike the beautifully engraved, gilded pair Paul had once seen in the Belvedere Palace in Vienna, these pistols were decoration-free killing machines. Their sole purpose was to fire a lead musket ball at a stationary opponent some 30 feet away.

"Each set comes with a powder flask, powder measure, rod for cleaning and loading, spare flints, bullets, patches and a bullet mould."

"I'll take them both."

"Yes, Your Excellency." The pawnbroker lowered his eyes. "That will be eight reichsthaler and twenty groschen, please."

Like Franz, Paul also decided to pay the full price. *Junker* did not bargain.

"Shall I wrap them up, Your Excellency?"

"Of course. What do you take me for?"

The pawnbroker kept his head down while tying the parcel and handing it to Paul, who grabbed the package and marched out of the shop. He returned to his room, where he showed Franz what second-hand clothing and an arrogant mien could accomplish.

"Well done." There was a note of exhilaration in Franz's voice that gave Paul a sense of genuine achievement.

"All we need now is some hair dye and convincing false facial hair, and we're done," he said to Franz.

"Actually, I've already taken care of some of that. While you were gone, I went to an apothecary. I've never been to that shop before and, for our safety, I'll never go there again. I told the apothecary that I wanted some water-soluble dyes to use in the classroom. I have here a variety of dyes that we can mix to get the hair colors we want."

"So all we need is the facial hair then. Any ideas?"

"Yes. Let's put on our *Junker* costumes and go to the Potsdam theatre," Paul suggested. "Maybe they can lead us in the direction of where to purchase a beard and a moustache."

***

The box office in the front of the building was closed, so they walked round to the stage door at the side. Paul knocked, and the stage door keeper flung it open. He was clearly about to yell at the intruders until he realized that two *Junker* stood before him. Jumping to attention, he politely invited Paul and Franz to enter.

They walked up a spiral staircase, where a harried-looking man in overalls stood with a puzzled expression on his face. "I'm Otto Lendler, the stage manager," he said. "May I help you?"

"I'm the Earl von Schloss Müller and this is the Marquis zu Braun und Weissburg," Paul said.

The presence of two such high-ranking members of the Prussian nobility stunned Otto so much that he did not notice the pair's ill-fitting, old clothing. He bowed low. "How can I help, Your Excellencies?"

"We have been invited to a costume ball," said Franz, laughing to himself. The schoolmaster's "costume party" had just become a "ball."

"We were wondering where in Potsdam we could buy convincing false beards and moustaches."

"Your Excellencies, please help yourselves from our costume department. Allow me to show you the way."

He led them to a large room with three chests of drawers. "This drawer contains beards," he said, pulling it open, "and this one over here has our moustaches. Let me get you each a bottle of spirit gum for fastening the facial hair. And please look in the other drawers, as well, just in case there's something that catches your fancy."

The earl and the marquis helped themselves to a variety of different items. They thanked the stage manager, who bowed even lower than before. Then they marched out. "Even our own mothers won't be able to recognize us," Paul said.

CHAPTER FIVE

"I think we need to recruit an out-of-work former soldier," suggested Franz. "If we can convince him that taking the letter to the hut is in the national interest, he'll do all he can to get it there. And if we throw in decent money, payable on his return, there's no question he'll make every effort to deliver the letter and come back for his wages."

"I agree. But where do we find him?"

"In a tavern, I reckon. Let's put on our *Junker* costumes and head for the north side of the city. We'll go into a tavern. If we see a likely candidate, we'll ask him to come with us into a quiet corner or a back room or something, buy him a beer, and present our proposition to him."

"But won't everyone in the tavern be surprised at seeing two *Junker* there?"

"I don't know. Let's find out. In the worst case, we won't find anyone willing to take our letter to the hut."

The two men, now *Junker* both inwardly and outwardly, strode toward the Judengasse. As they reached the street, they saw a ruggedly handsome young man dressed in tattered clothing, standing on the corner. He wore a grenadier's miter rotated a quarter turn to the left so that the metal plate, embossed with a coat of arms and ornaments, was positioned over his left ear.

"He looks like a suitable candidate," Paul said. "He's clearly an ex-soldier. Judging from the state of his clothes, he's out of work.

And he's slightly drunk, if you look at the way his miter is perched on his head."

"You!" Franz said, pointing. "I want to talk to you."

The soldier's Prussian discipline snapped him to attention. "Yes, Your Excellency." The fact that he was no longer a soldier made no difference—he was at the command of this *Junker* officer.

"What's your name?" barked Franz.

"Hoffmann, Your Excellency."

"Hoffmann, come with us."

The two Austrian secret agents marched into the nearest tavern with Hoffmann at their heels.

"Bring three beers to our table!" shouted Paul as he walked past the tavern keeper.

The tavern keeper quickly brought three tankards of beer, placed them on the table and scuttled back to the safety of the area behind his counter.

Franz raised his tankard and made a toast. "Long live King Frederick!" The other two repeated the toast and drank to the King.

"Hoffmann, are you a loyal Prussian?" Franz asked.

"To my last drop of blood!"

"Hoffmann," Franz continued, "are you prepared to undertake a mission for the Prussian people and our gracious King?"

"Of course!"

"In return for two days of work," Paul said, "His Majesty will reward you in two ways: with his gratitude and with 10 reichsthaler."

"Ten reichsthaler for two days of work? That's more than I've ever earned in two weeks. What do I have to do?"

"Hoffmann," Franz said, "we have a secret mission for you. You are to tell no one. Not your girlfriend, not your comrades, not your parents. Is that understood?"

"Yes, Your Excellency."

"Do you have your papers on you?" Franz asked.

Hoffmann put his hand inside his shirt and brought out a grubby piece of cardboard. He unfolded it and handed it to Franz. Franz determined that Caspar Hoffmann, resident of Potsdam, had been born in Potsdam 25 years before. He refolded the document and gave it back to Caspar.

"Hoffmann," Franz continued, "we have a letter for you to deliver to a place near Brandenburg an der Havel." He checked his pocket watch. "You are to leave right now. It will take you about eight hours to walk there. You will arrive after midnight. You will eat your evening meal there, sleep there, and return the next day."

"Now," Paul said, "where are you going to place the letter during your walk?"

"Here, under my shirt, with my papers. I'll keep the shirt buttoned up so the letter cannot possibly fall—"

"It had better not fall out," Franz said. "Do you know what will happen to you if you lose the letter before you get to the hut?"

Hoffmann shook his head.

"Anyone who loses a letter while in the service of King Frederick is placed in front of a wall and shot," he explained. "Do you understand?"

"Sh-shot?"

"Yes, shot. No excuses whatsoever will be accepted. None. So if you don't want to accept this secret mission, tell us now, and we'll find someone else to serve Prussia and our beloved King."

Franz suspected that Caspar Hoffmann was badly torn. On the one hand, he genuinely wanted to serve King and country—he was a dyed-in-the-wool patriot. He also clearly coveted the 10 reichsthaler. On the other hand, he was terrified of losing the letter and getting shot. After thinking deeply for a few seconds, Hoffmann nodded to indicate that he accepted the mission.

"You are now in the King's service, so no more beer until you've delivered the letter," Paul said, pulling away Hoffman's tankard. "Also, under no circumstances are you to stop at an inn on the way. Here's five groschen. Use the money to buy food here in Potsdam before you leave. When you've successfully completed the mission, return to this tavern. We'll be waiting for you here at this table. We'll give you your 10 reichsthaler and the grateful thanks of your King for your services to him."

Franz then explained to Caspar Hoffmann where to find the hut. "When you get there, leave the letter on the table. Spend the rest of the night there. Eat your breakfast and then walk back here. Do you have any questions?"

Hoffmann shook his head.

"One final remark—and this is very, very important." Franz said, "You've been a soldier, so you know that His Majesty keeps our glorious country safe via patrolling troops. You know that soldiers or police will stop you several times on the way, demand to see your papers, and ask you the purpose of your journey. When they ask you why you are traveling, what are you going to tell them?"

"That I'm walking to the hut to leave the letter there for the King, naturally," Hoffmann said with a note of pride in his voice.

"Weak-minded imbecile!" yelled Franz. "Didn't I just tell you that you're on a secret mission? Didn't I just tell you not to tell anyone, not your girlfriend, not your comrades, not even your parents? Didn't I?"

Hoffmann hung his head and said nothing. Clearly, his seven years in the Royal Prussian Army had taught him that silence was definitely the safest answer.

"Hoffmann, listen to me," Franz continued. "If soldiers or police stop you on the road between here in Potsdam and the hut near Brandenburg, you are to say that you are walking to Brandenburg to seek work. If soldiers or police stop you on the road from the hut on the way back to Potsdam, you are to say that you are walking to Potsdam to seek work. Is that completely clear?"

"Yes, Your Excellency."

"This is a secret mission for our King. No matter who asks you, no matter what they ask you, you are not to mention us, you are not to mention the hut, and you are not to mention the letter. All you are to say is that you are walking to seek work. Is that clear?"

"Yes, Your Excellency."

"You are on a secret mission for the King. If you betray his secrecy, you are a traitor to Prussia. And traitors are shot. Is that clear?

"Yes, Your Excellency."

Franz handed him the letter addressed to Max Hirsch in Vienna and watched Hoffmann place it inside his shirt next to his papers. Then Franz pointed to the door.

CHAPTER SIX

The first man handed the letter to the second man, who passed it on to the third man. The third man looked at the address written on the outside of the letter, and immediately handed it back to the second man, drawing his attention to the Austrian destination. Both the second man and the third man then drew their pistols, which they pointed at Hoffmann's head. The first man took out a pair of cuffs and secured Hoffmann's hands behind his back. The three men then proceeded to march him to police headquarters a few blocks away. Not a word was spoken.

Hoffmann had left the tavern and—under the influence of all the beer he had consumed before and during his meeting with the *Junker*—had forgotten that he had to buy provisions before leaving Potsdam. Instead, he had headed straight for the Brandenburg Gate. The first patrol he encountered comprised three plainclothes men waiting at the corner of Brandenburg Strasse and Lindenstrasse. They crossed the street. "Halt! Papers, please!" the first man barked. Caspar Hoffmann had unbuttoned his shirt and put his hand inside to rummage for his papers. Instead he pulled out the fictional letter and handed it over.

The men took Hoffmann to Commissioner Grün's office and forced him onto a chair. They did not remove the handcuffs. The second man, who was still holding the letter, now handed it to Commissioner Grün. The inspector broke the seal and opened the letter. He read it and turned visibly pale. This matter needed to be handled at once by police headquarters in Berlin, and preferably by

Baron von Hochenheimer himself. He turned to one of the plainclothes men: "Have this man taken to Berlin right now under heavy guard. He is not to be left alone for one instant. There are to be at least two armed policemen locked in the police coach with him. The handcuffs stay on, obviously, and I want his legs chained, as well. The coach is to be escorted all the way to police headquarters by a troop of six dragoons. Ask Colonel zu Meinratz to arrange this. No, make that eight dragoons. This is a most serious matter."

Commissioner Grün wrote a short note addressed to Baron von Hochenheimer. He explained that they had found the letter in the possession of a man arrested in Potsdam that evening. The man was being taken to Berlin for interrogation and would arrive shortly.

He turned to a second plainclothes policeman. "Make a copy of this letter and the address that's written on the outside. Arrange for the original letter to be taken to Minister von Hochenheimer in Berlin by armed courier at once, together with this note. The courier is to be accompanied by a suitable armed guard—talk to Colonel zu Meinratz about that. Impress on the colonel that this letter is unimpeachable evidence of a vast conspiracy against the King. You have my permission to show the letter to the Colonel, under cover of the strictest of strict confidentiality."

Both men left. Commissioner Grün ignored Caspar Hoffmann, who was in a state of shock. The effects of the beer he had consumed had worn off. He had no false illusions regarding his fate. He would serve Prussia by saying nothing at all. Even if the executioners asked for his last words, he would remain silent.

A few minutes later, two armed policemen came into the room. They fastened leg chains to Hoffmann's ankles and assisted him in walking to a police coach that was waiting in the courtyard. Eight dragoons rode up to the coach and positioned themselves pairwise in front, behind and on each side. The fortified doors of the courtyard opened, and the coach rumbled its way to Berlin.

At the same time, eight heavily armed hussars escorted a Royal Prussian Courier along the same route. In his saddlebag, the courier carried the fictional letter and Commissioner Grün's note. The courier and his escort arrived at police headquarters first. The courier dismounted from his horse, grabbed his saddlebag and rushed up the stairs. One of the guards at the door escorted him to von Hochenheimer's office.

Despite the lateness of the hour, von Hochenheimer was at his desk. The Minister of Police was a tall, gaunt, humorless man of about 50. His black hair was starting to thin at the temples but there was as yet no trace of gray. A Roman nose and angular cheekbones dominated his sallow, thin-lipped face.

The courier handed him Commissioner Grün's note and the fictional letter, saluted, and returned to his horse and escort. Von Hochenheimer picked up the letter and examined the Vienna address on the outside. He knew very well whom Max Hirsch was and grew concerned. The Minister of Police was known for his nerves of steel and placid demeanor. On reading the letter, however, von Hochenheimer exploded. He shouted for his aide to come at once.

"Kunersdorf, where's the prisoner from Potsdam?"

"What prisoner, Minister?" asked the aide, a short, plumpish man with long, fair hair combed straight back over his round head. Von Kunersdorf was sweating profusely. He had never seen the Minister like this, and he knew it meant trouble for him, lots of trouble.

"What do you mean 'What prisoner?' You know precisely what prisoner I mean—the man arrested in Potsdam this afternoon."

"But Minister, as far as I know no prisoner has arrived here from Potsdam this evening. But I'll go to the guards and find out."

He came back, panting. "No prisoner has arrived this evening from Potsdam, Minister."

In a state of panic, von Hochenheimer reread Grün's note—this time more carefully—and realized that the prisoner must still be en route to Berlin.

"Go downstairs again. Tell them that when the prisoner arrives, he is to be taken to the cellars, to Interrogation Room Three. And make sure that Sergeant Winterfeldt is in the room. I'm going to need his expertise tonight."

The aide rushed downstairs a second time, only to reappear a minute later in the Minister's office. "The prisoner has just arrived from Potsdam, Minister. He's on his way to Interrogation Room Three, as you have ordered."

"Excellent, Kunersdorf. Excellent." The Minister of Police had returned to his usual state of icy calm. "Come with me."

Taking the letter in his hand, von Hochenheimer descended to the cellars, followed by his aide. They entered the room. A large leather office chair and a desk stood against one wall. Von Hochenheimer marched to the chair and sat down, placing the documents on the desk in front of him. Next to the desk was a somewhat smaller chair behind a table furnished with writing materials for transcribing an interrogation. Von Kunersdorf sat there.

Opposite the desk stood Caspar Hoffmann, still cuffed and chained. Behind him stood burly Sergeant Winterfeldt and two jailers. To his right a wooden whipping bench and whip threatened.

"What is your name?" von Hochenheimer demanded.

"Hoffmann, Your Excellency. I was walking to Brandenburg to—"

"Silence!" said von Hochenheimer. "When I ask you your name, you give your name and nothing else. Sergeant, search the prisoner."

Sergeant Winterfeldt conducted a thorough examination, finding only Hoffmann's papers in his shirt and five groschen in his pocket. He placed the items on the Minister's desk and resumed his place behind the prisoner.

Von Hochenheimer unfolded the paper. "You are Caspar Hoffmann, age 25, born in Potsdam, and you live at 23 Herzogstrasse, Potsdam. Is that correct?"

"Yes, Your Excellency."

"Is that your letter?"

"No, Your Excellency."

"How did you get it?"

After a few moments of silence, the Minister of Police turned to Winterfeldt and said, "Make him talk."

The sergeant and the two jailers forced Hoffmann to stand in front of the whipping bench. They unlocked his handcuffs and leg chains and stripped him to the waist. Then the two jailers tightly pinioned Hoffmann to the bench and left the room.

Sergeant Winterfeldt took the long leather whip from the wall, stood to one side of the bench, took aim and—with all the force that his muscular body could exert—slammed the whip into Hoffmann's back. Hoffmann howled in pain.

As a Prussian, Hoffmann had no doubt been caned at school, and corporal punishment, often severe, was widely used to enforce discipline in the Royal Prussian Army. But no past beating could have prepared him for the sheer agony of this torture.

The sergeant stood back, waited a few seconds and then smashed the whip into Hoffmann's back a second time. A third blow followed, as vicious as the first two.

Von Hochenheimer signaled to the sergeant to suspend the beating. The Minister got up from his chair and walked over to Hoffmann, who sobbed uncontrollably.

"Hoffmann, can you hear me?"

"Yes, Your Excellency."

"Do you want the good sergeant to continue whipping you?"

"No, Your Excellency. Please let me go, Your Excellency. Please. I want to go home."

"Are you ready to answer my questions, Hoffmann, or should I tell the sergeant to continue?"

Silence. The only audible sound was the drip, drip of blood onto the bench.

"Fine. If that's your decision, I'll ask the sergeant to resume the whipping until you change your mind. Eventually you will talk. Everyone does. You can save yourself a lot of unnecessary pain if you talk now, rather than later."

No response.

"Sergeant!"

"I'll talk! I'll talk!"

Von Hochenheimer waited for a minute or so. "Where did you get that letter?" he began.

"Two *Junker* gave it to me. This afternoon. In a tavern."

"What tavern?"

"I don't know the name. I've never been there before. It's on the Judengasse."

"Don't lie to me. *Junker* don't go to bars on the Judengasse. Sergeant!"

"No, no, don't hit me anymore. I'm telling the truth. I was standing on the street corner on the Judengasse and these two *Junker* came up to me. They said they wanted to talk to me and they took me into this tavern and bought me beer. They said they had a secret mission for me, a mission for the King. And they gave me this letter and told me where to deliver it."

"And where did they want you to deliver it?" asked the Minister of Police. He looked sideways at Sergeant Winterfeldt as if to indicate the confession was a lie.

"A hut in the forest just outside Brandenburg," Hoffmann whispered, eyeing the whip.

At this, von Hochenheimer held up his hand to the sergeant. He knew that, regardless of the other lies Hoffmann may have been telling, this last statement was the truth. And he knew, with absolute and total certainty, that if he was to save the life of

Frederick II, King of Prussia, he had to extract every single fact from Hoffmann.

"Let's start again at the beginning," said von Hochenheimer. "You were standing on the street corner on the Judengasse. Two men came up to you. You said that they were *Junker*, which is impossible. What made you say that?"

"They were *Junker*. They dressed like *Junker*. They talked like *Junker*. They behaved like *Junker*. Your Excellency, I was in the Royal Prussian Army for seven years. All the officers are *Junker*. These men were officers, for sure. Their behavior, with one exception, was that of *Junker* officers."

"And what was that one exception?"

"They ordered me to sit at their table, they bought beer for me, and they drank beer with me."

"And didn't that make you suspicious?"

"Of course not, Your Excellency. The *Junker* are our masters. They can do whatever they like and they can do whatever they like to us. If a *Junker* tells me to go into a tavern and drink beer with him, I obey him, no matter how strange it is."

Von Hochenheimer considered what Hoffmann had just said. It was true that the *Junker* ruled Prussia. All the officers were from the *Junker* class, and the Army *was* Prussia. The word of a *Junker* was essentially law. It was possible that Hoffmann was telling the truth. Von Hochenheimer decided to withhold judgment until he had heard more.

"You don't know the name of the tavern, but you're sure that it's on the Judengasse. Is that correct?"

"Yes, Your Excellency."

"Describe the tavern. Where is the door? Where is the counter? Where did you sit? Is there a back room? Is there an upstairs?"

He motioned to von Kunersdorf to approach the whipping bench to which Hoffmann was tightly fastened. "My aide here will write down every word you say. Your statement will be taken to Potsdam, where it will be used to identify the tavern. Then we'll find out just who was in the tavern this afternoon. I strongly suggest that you tell the truth. One lie, just one tiny little untruth, and I'll have you whipped to death."

Von Kunersdorf returned to his table and picked up his quill. He dipped it in the ink and waited for Hoffmann to speak.

"I'm telling the truth, Your Excellency. The tavern is, as I said, on the Judengasse. I don't know the name of the tavern. I'd never been there before. It's quite small. The room is long and narrow, about 10 feet wide and about 20 feet deep. I'm not sure about the exact dimensions. It's quite dark inside. The door is in the middle of the wall and is flanked by small windows, one on each side. The counter is on the left as you come in. The tavern keeper was there. He brought the beer to our table, and he'll tell you that the two men were *Junker*."

"Where were you sitting?"

"We were at a table for four in the far corner. There were a few other tables. I don't remember how many. Perhaps two or three."

"Were there other people in the tavern?"

"Not many. Most people were still at work. I remember one old man sitting at the counter. Maybe there was someone else."

"Anything else you can tell us about the tavern?"

"No, Your Excellency. Wait, there was one strange thing."

"Go on."

"Well, when you go into a tavern, you tell the tavern keeper what you want to drink. He then puts what you ordered in front of you. You pay him, and then you take your beer."

"Yes. So what?"

"Well, these *Junker* walked into the tavern ahead of me. As he passed the counter, the first *Junker* shouted to the tavern keeper to bring three beers to our table. We sat down. The tavern keeper brought the tankards of beer. But he didn't ask for money, and the *Junker* didn't pay him. That's not how things are done in a tavern."

Von Hochenheimer took von Kunersdorf by the arm and led him to the far corner of the room, away from the bench. He spoke in a low voice. "I'm convinced about two things. First, I believe he's telling the truth. Second, I am absolutely convinced that the two men in the tavern were *Junker*. Do you agree?"

"I definitely agree," his aide said.

"We need to get more information about the *Junker* from our friend here. You will arrange for everything he has said to be copied and taken to Potsdam as soon as physically possible. The police are then to comb the city for the two *Junker*. If necessary, the whole country will be searched.

"The situation is utterly incredible. If you'd told me that one *Junker* is conspiring with Austria to assassinate our King, I'd dismiss you on the spot for insanity. But here we have two of them—two *Junker*—trying to kill King Frederick II."

"And what about the third man, Minister?"

"What third man? Do you mean Hoffmann here?"

"No, Minister. The letter appears to come from three secret agents—look at the bottom of the page. Hoffmann says that two men gave him the letter in the tavern. Who's the third man? Is he another *Junker*? I sincerely hope not, but after reading this letter, anything is possible. And where's the third man? He wasn't in the tavern. Could he be waiting at the hut?"

"Now there's a thought," said von Hochenheimer. "When you've sent my instructions to Potsdam, send further instructions to Brandenburg an der Havel to tell them to search the hut where the dead poacher was found and keep it under constant observation. No, those provincial fools at Brandenburg will mess it up. They always do. Send a second set of instructions to Potsdam regarding the hut."

"Yes, Minister."

"Now let's find out more about those *Junker*."

The Minister returned to the whipping bench. "Hoffmann, I want to know everything you know about those two *Junker*. Describe them to me. And when you do, remember at all times what's going to happen to you without fail if you dare lie to me."

"Yes, Your Excellency. There were two *Junker*. One was of medium height and thin. He wore a blue suit. Dark blue, but not Prussian blue. More like navy blue, perhaps. Or royal blue? I'm not too good with fancy colors. Let me just say that his suit was blue. He had red hair and a large red beard, and he had an eye patch over his eye. The left eye, I think. No, no, it was his right eye."

"And the other *Junker*?"

"His suit was red, no, maroon, Your Excellency. That's it, maroon velvet. Very fine. He was quite a big man. Eats a lot, I think."

"And his hair?"

"His hair is pitch black, and he has a huge black moustache. One of the largest moustaches I've ever seen—it extends on both sides, and it's quite wide. The part under the nose is the narrow part. As it gets beyond the mouth, it grows up and down. It's almost like a full beard that's been shaved below the mouth, if you know what I mean."

"The color of his eyes?"

"I'm afraid I didn't notice that, Your Excellency. But I did notice one other thing: Large, black moles surround the area around one eye. There must have been four or five, maybe more."

"Which eye?"

"Now I'm not sure. I'd rather not say than get it wrong."

"Anything else about the appearance of the *Junker*?"

"No, Your Excellency."

"Anything else at all about them? Their behavior, their demeanor, anything?"

"Nothing, Your Excellency."

Von Hochenheimer escorted von Kunersdorf back to the far corner of the interrogation room a second time.

"Did you notice anything unusual regarding what Hoffmann has just said about the appearance of the two *Junker*?"

"Nothing exceptional, Minister."

"Are you sure?"

"Yes, Minister."

"It doesn't seem strange to you that one *Junker* has a huge red beard and a black eye patch, and the other *Junker* has the biggest moustache you've ever seen and several big, black moles around his eyes? You're a *Junker*. Does either description sound like any *Junker* you've ever met?"

"No, Minister, but I haven't met all the *Junker* in Prussia."

"Let me put it more directly. What do the following things have in common: one, a huge red beard; two, a black eye patch; three, the largest black moustache you've seen, almost like a full beard that's been shaved below the mouth; and four, a clump of large black moles?"

"You mean: The *Junker* wore disguises?"

"Precisely, my dear Kunersdorf. So now we have to look for two, or perhaps three, *Junker*. And what do we actually know about them? One is of medium height and thin. And that's it."

"Don't we know that the other was fat?"

"Do we know that? Could he have been another thin *Junker* wearing a large suit with padding?"

Von Kunersdorf was silent.

"Let's go back to Hoffmann and see if he knows anything else."

They returned to the whipping bench.

"Hoffmann," said von Hochenheimer, "you've been most helpful. You've told us everything you know about the tavern; you've told us everything you know about the *Junker*. As a loyal Prussian and subject of the King, is there anything else that happened that you haven't mentioned yet?"

Hoffmann cocked his head to the side and winced at the pain from the lacerations. "They told me that I'd been chosen for a secret mission. I'd be serving the King, who would reward me not just with his gratitude, but also with 10 reichsthaler. They gave me five groschen to buy food for the journey before I left—they instructed me not to stop at an inn."

"Anything else?"

"No, Your Excellency. Wait! I've thought of something. They warned me that I'd be stopped several times by soldiers, that they'd want to see my papers and that they'd ask me why I was traveling. They repeated that this was a secret mission, so I was to tell the soldiers that I was looking for work—I was to say nothing about the letter, the *Junker* or the hut."

"Ah, yes, the hut. What did they tell you about the hut?"

"It's just before you get to Brandenburg. There's a huge dead tree on the right of the road. You turn right when you reach the tree, you walk about 500 feet into the forest, and there's the hut. I was told to put the letter on the table, sleep in the hut, eat my food there and then walk home."

"And that's all you can tell us?"

"Yes, Your Excellency."

The Minister turned to von Kunersdorf. "You know what to do. Time is of the essence."

Von Kunersdorf got up and left the interrogation room. As he did so, a thought struck von Hochenheimer.

"Hoffmann, you said that the *Junker* promised you 10 reichsthaler. How were you going to receive your pay?"

"Back at the tavern on the Judengasse, Your Excellency. They said they'd be waiting at the table with my money when I returned from the hut."

Von Hochenheimer rushed to the door. "Kunersdorf, come back! Come back! Guards, fetch my aide."

Von Kunersdorf ran back into the interrogation room, panting again. "The guard said you called me back."

"Yes, yes. Come into the next room so that we can talk privately."

The Minister led his aide into an adjoining interrogation room, furnished identically in every way to Interrogation Room Three. After shutting and locking the door, von Hochenheimer sat at the desk and indicated that von Kunersdorf should sit, as well.

"Wonderful news! Hoffmann says that the two *Junker* will be back in the tavern to pay him when he returns from the hut. You and I are going to Potsdam at once. We'll order plainclothes policemen to surround the tavern. When the two *Junker* return to the tavern to pay Hoffmann, we'll have them."

"Shouldn't we take Hoffmann with us, Minister?"

"Hoffmann? Why Hoffmann? What's he got to do with it?"

"With the greatest respect, Minister, I doubt if the two *Junker* are going to sit in the tavern waiting for Hoffmann. Surely they'll send a servant to the tavern on the Judengasse to watch out for him. When Hoffmann arrives, the servant will either summon the *Junker* or more likely escort Hoffmann to where the *Junker* will really be waiting."

"That's brilliant! Of course, we'll need to take Hoffmann with us. And furthermore, it's vital that we don't tip off the tavern keeper or anyone in the tavern—that would spoil everything. We'll go to Potsdam now so that I can supervise the whole operation personally. We'll have to locate the tavern discreetly and surround it equally discreetly. If the two *Junker* come in person, we'll have them. If not, we can work out when Hoffmann should arrive back at the tavern. At that time, we'll send Hoffmann inside to collect his money. In fact, we can work it out now: Eight hours to walk to the hut, eight hours to sleep, eight hours to walk back. So Hoffmann should be back at five. If the *Junker* haven't arrived at the tavern by then, we'll send Hoffmann in. As you cleverly worked out, the servant will lead us to his masters, and we'll have them.

"I want you to order my coach. You and I will leave immediately for Potsdam—we'll try to get some sleep on the way. I'll go back next door and give instructions to Sergeant Winterfeldt regarding Hoffmann."

The Minister unlocked the door of Room Four and went back into Room Three. His aide followed him out and went back upstairs to make the necessary arrangements.

Von Hochenheimer approached Hoffmann. "I'm sorry that we had to whip you, but it was the only way to get you to talk. You've behaved like a true Prussian. Tonight you have served your country and your King, and both of them are proud of you."

Hoffmann said nothing.

"I believe that you've answered every question honestly and to the best of your ability. As a reward, tomorrow you will get your 10 reichsthaler from the two *Junker* in the tavern on the Judengasse."

The Minster turned to Winterfeldt. "Sergeant, have the prisoner cleaned up—get him some medical attention for his back. Then put his shirt and coat back on and escort him to Potsdam in a police coach with a military guard. You know what to do. And Sergeant: I want Hoffmann to be treated well at all times. I'm going to Potsdam, too. When you get to police headquarters there, ask for me and I'll give you further instructions."

CHAPTER SEVEN

The surprise arrival of von Hochenheimer and his aide in the early hours of the morning threw Potsdam police headquarters into an uproar. The Minister rarely arrived unannounced, and never in the middle of the night. Night staff who had been taking an unauthorized nap were hurriedly shaken awake. Uniform jackets that had been removed for comfort were hastily replaced. Buttons were done up. Books and newspapers were quickly tucked in desk drawers. And bottles of schnapps, now half empty, were swiftly hidden at the back of filing cabinets.

Von Hochenheimer went to his office and sat down. He told his aide to summon the duty commander. Within seconds, Police Commissioner Magdeburg came into the room.

"Magdeburg, we have work to do. First, I want you to send men right away to that hut in the forest outside Brandenburg an der Havel. They are to maintain a discreet, 24-hour surveillance on the place, and to arrest anyone who even approaches it. Choose only men who have the skill to hide in a forest without being detected—the person whom we expect to catch is a highly trained Austrian secret agent. He'll be extremely careful and will approach the hut circumspectly. Impress on your men that they should wait until he gets inside the ring of watchers, so that he doesn't escape. And you need to warn your men that there is a remote possibility that the agent may be disguised as a Prussian policeman or even an army officer. But whether or not in disguise, everyone who approaches that hut is to be arrested and brought to me. Second, what time in the morning do the taverns open?"

"Officially at ten, Your Excellency, but there are always tavern keepers who open early. We try to arrest anyone who—"

"Yes, yes, I know. But I'm not concerned about the licensing laws now. We have a matter of national security on our hands. I want you to arrange for two of your best detectives to dress as out-of-work manual laborers and go into a tavern on the Judengasse this morning at about a quarter past ten. I don't know the name of the tavern, but it's apparently quite small, about 10 feet by 20 feet. The door is in the middle of the street wall, with a small window on each side. The counter is on the left, and there are a few tables in the room.

"The job of your men is to identify the tavern, then go in and order a beer. While drinking, they are to look around discreetly and see if there are any exits other than the front door. When they leave the tavern, they are to go across the street and find a room with a window from which we can watch the tavern. If necessary, we'll arrest the people living there and keep them in the cells until the operation is successfully concluded. As I said, this is a matter of state security.

"After your detectives have reported back to you, the tavern is to be placed under close but discreet surveillance. There'll be watchers in the room across the way that your detectives will find for us, including me and members of my staff. There'll also be a prisoner there, but he'll be under the watchful eye of Sergeant Winterfeldt, whom I think you know. I want plainclothes policemen in the street. In the strictest confidence, we are looking for two *Junker*."

"*Junker*, Your Excellency? Did you say *Junker*?"

"Yes, *Junker*. Even stranger, the *Junker* may be in disguise. But under no circumstances should you share the fact that our targets are *Junker* with anyone below the rank of Police Commissioner. Is that understood?"

"Perfectly, Your Excellency."

"Your men are not to prevent anyone from going into the tavern. Anyone who leaves the tavern, however, is to be tailed or arrested when out of sight. I will signal from the window if the person is to be arrested by moving my open hand downward like this. Clearly, you'll need to have plenty of men in the area to do all the necessary tailing.

"Third, Sergeant Winterfeldt will soon be here with a prisoner named Hoffmann. Hoffmann is to be put in a cell for now, but he is to be given the best possible treatment. We're going to need his cooperation this afternoon.

"Report back to me at noon, by which time both surveillance operations need to have commenced. Any questions?"

"Not at this time, Your Excellency."

***

Promptly at noon, Police Commissioner Magdeburg came to the office, accompanied by Police Commissioner Schnittler who had taken over as duty commander at eight. Nevertheless, it was Magdeburg who reported on the latest developments.

"Your Excellency, regarding the hut in the forest: I have sent two teams of six men each to the area. They were all brought up in forests and therefore have the necessary skills. They understand what they are to do. The teams will watch for 12 hours in turn. Two mounted policemen will handle communications; one of them will vigilantly approach the area every four hours. If necessary, he will then ride here to report.

"All 14 men are now based in Brandenburg an der Havel. For obvious reasons, I've told the locals nothing, other than that the men are under my direct command. And the men have been ordered to keep their mouths shut."

"Good work," replied the Minister.

"I turn now to the other matter," the Commissioner continued. "This morning, two detectives went to the Judengasse, disguised as out-of-work laborers. They found that there's only one tavern on the Judengasse and that it meets the description you gave me. There's no back door or upstairs—the only way in or out is the door on the Judengasse.

"My two detectives drank their beers and left. Across the street, they found a second-floor apartment with a window that directly faces the door of the tavern. As you ordered, they arrested the woman living there. Her husband is currently at work, and we will arrest him. In that way, there's no possibility of the suspects being alerted to our presence in the apartment.

"My men are arrayed in the vicinity of the tavern on the Judengasse and the surrounding streets. I passed along all of your orders, of course. In addition, I have arranged for at least one of my men to be inside the tavern at all times. Each man will stay for

30 or 40 minutes, then drink up and leave when the next man enters. All my men are armed, so that will provide additional firepower if the two suspects should enter the tavern."

"Again, good work. Please make the necessary arrangements for my aide and me to be taken to the surveillance room to arrive there at half past four this afternoon. And now I want to see Sergeant Winterfeldt and the prisoner, Hoffmann."

The two men left the office. A few minutes later, Winterfeldt and Hoffmann entered. Von Hochenheimer noticed that Hoffmann did not look too unhappy—undoubtedly, the orders to treat him well had been obeyed. In particular, the handcuffs and leg irons had been removed.

"Hoffmann, as I promised, you are going to receive your 10 reichsthaler. You will be taken to a room opposite the tavern on the Judengasse. You will sit by the window and observe the pedestrians meticulously. When you see the two *Junker* arrive, you will wait a few minutes and then go into the tavern to receive your money.

"If the *Junker* haven't arrived by five o'clock, you will go into the tavern, order a beer, and sit at the same table as yesterday, but facing the door—Kunersdorf, give him some money. If someone comes up to you and asks you to come with him to his masters, go along with him. He will take you to where the *Junker* are waiting to pay you. Is that clear?"

"Yes, Your Excellency."

"Sergeant, take Hoffmann to the Judengasse."

***

At precisely half past four, von Hochenheimer and von Kunersdorf entered the second-floor apartment and walked over to the room that overlooked the Judengasse. Hoffmann was seated in a straight-backed chair, totally engrossed in watching the street below. Behind him stood Police Commissioner Schnittler and Sergeant Winterfeldt. The Police Commissioner was watching the scene below as intensely as Hoffmann; Winterfeldt was watching Hoffmann. None of the three men were aware that the Minister of Police and his aide had entered the room.

Finally, von Hochenheimer spoke. "Commissioner, what's happening now?"

The heads of the three men at the window spun round as one. Hoffmann sprang to his feet; all three men jumped to stiff attention.

Schnittler seemed utterly nonplussed by the unheralded arrival of his chief, but he soon regained his composure. "Your Excellency, very little has happened so far," he reported. "Only one person has entered the tavern, an old man, probably a retired soldier. Hoffmann told us that he saw that old man in the tavern yesterday—he might come there every afternoon.

"Other than the old man, the only people who've come into the tavern have been my men. They've entered one at a time, stayed for half an hour or so, and then left a few minutes after the next man arrived.

"Furthermore, the Judengasse has been all but deserted this afternoon. My men have been virtually the only people seen on the street. One middle-aged man walked into the pawnshop, stayed for about 10 minutes, and left. One of my men tailed him; he'll report back later this afternoon, once the operation has been concluded."

"Very good. Let's continue the surveillance."

They watched until five. No one came into the Judengasse, let alone entered the tavern. There were only three people in the tavern: the tavern keeper, the old man, and a plainclothes policeman.

Von Hochenheimer turned to Hoffmann. "It's time. Sergeant Winterfeldt will escort you downstairs. You will exit the building, cross the road, and go into the tavern. Order a beer and pay for it with the money that von Kunersdorf gave you. Take your beer to the table where you sat yesterday with the two *Junker*. Choose a chair facing the door so that you can see if anyone enters the tavern.

"As I said earlier, if someone comes into the tavern and asks you to come with him, do so. He will take you to the *Junker* who will give you your money. Oh, one other thing. Hoffmann, if you were thinking of escaping, may I remind you that the street below is filled with armed policemen. And if you don't carry out—to the letter—the orders I have just given you, I will arrange for Sergeant Winterfeldt to punish you extremely severely. Do you understand me?"

"Yes, Your Excellency."

Hoffmann and the sergeant left the room. Winterfeldt returned a few minutes later and reported that Hoffmann was on his way. Schnittler, now watching intently at the window, added that Hoffmann had entered the tavern.

"Sergeant, with the Minister's permission, would you mind waiting for us downstairs?" von Kunersdorf asked.

When they were alone with Police Commissioner Schnittler, von Kunersdorf turned to the Minister and said, "I've just realized—they're not coming."

"Who's not coming?"

"The *Junker*. They're not coming."

"How can you say that? We've not caught Hoffmann in a single lie. Every fact that could be verified has been verified. And did you see the look on his face when I told him what would happen to him if he disobeyed? No, Hoffmann is understandably terrified of Winterfeldt's whip. As far as I'm concerned, in order to avoid further punishment, he's told us the truth."

"You're quite correct, Minister. Hoffmann has been totally truthful in every way. But the two *Junker* have lied to him. They told him to come back to the tavern this afternoon to receive his money. But there's no reason at all for them to return to the tavern, and many good reasons for them to stay away—permanently."

"Go on."

"If the *Junker* come back to the tavern, there's a risk that they'll be arrested. In my opinion, they've already burned the clothes they wore yesterday, as well as the false facial hair and the black eye patch. If they never return to this tavern, there'll be nothing to link them to the letter. They'll be completely safe.

"The same thing holds if they send a servant. Hoffmann could be followed, leading to their discovery. Or he could tell us afterward where the *Junker* are hiding out. So, they won't send a servant, either."

"But they promised to pay Hoffmann. A *Junker* is invariably true to his word."

"Minister," von Kunersdorf replied gently, "a *Junker* who plots with the enemies of Prussia to assassinate his King cannot be trusted."

There was silence while von Hochenheimer thought about what von Kunersdorf had just said. "So what do you suggest we do?"

"We have to wait at least an hour. After all, I may be wrong. But if no one has approached Hoffmann by six o'clock, we may have to call off the whole operation."

They waited in silence for an hour. Then von Hochenheimer went to the door of the apartment and summoned the sergeant waiting below.

"Winterfeldt, I want you to go into the tavern and take Hoffmann back to our headquarters here in Potsdam. I want to be quite sure that he was telling us the truth. So, when you arrive there, take him to Interrogation Room One and fasten him to the whipping bench. But don't hurt him in any way." He turned to Schnittler. "Commissioner, thank you for your help this afternoon. Would you please call off the operation now? Also, I would like you to pass on my personal thanks to all the police personnel involved here this afternoon. And please be so kind as to arrange transportation for me back to headquarters. One other thing: Would you ask your men to take the tavern keeper and the old man to headquarters? I want to ask them about the *Junker*."

***

When von Hochenheimer arrived back at his office, the tavern keeper and the old man were waiting outside. He sat down at his desk and asked von Kunersdorf to bring in the tavern keeper.

"Describe the two men who were in your tavern yesterday afternoon."

"*Junker*, Your Excellency."

"Is that all you can say about them?"

"Yes, Your Excellency."

The Minister dismissed the tavern keeper and asked von Kunersdorf to bring in the old man.

"What can you tell me about the two men who were in the tavern yesterday?"

"Do you mean the two *Junker*?"

And that was the end of that interview, too.

"Like you," von Hochenheimer said to von Kunersdorf when he came back in, "I'm 100 percent certain that Hoffmann was telling the truth. The tavern keeper and the old man made me even more certain, if that were possible. Nevertheless, I need to make sure that I haven't overlooked something. I'm going to interrogate him once more, from the very beginning. There's no need for you to come. I shan't need a new transcript; I'm going to use the one you made yesterday."

Von Hochenheimer opened the door to Interrogation Room One, walked inside, and closed the heavy door. Sergeant Winterfeldt was standing next to Hoffmann, who was once more tightly fastened to the whipping bench, his raw wounds from the beating exposed. Von Hochenheimer walked up to him. He asked Hoffmann to repeat his account of the preceding day. Caspar Hoffmann's answers were all but identical to what he had said the previous evening, as reflected on the transcript. The Minister of Police was about to order the Sergeant to release Caspar Hoffmann when a thought came to him.

"Hoffmann, I have one further question to ask you. You were found with five groschen in your pocket. You told me yesterday that the two *Junker* gave it to you to buy food for your journey."

"Yes, Your Excellency."

"They told you to buy provisions in Potsdam before you left for the hut. Correct?"

"Correct, Your Excellency."

"You are an obedient fellow. You did everything you were told to do, except for one thing: You didn't buy provisions before you left for Brandenburg an der Havel. Why not?"

"I don't know, Your Excellency. I just didn't."

"You are lying, Hoffmann. Why did you disobey the *Junker*? Why didn't you buy food before you left?"

Hoffmann started to panic. "I don't remember, Your Excellency; I just didn't buy food. I must have forgotten my orders."

"Forgotten your orders, Hoffmann? Forgotten? What else have you forgotten? Is your whole story a pack of lies? Have you forgotten the truth?"

"No, no, Your Excellency, I'm telling the truth. But I don't know why I didn't buy food. I just don't know."

Von Hochenheimer nodded to Sergeant Winterfeldt. Hoffmann's screams were heartbreaking. But the endless shrieks of agony did not move Baron von Hochenheimer; his sole concern was the safety of the King. So he just kept repeating, "Why did you disobey your orders? Why didn't you buy food before leaving the town of Potsdam?" Finally, Caspar Hoffmann sagged into merciful unconsciousness.

CHAPTER EIGHT

"Your Majesty, thank you for agreeing to see me on such short notice," von Hochenheimer said. He bowed low and then took the proffered seat in King Frederick's study in Sanssouci.

"Baron, over the years I've come to learn that if you ask to meet without an appointment, there's invariably an extremely important reason. Why have you come to see me today?"

"Your Majesty," he began, "two days ago, my men stopped a young man named Hoffmann here in Potsdam. He was found to be carrying a letter." Von Hochenheimer handed him the letter. He paused while the King examined the address written on the outside and then read the letter itself. "As you can see, it's addressed to Max Hirsch in Vienna. Hirsch is in charge of many of the Austrian secret agents who have come to Prussia to try to kill you. And we both know who's behind all this—Maria Theresa, the Empress of Austria."

"There have been many letters like this before, and your spy network has always found the Austrian secret agents quickly. Why is this letter different from all other letters?"

"Your Majesty, this letter is not from Austrian secret agents. It grieves me greatly to say this, but at least two of the conspirators are *Junker*."

Frederick had not had an easy life. He had been brought up with great cruelty, so much so that at age 18 he had tried to flee to England with his childhood friend, Hans von Katte. They were caught. Frederick's father imprisoned his son and forced him to watch von Katte's decapitation. But clearly nothing that he had suffered in the past had adequately prepared Frederick for the shock of learning that two of his own nobles were conspiring to kill him.

He grew pale. "Give me their names."

"Your Majesty, unfortunately we don't know who they are yet. All we know so far is that two *Junker* in disguise handed this letter to Hoffmann."

"In disguise?"

"One was wearing a false red beard and a black eye patch. The other sported a huge black moustache and several large, black moles near one eye."

"And Hoffmann didn't realize that these *Junker* were in disguise?"

"Your Majesty, Hoffmann is a simple man. The idea of *Junker* being in disguise would never have occurred to him."

"How sure are you that the two men were really *Junker*?"

"Hoffmann was absolutely adamant on that point. He mentioned their clothes, their accents and, above all, their attitudes and mannerisms. He served for seven years in Your Majesty's Royal Army, so he's had the opportunity to observe many different *Junker* up close. When he stated that the men were *Junker*, I was inclined to believe him. But one man's word is never enough, no matter how certain he may be. So, yesterday when I came to Potsdam, I interviewed the tavern keeper myself."

"What tavern keeper?" Frederick asked.

"The two *Junker* encountered Hoffmann on the Judengasse, and took him to the nearest tavern, where they all drank beer."

"Preposterous! *Junker* don't drink beer in a tavern on the Judengasse with a young ex-soldier."

"Agreed, Your Majesty, agreed. And *Junker* don't plot to assassinate their King either. But both things happened."

"And what does the tavern keeper say?"

"Like almost all your male subjects, he's a former soldier, too. I asked him to describe the two men who came into his tavern with Hoffmann. The first word that came out of his mouth was *Junker*.

"In addition, there's an old man who spends every afternoon in the tavern. He, too, is a former soldier. My men brought him in, and I asked him the same question. His reply was: 'Do you mean the two *Junker*?' So we have three men, all former soldiers, all absolutely inflexible and obdurate that the two men with Hoffmann were *Junker*."

The King sat back in his chair, clearly stunned. "Do you have a description of the two *Junker*?"

"That's the whole problem, Your Majesty. The descriptions we have all center around the disguises: the facial hair, the eye patch and so on. These two *Junker* are extremely clever. By wearing such preposterous disguises that would never fool a fellow *Junker* for one split second, they've forced the workingmen who'd seen them to focus on their false features. It doesn't help me to be told that the day before yesterday, a man had red hair, a huge red beard and a black eye patch when I know with almost total certainty that today his hair is back to its natural color, he's clean-shaven and both eyes are visible."

"You have a huge police force. My army of 150,000 men is at your total disposal, and you have a vast array of spies working for you, particularly in Potsdam where the *Junker* were yesterday, and in Berlin where they propose to kill me. How do you rate your chances of finding these men?"

"Regrettably zero, Your Majesty. All we really know about the two *Junker* is that one is thin and of medium height."

"And the other man?"

"He gave the impression of being a large man, Your Majesty. But he could just as easily have been a thin man wearing a large-size padded suit."

"So what you're saying, Baron, is that all you can do is arrest every thin *Junker*, and interrogate him under torture to determine if he is one of the two men in the tavern. Is that correct?"

"Essentially, yes. But there's another problem. The letter is from Secret Agent 79, Secret Agent 312, and Secret Agent 85. It seems reasonable to assume that two of the three signatories are the two *Junker*. But what about the third man? Who is he?"

"Could it be a woman?" the King asked.

"I hadn't thought of that. None of the many Austrian secret agents we've captured so far have been women, but then none of them have been *Junker*, either. As Your Majesty suggests, we need to consider all possibilities."

"Do you have any further information at all?"

"Well, we have one clue. A few days ago, a poacher was stabbed to death with a stiletto in a hut in a forest just outside the town of Brandenburg an der Havel. 'Long Live Empress Maria Theresa!' had been scribbled on one wall of the hut. We assumed that this was the work of Austrian secret agents, though why a foreign agent would bother to kill a poacher is beyond me, let alone why the killer would disclose his Austrian connections. The key point is that the *Junker* instructed Hoffmann to leave the letter on the table in that hut.

"I've instructed the police to watch that hut day and night and to arrest anyone who even approaches the hut. That may result in our finding the third secret agent, but I'm not optimistic."

"So what are we to do?" the King asked.

"Your Majesty, I've explained the situation to you in the greatest of detail so that you will appreciate why I say that, for the first time—and, I hope and pray, for the last time—I do not feel confident that I can protect you against an assassination attempt. Not only do I know nothing about these three secret agents—other than the fact that two of them are *Junker*—but also it appears that they're going to disguise themselves as policemen. Just as I cannot arrest every thin *Junker*, I cannot possibly arrest every policeman on the day of the parade. So, unless I can find the three secret agents in time, with the greatest of respect, I have to request you to cancel your birthday parade this year."

"Baron von Hochenheimer, I fully appreciate that, as always, you have my welfare at heart. But I have my people's welfare at heart, and I cannot cancel the parade under any circumstances. What would they think?"

"But, Your Majesty—"

"No more, please, Baron. No more. I understand your deep concern, and I am most grateful for it at all times, but the parade will take place as planned. I know you will do your very best to protect me, as always."

The Minister of Police rose from his seat, bowed low, and left the King's study. He realized that he had to find the three Austrian secret agents and quickly.

Returning to his office, he summoned von Kunersdorf.

"I spoke to His Majesty," he reported. "It's no use; he won't cancel the parade. So we have to do something. But what?"

"Let's reread the letter. Maybe we've overlooked something."

"You're just grasping at straws, aren't you?"

"Certainly, Minister, but all we have left are straws."

"There's no need to get the letter out of the file," said von Hochenheimer. "We both know it by heart. I've even dreamt about it, on the one occasion that I managed to sleep briefly since the letter was found. The key part is this:

We have come up with a plan to kill King Frederick on his birthday parade. The three of us will acquire Prussian police uniforms. We will kill him with hand grenades as he rides into Lustgarten Park.

"Actually, my reciting that paragraph has given me an idea. The secret agents need to do two things. First, they have to bribe a policeman to get three uniforms."

"They can also get uniforms from a tailor," von Kunersdorf said.

"Yes, that's so. In fact, it's probably easier to get uniforms in the correct sizes by paying a tailor than by bribing a policeman. After all, how many policemen have three spare uniforms in the appropriate sizes? No, the Austrians are going to have to find a tailor to make their uniforms."

"Agreed."

"Now, what about the hand grenades? As far as I can see, the only place to get those is from a grenadier regiment."

"Perhaps," von Kunersdorf said. "But surely the grenades are carefully guarded. An Austrian can't walk up to an armory and say to the sergeant in charge, 'Sell me three grenades, please.'"

"No, but a *Junker* officer can acquire anything he wants in the way of weapons, particularly if he's an officer in a grenadier regiment."

There was silence. Then von Kunersdorf finally spoke. "Does that mean that one of the secret agents is an officer in a grenadier regiment?"

More silence, then the Minister quoted:

Does this plan meet with your approval? If so, please send us another 1,000 reichsthaler via this route—we need it for bribes to get the uniforms and the hand grenades.

"That paragraph contradicts what we've been saying. The key word is 'bribes.' When you buy a uniform from a tailor, you pay him—you don't bribe him. You don't bribe him even if you buy three uniforms. Perhaps you could bribe him to keep quiet about the transaction, but that's not what the letter says; it speaks of 'bribes to get the uniforms.'

"And the same thing applies to the hand grenades. If a grenadier officer wants hand grenades, he requisitions them—he doesn't need to bribe anyone. On the contrary, the natural thing to do is just to order what he wants; bribery will only raise suspicions.

"And another thing. *Junker* are landowners. They generally have plenty of money. These secret agents are pleading for 1,000 reichsthaler for bribes. So, at last, we have something. These *Junker* are short of money. After all, 1,000 reichsthaler isn't very much money, but the secret agents are asking Max Hirsch to send them that amount. So, we know that we're dealing with poor *Junker*. That should reduce the field more than somewhat."

"So, Minister, what you're saying is that we're dealing with two *Junker;* we know nothing about the third individual. The two *Junker* and the third secret agent together are short of funds. They're going to obtain police uniforms with bribes, not by paying a tailor to make them. And they're going to get hand grenades with bribes, rather than using their military connections to acquire them. Minister, we're dealing with two weird *Junker*."

"You forgot to mention that these *Junker* are plotting to assassinate their King. These *Junker* are more than just weird. But all this may not even matter. That second paragraph asks: 'Does this plan meet with your approval?'"

"In other words," von Kunersdorf said, "the assassins aren't going to do a thing until they get permission from their spymaster in Vienna. Hoffmann was to carry the letter to the hut. Then it was to be taken somehow to Vienna, a distance of about 400 miles. The post coach would take four days. Then the answer would have to come all the way back to the hut, and the three Austrian secret agents, presumably based in Potsdam, would have to pick it up from the hut. So, it would surely take about two weeks just to get an answer, after which the plan could be initiated. But the parade is in less than a month."

"We're obviously overlooking something important," the Minister said. "But what is it?"

CHAPTER NINE

"What's bothering you now?" Franz asked his friend, who held his head at a strange angle.

"Just this: What happened to the fictional letter, and how can we find out?"

"Well, one possibility is that Hoffmann lost the letter. If that's what happened, the only way we can find out is to get hold of Hoffmann and ask him."

"Which we cannot do," Paul said.

"Which we certainly cannot do," Franz replied. "We have no idea how to find him. And it would definitely not be a good idea to hang around the Judengasse in our *Junker* costumes. Sooner or later, one of von Hochenheimer's spies will report us to the authorities, and that will be that. And if Hoffmann sees us, he's liable to get very angry indeed, because we owe him quite a bit of money."

"A second possibility," Franz added, "is that Hoffmann got himself arrested on his way to the hut, inside the hut or on his way home. And if that's the case, the only way we can find that out is to go to police headquarters and ask them if they arrested one Caspar Hoffmann and found a letter on him."

"Which we cannot do," said Paul, once more.

"Which we certainly cannot do," Franz replied again. "And there's no need for me to explain why."

"A third possibility," Franz continued, "is that the letter is laying on the table in the poacher's hut. And if it's there, the only way we can find out is to travel to the hut and check."

"Which we cannot do," said Paul for the third time.

"Which we certainly cannot do," Franz replied for the third time. "I scribbled 'Long Live Empress Maria Theresa!' on the wall specifically so that we could use the hut as a conduit for fictional material. I did it in the hope of ensuring that the hut would be under Prussian police surveillance night and day. There's no way that either of us should venture anywhere near that hut. In fact, we probably should stay well away from Brandenburg an der Havel."

"And that's why this deception business is even more complicated than I thought," Paul responded. "We carefully produced a fictional document intended to achieve a certain effect. But we don't know whether it's even in the hands of the Prussian police, let alone whether they fell for it."

"And there's another possibility," Franz noted. "What if they have the letter and realize it's fictional? In that case, the guard around King Frederick at Viereck, at the beginning of the parade, is likely to be even heavier than it would've been before we decided to deceive von Hochenheimer with our letter."

"So what do we do?" asked Paul.

"I don't know. My first reaction is to call off the real plan as a consequence of all this uncertainty—uncertainty my 'clever' idea has caused. But we've put so much time and effort into the real plan that I'm hesitant to abandon it."

"What alternative do we have? We were sent here to assassinate Frederick, and we came up with a way of carrying out the killing, but with a relatively low chance of success. So we determined to increase our chances by deceiving von Hochenheimer. Now we don't know if the chance of success is more, less or the same as before. It's utterly frustrating."

"Maybe you're wrong," Franz said. "Maybe we *can* find out whether we've deceived von Hochenheimer."

"How? We've just been through all that and decided we can't determine anything."

"Our fictional plan talks about acquiring police uniforms and hand grenades through bribery. If our deception has fooled the Prussians, they'll make it impossibly hard for us to do this. They'll warn policemen and grenade owners that a bribery attempt is going to be made, and promulgate draconian regulations describing the awful things that will happen to anyone who accepts a bribe of that kind. So all we have to do is walk around the city tomorrow and look for warnings against bribery in general, and against uniform and grenade bribery in particular. If we find public notices of that kind, we'll know that von Hochenheimer has fallen for our deception."

The next morning, the two agents separated in order to cover as much of Potsdam as they could. They returned in the late afternoon, tired and discouraged. Potsdam was poster-free.

"We don't want to do this again for a while," said Franz over their evening meal. "It's essential that we keep a low profile. There are too many spies in Prussia, and far too many here in Potsdam. Let's look once more in a few days' time."

***

Three days later, Paul went to buy bread from the bakery near their rooms and found a poster pasted to a wall warning against accepting bribes of any kind. He returned to the room as quickly as he could to tell Franz. They combed the city and—much to Paul's surprise and to Franz's satisfaction—they found copies of the poster on walls all over Potsdam. The notices specified long periods of imprisonment for malefactors. They did not mention specific acts of bribery, but they made it abundantly clear that all types of bribery were totally forbidden. Furthermore, any bribery attempt was to be immediately reported to the appropriate authorities.

"We did it!" said Franz when they were back at Paul's lodgings. "Von Hochenheimer has fallen for our fictional letter—hook, line, and proverbial sinker. Tomorrow we leave for Berlin to prepare for the parade. But we have to be careful. We may need to come back here, so you need to pay your landlord a month's rent in advance. Also, while we're gone, the police may search this place. As the birthday parade nears, more and more searches will take place, with or without a reason. The last thing we want is for our plans to go awry because the police conducted a random search and found an incriminating piece of paper here. So, the next thing we do is to go through this room and look for papers that we should've destroyed. We've been hiding our plans in books, so we need to look carefully through every book we have. And when we've found every piece of paper that needs to be burned, we'll burn them one at a time in this ashtray—all we need is the fire brigade bursting in."

"Are we going to leave our possessions in this room?" Paul asked.

"Here in Potsdam, people think that I'm a schoolmaster, and they've seen you working as a stevedore. So we'll leave behind everything that supports those roles. We've still got enough money from Max, so let's go to yet another pawnshop and garb ourselves as stolid members of the middle class. We are now the owners of a small import/export business in Brandenburg an der Havel, doing business with France, our glorious ally in the recent war against Austria."

"But why Brandenburg?"

"Because that town has the most inefficient police force in the whole of Prussia. Their records are incomplete and contradictory. Innuendo is recorded as fact, and vague supposition as gospel truth. Facts as such are systematically deleted from their files. Any inquiry made about us will lead precisely nowhere, not that any sane person would try to get information out of Brandenburg."

"Do you really think we can get away with it?" Paul asked.

"Remember what Max taught us about disguises," replied Franz. "If you really believe that you're the coowner of a small import/export business, then you'll successfully convince others of that fact."

"What'll we take with us?"

"Obviously we're going to have to travel to Berlin by post coach—we're import/export merchants. We'd better buy a trunk for our *Junker* outfits and our dueling pistols, the kind of well-used, well-traveled, sturdy trunk that import/export merchants would have with them in a stagecoach. We may be searched en route—in fact we probably will be searched—so no papers, please."

"And how will we explain the *Junker* costumes and dueling pistols in our trunk?" Paul asked.

"We're import/export merchants. We're on our way to France with samples of what we propose to export there, thereby boosting the economy of Prussia. We shouldn't have any problems."

"Let's buy a few more Prussian products at the pawnshop, to add verisimilitude. A flute would be an excellent idea to show our deep loyalty to Frederick the Flautist."

"That's a great suggestion. Maybe we should include two, a transverse flute and a recorder, say. That would certainly convince any Prussian policeman of our undying fidelity."

***

Two days later, they left Potsdam in a coach bound for Berlin. Wearing their recently purchased clothes, they were not masquerading as import/export merchants—they *were* import/ export merchants, and from Brandenburg an der Havel, no less.

The rickety coach creaked and groaned all the way to Berlin. From time to time, it sounded as if it might fall apart, so it came as a pleasant surprise to all the passengers when the stagecoach not only reached the outskirts of Berlin, but also stopped at an inn that fronted on Viereck. All the passengers alighted; it seemed to be the end of the line.

Franz and Paul lugged their heavy trunk to the side of the square, which turned out to be a large parade ground. Their luggage had not been inspected. Franz told Paul that the fact that the coach company's terminus was Viereck—the site of their assassination attempt—was an auspicious sign.

"We're going to need somewhere to stay," he continued. "We have two basic choices. We can either find a room close to Viereck, which will aid in planning but add to the risk, or we can get a room on the other side of Berlin."

"I suggest we find something here," Paul said. "We're certainly going to have to flee after killing Frederick, and the more familiar we are with the neighborhood, the greater our chances of getting away."

They found a room in a house two blocks from the square. Frau Deitel's husband had been a successful Berlin furniture manufacturer whose business partner had embezzled the firm's money. Herr Deitel died soon after the theft was discovered, leaving his widow with a large, beautifully furnished home but no money. To survive, she was forced to take in lodgers. She gave the two Austrian secret agents a large room on the first floor, the former dining room. It contained two beds plus the dining room furniture, which Frau Deitel was loath to sell.

The dining room table served as their writing desk, but the 12 dining room chairs invariably got in their way. They were tempted to place the chairs on the table, but were concerned that Frau Deitel might take offense and ask them to leave, so they continued to stumble around the room, stubbing their toes and bruising their arms.

***

The day after they arrived, Paul and Franz started to make a careful study of the streets in the vicinity of Viereck. They had two objectives. First, on Frederick's birthday they would walk from their lodgings to Viereck with pistols in their pockets. On the one hand, it was highly unlikely that a *Junker* would be stopped and searched. On the other hand, von Hochenheimer might have gotten word of the two *Junker* who had met with Hoffmann in the Judengasse tavern, especially if Hoffmann had been arrested. Accordingly, they wanted to find a route with a minimal number of checkpoints.

Second, although they were certainly willing to give up their lives in exchange for killing Frederick, they much preferred to flee to Vienna after the shooting. So they assiduously combed the streets around Viereck, trying to decide which would be the least-guarded exit routes.

Franz came back in the afternoon. He had been walking the area for two days now and was extremely tired. He entered their room, greeted Paul unenthusiastically, and flopped onto his bed to rest. Suddenly he sat upright, all his energy having returned. "Paul, I've just realized something. For two days, we've explored every street in the area, most of them several times. Did you notice anything strange? Or, more specifically, did you notice anything that wasn't there but should've been there?"

Paul had been lying on his bed, equally worn out. In fact, he had been asleep when Franz had called out to him. Slowly waking, he asked Franz to repeat the question.

"No, everything seemed correct. What's missing from the streets of Berlin?"

"Posters."

"Posters?"

"When we left Potsdam two days ago, there was an anti-bribery poster on every official notice board. Furthermore, there were even posters pasted on walls directly under signs saying 'Do Not Affix Posters Here.' For two days, I've walked up and down street after street here in Berlin, and I haven't seen a single anti-bribery poster. Have you?"

Paul was suddenly wide-awake. "Come to think of it, no, I haven't seen a single poster either. What's going on?"

"Obviously von Hochenheimer has seen our fictional letter. Our letter makes it clear that bribery is an integral part of our fictional assassination plot, so he had the posters put up to deter the good citizens of Potsdam from being bribed by us. But there are no posters in Berlin. Ergo, von Hochenheimer knows that the assassins are in Potsdam or, rather, he knew that we were in Potsdam."

"But how could he know that from the letter?" Paul asked. "It was found in a hut near Brandenburg. Surely it was more likely that the assassins were in Brandenburg?"

"Not if the letter never reached the hut. Suppose that guards stopped Hoffmann and searched him at a checkpoint on the way to the hut, and soldiers found his fictional letter on his person. He'd tell them that he was given the letter in a Potsdam tavern."

"But we told him that he was on a secret mission," Paul protested. "Why would he tell them anything?"

"One word: torture. And I'm sure that, under torture, he told them everything, including the fact that he was given the letter by two *Junker*."

"But von Hochenheimer's men couldn't possibly identify us. We had those beards and the eye patch and everything."

"They can't identify us from what Hoffmann has told them," Franz explained. "But the Minister of Police knows that there's a plot to kill the King during the birthday parade. He knows that three secret agents are involved, and that at least two of those secret agents are *Junker*. He's probably worked out that we disguised ourselves when we met with Hoffmann, and he may even have worked out where in Potsdam we obtained those disguises. The stage manager has probably given him a description of 'the Earl' and 'the Marquis' and, being a theatrical professional, he probably took close note of our clothes—costumes are an integral part of the theatre. My guess is that von Hochenheimer has circulated a detailed description of the two *Junker*. In fact, I'm certain that we'd be arrested on the spot if we were to be seen anywhere near the birthday parade in those suits."

"So what do we do now?" asked Paul.

"We get rid of those outfits. If this room is searched and the precise suits of clothing that the stage manager has described to von Hochenheimer are found, our mission is over, and we're dead meat. We need to revise our real plan. We're going to have to get to Frederick while wearing our current outfits. Yes, it would be much easier for a *Junker* to get close to the King than an import/export merchant, but we have no choice—those clothes have been compromised."

"On the one hand," Paul said, "we've successfully convinced the Prussians that the assassination attempt will be in Lustgarten Park, at the eastern end of Unter den Linden, whereas we're going to kill him here at the Viereck end, more than a mile away. That should make it easier for us to penetrate the protective cordon. But on the other hand, as a consequence of our plan to deliver our fictional letter, the stage manager has seen us and given a detailed description to von Hochenheimer. Also, we can no longer masquerade as *Junker*. That means that access to the King will be much harder. Also, the chance of being searched at a checkpoint and the guards finding our pistols has significantly increased."

"On balance, I think we're ahead," Franz said. "Or maybe we're just even. Let's revise our real plan to take into account that we'll be middle-class businessmen. How are we going to get our pistols past the protective cordon?"

"Let me think about that." Paul paused for a moment before continuing. "There's got to be a way. In any event, we have plenty of time; the parade isn't scheduled to take place for three weeks. By the way, there's a full-scale dress rehearsal two weeks from now. We'll certainly observe the dress rehearsal from Viereck."

CHAPTER TEN

"I think I've solved the pistol problem," Paul said.

It was nearly midnight, three days later. The two Austrian secret agents had spent every waking moment trying to come up with a way that they could each smuggle two loaded pistols to within shooting distance of King Frederick at the start of his birthday parade.

"I've heard those words about 50 times from you so far," Franz said, shaking his head. "And each suggestion, I'm sorry to say, has been as preposterous and unrealistic as the last. What's your new idea? Are we going to soar to the heavens in a hot air balloon and descend on Viereck at the right moment? Are elephants involved this time?"

"We're going to leave for Paris," said Paul, ignoring Franz's sarcasm. "At least that's what we want people to think. Here's the plan: We've been telling people that we're import/export merchants on our way to France. So, let's follow through on it. On the morning of the parade, we'll hire a porter to carry our trunk to that inn from where all the coaches leave. He'll carry the trunk from here to the inn. If we're stopped and searched at a checkpoint, nothing will be found, because we're going to add a false bottom to the trunk. Under the false bottom, we'll put the two pistol cases containing the loaded pistols. On top of the false bottom, we'll put a few items, not so many that they'll ask us to empty the trunk for searching, but enough to cover the false bottom thoroughly. Unless someone has tipped off the security forces, they won't even think of looking for a hidden compartment under the floor of the trunk.

"When we reach the inn and the porter puts the trunk on the ground, we pay him, thank him, dismiss him, and then open the trunk, retrieve the pistol cases, take out the loaded pistols, and rearrange the contents in such a way that it'll be easy to reach the pistols when the time comes. Then we close the trunk again.

"Finally, when the King's coach comes into sight and everyone starts cheering, we open the trunk. We grab the pistols. We rush forward as far as the protective cordon around the King permits. And then we shoot him."

When Paul was finished, Franz remained silent. But after a few minutes he said, "Let's go to a café and have a drink to celebrate."

Despite their elation, both men were careful to drink only one glass of schnapps each. They were only too aware that alcohol lubricates the tongue. Now that they had found the solution, they had to be sure that they did not inadvertently share it with the Prussian security forces.

"Your plan is brilliant," Franz said to Paul on the way home. "But I strongly suspect that you can improve it."

"Not tonight," replied Paul. "My brain is worn out. Maybe after some sleep."

***

In the morning, Paul suggested to Franz that the next step should be to take their trunk to an expert. Obviously they could not ask anyone how to hide four loaded pistols in the trunk, but perhaps they could get some advice without giving away the purpose of the hidden cavity. So they went to Frau Deitel and asked her to suggest someone who could repair the inside of their trunk. She told them to take the trunk to Fritz Apfelkern's workshop, located at the southern end of Charlottenstrasse.

They emptied the contents of their trunk onto the dining room table, taking the greatest care not to scratch its polished wooden surface. Together they carried the empty trunk to the workshop. As they entered the room, a tall, well-built man with graying hair greeted them. Thick lenses hid his eyes. Beneath a generous mouth, he had a neatly trimmed gray beard. "Can I help you?" he asked.

"We're traveling to France," replied Paul, "and in order to protect our valuable goods, we'd like a false bottom for our trunk. We need a compartment about this size." He handed over a piece of paper showing the dimensions of a cavity large enough for the two pistol cases.

Fritz laughed. "Don't you know that false bottoms are a dead giveaway? Everyone and his brother has a trunk with a false bottom. It's the first place any thief would look, especially a French thief. Also, every customs inspector today has a stick to measure the interior height of a trunk and compare it with the exterior height. If the difference is too large, the existence of the false bottom is obvious."

Franz and Paul looked at each other carefully, but before either one could reply Fritz continued.

"There's another thing. Your trunk isn't new. No matter how much I try to age the appearance of a false bottom, someone who's looking for a hiding place in your trunk will see that the false bottom looks different from the sides and the top. Your trunk is lined with thin wood. If you look here and here, you'll see water stains starting on the sides and extending to the bottom. If I were to put in a false bottom, the water stains would end abruptly at the level of the false bottom.

"So, gentlemen, I'd be delighted to take your money and put a false bottom in your trunk, but it won't do you any good. On the contrary, it would invite suspicion."

"Do have a better suggestion?" Franz asked.

"I thought you'd never ask." A broad grin lit up Fritz's whole face. "If this were my trunk, I'd strip the inside down to the pine box. After that, I'd cut out cavities in the sides at both ends. Each cavity will be about half the size shown in your drawing. Obviously, this will weaken the wooden box, so I'd screw in strengthening bars made of iron. I'd line the whole trunk with some old thin wood I've got, add a water stain and possibly an oil stain or a wine stain, and there you are. The trick is in the panels at the ends. If you press on two nails at the same time, the whole panel opens."

"How much would you charge for the job?" Paul asked.

Fritz named a fair price. It was clear that he had no idea that the two men in his workshop were anything but import/export merchants who wanted to bring valuable Prussian goods into France without being robbed. If he had suspected that the trunk was a key component of a plot to shoot the King of Prussia and he was an honest man, he would summon the police; if he were a rogue, he would charge them an arm and a leg for the job.

"Can you have the job finished in a week?" Franz asked. "We're in a hurry to leave for Paris."

"I can try. Some of the work is straightforward, but the glue from one step has to dry completely before I can start the next step. Here's what I suggest: Pay me half the cost now and come back in a week. I'll do my best to meet your deadline."

They shook hands and the Austrian secret agents left.

***

"There was one thing that I wanted to ask Fritz," Franz said when they had returned to their lodgings, "but I obviously didn't dare: What's the best way to get the pistols out of the side cavities quickly? We obviously have to store one case with two loaded pistols on the left side and the other case with two loaded pistols on the other side so that the trunk is balanced. But how are we going to get our hands on the pistols quickly when the King's coach arrives?"

"I think I have a solution to that, too. We wait until the porter has left. Then, if no one is staring directly into our trunk, we can rearrange the contents of the trunk so that there's a blanket covering everything else inside. We can then quickly open the two panels, take out the loaded pistols, place them on top of the blanket and close the trunk lid. When the coach arrives, we open the trunk, grab the pistols, and run toward the King."

A week later, they returned to the workshop.

"I'm glad you've come," said Fritz Apfelkern. "I've encountered a problem. I took out the lining, as we agreed, and look what I found—part of the pine frame is rotten. I can easily replace it and make it as good as new, but it's going to cost a few extra pfennigs. Not much, not much at all, but I didn't want to proceed without your permission."

As they left the workshop, having readily agreed to the minor additional charge, Franz said, "Confound it, his honesty has cost us a week. He's done nothing other than remove the lining."

"Don't worry, we don't have to have the trunk for the dress rehearsal. In fact, leaving Frau Deitel's place with our trunk to go to Paris and then returning with it later in the day might arouse some suspicion. Also, the porter might want to put our trunk directly onto the Paris coach, which wouldn't help matters. Not having the trunk for the dress rehearsal isn't going to be a problem."

"Unless he finds some other minor issue and does nothing for a second week," Franz said, rolling his eyes. "I did try to impress upon him that we have to leave for Paris in a week's time, and the trunk has to be ready by then. You'll no doubt recall that I also told him, as politely as I could, that we didn't mind paying a bit more if he encounters any other problem. But this man seems so thoroughly honest that I doubt if he'll do anything else at all without our explicit authorization."

"What are we going to do if the trunk isn't ready in time for the actual parade?" Paul asked.

"I hope it won't come to that, but we may need to take the trunk back from Fritz, no matter what its interior is like at that time, and take a chance that it won't be opened at a checkpoint on the way to Viereck, or by an officious policeman when we reach the square. We have no alternative. We're here on a mission, and I don't know when we'll have another chance as good as this to shoot Frederick."

CHAPTER ELEVEN

The day of the dress rehearsal dawned brightly. On their way to Viereck, they saw that the parade had drawn up on Mittelstrasse in preparation to march behind the King once he had reached the square. For obvious reasons, the King himself did not take part in the rehearsal—his substitute was a Hussar officer, Lieutenant Sigismund Hasenpfeffer. Hasenpfeffer had heard just one too many jokes about his unfortunate last name, and one evening he had lost his temper in the officers' mess. His colonel punished him by making him ride at the head of the parade, knowing that the passersby would make many snide comments at the expense of the Lieutenant.

When they reached the square, they were delighted to find that the protective cordon of police allowed them to come within 30 feet of where Lieutenant Hasenpfeffer's horse was waiting. Standing there in the square, both secret agents independently imagined themselves on the day of the actual parade, rushing forward from the footpath in front of the inn to the security cordon—a pistol in each hand—and blasting away at Frederick.

Then the coach arrived. A groom opened the door, put the stairs in place, and Hasenpfeffer appeared, resplendent in the full dress uniform of a Hussar officer. He alighted from the coach, walked down the red carpet to his horse, and mounted it. The rest of the parade had started to march from Mittelstrasse when the coach came into view. Hasenpfeffer waited on his horse for the parade to reach him. During this pause, the secret agents could easily have shot him, had they so wished. Soon the men of the leading regiment reached the square, and 30 seconds later, they were just behind the "King."

Lieutenant Hasenpfeffer now started moving forward at a slow pace. The spectators studiously refrained from cheering, because that would have been interpreted as an insult to their beloved King. However, fear of committing the crime of *lèse majesté* did not deter them from making snide jokes as the Lieutenant rode past. Judging from the expressions on certain women's faces, some of those jokes were ribald in the extreme. Notwithstanding his inability to hear the actual words that were said, the Lieutenant quickly realized that he was the butt of a torrent of risqué humor, and he blushed a bright red. This had the effect of intensifying the mocking. Now he could hear tittering as he passed.

Once the first ranks had gone by, Franz and Paul saw no point in hanging around Viereck any longer. On the contrary, they did not want a policeman to remember them when they returned for the parade itself. So they headed back to their lodgings as inconspicuously as possible.

Four days later, their trunk was ready as promised. Fritz Apfelkern smiled broadly as he showed off his handiwork. Detecting that the left and right sides of the inside of the trunk concealed cavities large enough for their pistols was nearly impossible. Fritz showed how—by pressing simultaneously the heads of two protruding nails—a panel opened and a cavity appeared. His workmanship was excellent, and the price that Fritz charged was more than reasonable.

They paid him, thanked him profusely, and carried their trunk back to Frau Deitel's house. There they played endlessly with their new toy, trying different ways to quickly remove the pistols from the cases that would be stored in the cavities. Finally, they were satisfied.

***

The weather on the day of the parade was most auspicious; not a cloud could be seen in the blue sky. The secret agents rose early, ate a hurried breakfast, carefully loaded their pistols and then Franz went outside to wait for the porter they had ordered.

The porter arrived slightly before the appointed time. Franz escorted him upstairs to take their trunk. The porter carried the trunk outside and placed it on his handcart, which he proceeded to wheel to the terminus of the Berlin–Paris coach. The two secret agents closely followed him.

As they reached Viereck, Franz nudged Paul and pointed. The cordon had been widened to the full width of the square. In fact, the porter was having difficulty finding room on the footpath to wheel his handcart. They both quickly realized that their assassination plan had been totally foiled—there was no way now that they could get close enough to King Frederick to shoot him.

Astonished and in a state of disbelief, they followed their porter to the inn. There they found that, because the cordon extended right to the footpath, there was no way for a coach to enter the square. A man standing outside the inn told them that the Paris coach was now leaving from Behrenstrasse.

The only thing they could do was to follow their porter as he walked the one block from Viereck to Behrenstrasse. They stood dumbly by as he and the coachman tied their trunk, loaded pistols and all, on top of the coach. They paid the porter and boarded the coach.

When the porter was out of sight, Franz got out and asked the coachman, "Do you stop at Potsdam?"

"Of course."

"Can we travel as far as Potsdam?"

"If there aren't enough passengers for the five-day ride to Paris then you certainly may."

Four hours later they arrived back in Potsdam. The coachman untied their trunk from the top of the coach, and they carried it back to the room they had left a month before.

They sat in silence for a few minutes. Then Franz turned to Paul, "What happened?"

"I don't know. Could it be that our deception was turned against us?

"Maybe. We don't know if von Hochenheimer received the letter, but the bribery notices in Potsdam (but not Berlin) are pretty conclusive evidence that he did. We stated in our fictional letter that three men masquerading as police would kill King Frederick at the Lustgarten end of Unter den Linden. If he believed us, then he widened the cordon to keep the police further from the King. In other words, our clever fictional letter rebounded on us."

"But that means that he believed the letter," said Paul. "However, if he believed the letter, he would've widened the cordon not at the Viereck end but rather at the Lustgarten end—

that was where the policemen were going to kill the King with the grenades."

"What if he smelled a rat? What if something in our fictional letter told him that we were trying to deceive him? Then he would do the opposite of the letter. In particular, he would strengthen the Viereck end, not the Lustgarten end."

"But if he didn't believe the letter, that would mean that the assassins wouldn't be three men masquerading as policemen. So there was no need to move the cordon back anywhere."

"So it seems that he believed us and also didn't believe us."

"That's the whole dilemma," Paul replied. "If he indeed received the letter, then he seems to have believed only those parts that he chose to believe. In fact, he may not have believed any of our letter. He may have read the fictional letter and decided to ignore it completely. The action that he took at the Viereck end may have been because one of his hundreds of spies had uncovered some other plot, real or fictional."

"I wish I'd never thought of this deception idea," Franz said. "It's caused us nothing but trouble. If I could turn the clock back, I would never have written that letter."

"It's too late for regrets," Paul said, "and recriminations are a waste of time. Here's the situation: We're in Prussia to kill King Frederick. At this time we have no plan, we're running somewhat low on money, but we probably have achieved one thing: We've established a communications route to von Hochenheimer.

"I fully realize that the hut is out of bounds to us," he went on, "but once we've come up with another plan, we can again send someone else to the hut on our behalf."

"It's been about a month since we paid Hoffmann to go there. Do you really think that the Prussians are still watching the hut?" Franz asked.

"If von Hochenheimer believed the letter, then I've no doubt that the hut is still under surveillance as a source of reliable information, which is so hard to come by. If von Hochenheimer thought that the letter was intended to deceive him, then the hut is equally certainly still being watched—false information that is known to be false is as valuable as reliable information."

"There's a third reason why the hut is probably being watched day and night. Our fictional letter said: 'Does this plan meet with your approval? If so, please send us another 1,000 reichsthaler via this route.' In other words, Max was going to reply via the hut and, if he approved our plan, he'd send the money that way, too. So, unless von Hochenheimer thought that our letter was fictitious through and through, his men would be waiting for the answer from Vienna. We both know that there'll never be an answer from Max. So the watchers are probably still in position, waiting for a courier from Austria. Yes, the hut is still available for further deception."

CHAPTER TWELVE

"It seems that the birthday parade went off without a single hitch," said Baron Manfred von Hochenheimer to his aide. "His majesty was most grateful. What we don't know is whether or not our extra precautions were needed. By the way, that suggestion of yours to put the letter on the table in the hut was brilliant. The latest report I've received is that the letter from the two *Junker* is still sitting there, untouched. So there's no way that that *Schweinehund* Max Hirsch could've given permission to the three secret agents disguised as policemen to kill our beloved King with hand grenades. The request for approval never reached him."

"With all due respect, Minister," replied von Kunersdorf, "there might have been more copies of that letter to Hirsch that were sent via other routes. In particular, another letter sent earlier might have been received in Vienna, and those three secret agents might have received a response that came via a different route."

"Yes, that's perfectly true, and that's why I acted on that letter. I moved the police cordon back along the entire route, just in case Hirsch had sent a reply ordering the attack by bogus policemen to be made elsewhere on Unter den Linden, particularly at Viereck, where King Frederick was most exposed and vulnerable.

"Also, I took your advice regarding bribery. I sent a communiqué to the commanders of every grenadier unit, ordering them to guard their grenades even more carefully than usual. And I ordered posters to be printed and affixed all over Potsdam."

"But why didn't you have them put up all over Prussia?" von Kunersdorf asked.

"That was a bad mistake," von Hochenheimer admitted. "At the very least, I should've plastered Berlin with them. I slipped up because the two *Junker* approached Hoffmann in Potsdam, even though the parade was to take place in Berlin. So I assumed, probably wrongly, that they operated only in the Potsdam area."

"Did you ever decide whether the letter was genuine or deliberately intended to confuse?"

"No, and I still don't know. So I did two things. One, I acted as if the letter was genuine, arranged for the posters to be printed, ordered all grenades to be meticulously guarded, and moved the cordon back along the entire route—just in case the three secret agents managed to get hold of police uniforms. And second, I also acted as if the letter was deliberately put into my hands to deceive me. I assumed that there would definitely be an attempt made on the King's life during the parade, but not necessarily by bogus policemen using hand grenades. So I tried to tighten up security even more than usual. In particular, I sent word to my spies to look out for the two *Junker*. That was the one thing I did believe, by the way. Hoffmann, the tavern keeper, and the old soldier were all so emphatic on that point. So far, no one seems to have sighted either of the two *Junker* anywhere. I've even had bankers interviewed to find out about *Junker* who are short of money. Unfortunately, that approach didn't lead anywhere, either. By the way, where's young Hoffmann now?"

"He's still in jail, Minister."

"Is he, now? Well, in the light of the successful outcome of this whole letter business, I'm going to interrogate him just one more time, in the hope that—after a month or so with nothing to do but think about what has happened—he may have recalled something that he couldn't remember before. Please make arrangements with Sergeant Winterfeldt. I want the interrogation to take place downstairs in Room One at nine. There's no need for you to be present; I'm not going to require a transcript. I'll make notes on the previous transcript if there are any changes or additions. If all goes well, I'll have him released after the interrogation. For his sake, I hope he's remembered why he forgot to buy food before he left Potsdam."

CHAPTER THIRTEEN

"I bumped into Kurt Kluge this afternoon in the street," Franz said to Paul. "You remember him, don't you? He's the Austrian secret agent who was always asking for more money at our meetings. Surely you remember him: tall, fair hair, deep blue eyes? I went with him to his lodgings to talk about old times and new developments."

"Are you crazy?" Paul asked. "How do you know that he wasn't the double agent who turned us in to the police?"

"Well, he'd seen me, so there wasn't much else I could do. In any event, if he is a double agent, he's a particularly rich double agent. He gave me 1,500 reichsthaler, almost all of it in the new five thaler gold pieces."

"Where did he get all that money, and why did he give it to you?"

"He told me," Franz replied, "that after the police raid on the Taverne zum Schwarzen Adler, our group in Brandenburg an der Havel fell apart. Fortunately the meeting ended much earlier than usual, so almost everyone escaped the police raid—everyone except you and me, that is. However, there was no way to communicate with me because I'd disappeared. Kurt felt that there was no point in hanging around Potsdam with no one to report to. He couldn't set up a group with any of his colleagues, because one of them was a double agent, maybe more than one, but there was no possible way he could tell friend from foe. So he decided to go back to Vienna. He couldn't take a coach in case the police were after him, so he walked from Potsdam to Dresden. It took him nearly a week to get to Dresden, traveling only at night and hiding by day. From there he used the last of his money to travel by coach to Vienna. He refused to tell me how he crossed the border from Prussia into

Saxony, but he did say that he'd never felt so relieved as when he was safely on Saxon soil.

"He also told me that Max was delighted to see him, but horrified to hear of the raid. Max provided Kurt with a new identity (but Kurt hasn't told me his new name) and then sent him to Potsdam to set up a network with newly trained secret agents that Max will send to Prussia in due course. And, most interesting of all, Max provided Kurt with the necessary funds."

"But why did Kurt give the money to you?" Paul asked.

"Max made it clear that I was supposed to lead the new group. Only if he couldn't find me was Kurt supposed to organize things. Finding me was probably a mixed blessing for money-loving Kurt. The fact that he handed over Max's money has convinced me that he isn't a double agent. Kurt is certain that Gerhard Schuster is the double agent. You remember Gerhard, don't you—the bald-headed man with a big reddish nose and big red ears? Kurt has no evidence to back up his claim—at least none that he was willing to share with me—so I don't know how seriously to treat his suspicions. Furthermore, there may have been more than one double agent. All in all, I'm happy to work with Kurt and any new secret agents that Max sends me, but that's it. I don't want to have any contact with any other members of our old group.

"By the way," Franz added, "I've arranged for the two of us to go to Kurt's place this evening. There's a lot to talk about."

Kurt's landlord was a lawyer who was just starting off in practice and needed the rent, so Kurt's lodging was located in a nice part of the city. That evening, Franz and Paul climbed the two flights of stairs to their colleague's large bedroom.

"There's something I don't quite follow," said Paul when the three of them were seated at a small table. "Why does Max want us to continue working here in Potsdam? A double agent undermined our previous group, so the security forces know about us. You, Kurt, have a new identity, but Franz and I still carry papers bearing the names that the police definitely have on file somewhere. Surely it would make more sense for us to work in Berlin, the capital of Prussia?"

"The answer is quite simple," replied Kurt. "Old Bach. Ever since Johan Sebastian Bach came to Sanssouci, Frederick has spent as much time as he could with him. Granted, Old Bach is the greatest composer who has ever lived, and Frederick is a music connoisseur of the highest order, but it seems to go beyond that, almost to a form of hero worship.

"For example, ever since Old Bach arrived, Frederick's orchestra has played nothing but Bach's music, day in and day out, with an occasional flute concerto by Frederick himself. Even that has stopped now—the King is so cowed by Bach's genius as a composer that Frederick no longer plays his own works. And look what happened on Frederick's birthday. The day began early with a choral mass in Frederick's chapel. Old Bach wrote the mass and directed it at the organ. Then Frederick raced to Berlin for the parade, arriving just in time. And the moment the parade was over, Frederick came straight back to Potsdam—the same day—so that he could celebrate his birthday with a special concert Old Bach conducted at the fortepiano."

Kurt went on, "I have to make it clear that Frederick isn't neglecting his affairs of state in any way. He meets regularly with his generals. He also meets with his ministers all the time, thereby ensuring that Prussia is being governed effectively and that people like us are under almost constant surveillance. But he's spending every spare moment with Bach here in Potsdam. So, if we're to kill him, we need to be based here in Potsdam because our target is currently based here. And it looks like he's going to be based here until Old Bach decides that it's time to go back to Leipzig."

On that note, the meeting broke up.

***

Franz and Paul returned to their room. Kurt hadn't volunteered his new name, and Franz hadn't mentioned where he and Paul were staying. Also, Max Hirsch had arranged a dead letter drop that new agents would use for communicating with Kurt when they first arrived in Potsdam. Even though Kurt had made it clear, by handing over that money, that he considered Franz to be their unchallenged leader, he nevertheless hadn't divulged the address of the dead letter drop. It wasn't that there was mistrust among the three Austrian secret agents—quite the opposite. All three knew that, because of the risk of arrest and torture, the less each of them knew about the others, the better.

"It seems to me that there are three approaches we can use," said Franz, opening a fresh discussion between him and Paul. "One, we can try to get inside Sanssouci and kill him in the palace. Two, we can waylay him outside the palace and kill him there. And three, we can persuade a third party to kill him. Penetrating Sanssouci is going to be hard. There are two perimeters. The outer perimeter, the boundary of Sanssouci Park, is patrolled at all hours of the day and night. And if we manage to get into the park, we then have to penetrate the inner perimeter, the boundary of Sanssouci Palace itself. Furthermore, there are armed guards inside the palace, as well. So it's not going to be easy to assassinate Frederick in his palace. The second alternative—attacking him outside the palace—is also hard," Franz continued. "As Kurt pointed out yesterday, the King doesn't leave the palace very often, and when he does, a large number of his soldiers guard him. We'd have to know when and to where he's traveling, and we'd need to know far enough in advance to be able to plan an ambush. When we do it, there'll be the three of us against perhaps a hundred guards of one kind or another, all trained to be constantly on the lookout for Austrian secret agents. Again, I think that the chances of success along that route are minimal. The third way—finding someone else to kill Frederick—means that we have to find someone in the palace who wants to kill Frederick and who has regular access to the King, and provide that person with a suitable weapon. If you think that the first two ways are hard, the third is all but impossible." Franz shook his head. "I suggest that we meet every day to exchange ideas. If we continually exchange ideas among the three of us, something will come up."

"What about Guy Fawkes?" Paul asked.

"Who?"

"Guy Fawkes, the English leader of the Gunpowder Plot. Around 1600, he and a group of fellow Catholics tried to blow up the English House of Lords. They rented a cellar under the building and filled it with dynamite. But one of the conspirators sent an anonymous letter to Lord Monteagle, a Catholic Peer, warning him to stay away from the House of Lords. Monteagle immediately showed the letter to the English authorities, and they found the gunpowder just before Guy Fawkes was going to light the slow fuse."

"So," asked Franz, "are you suggesting that we rent a cellar under Sanssouci Palace, fill it with dynamite, and blow up the palace and everyone in it? That sort of behavior is unlikely to win friends for Austria. Old Bach is considered the greatest composer of all time. Killing him would definitely not be a good thing to do."

"No, that's not what I'm suggesting," Paul said. "You suggested that one of the three ways of assassinating Frederick is to waylay him outside the palace. You correctly pointed out that he's heavily guarded when he leaves Sanssouci. But what if he has to leave the palace in a hurry, to save his life? What if a fictional letter is received that the cellars of Sanssouci are filled with dynamite and will explode any minute? Frederick will be rushed out of the palace with the greatest urgency, with only a few guards to protect him. Maybe we can kill him while he's fleeing the palace."

"Where would he flee?" Franz asked.

"Clearly, Berlin. Berlin is his capital, the Winter Palace is there, and I'm sure you haven't forgotten that it's situated in Lustgarten Park at the eastern end of Unter den Linden. So, if we can induce Frederick to rush from Sanssouci to Berlin because of an impending explosion, the three of us may be able to stop his coach on the road to Berlin and kill him."

"Go on."

"As I see it," Paul continued, "there are numerous problems with my plan. First, we have to find a way to alert the Prussian authorities that there's dynamite in the cellars of the palace. Second, once they receive the letter, they'll search the cellars. We'll have to find a way to convince the palace guards that there is indeed gunpowder in the cellars. Third, we need to know when the alarm is sounded for Frederick to flee to Berlin. Fourth, we need a way to stop his coach to be able to shoot him."

"I agree," Franz said. "It's not an easy plan to carry out. The only easy part is the first issue: Telling the Prussians that there's dynamite in the palace cellars. We can use the hut in the forest for that. But the real problem is that the Palace of Sanssouci has no cellars."

"What?"

"No, there are no cellars. The King made it very clear to his architect that he wanted an 'intimate palace,' a ground-level building built directly on *terra firma*, with almost no steps. He likes the idea of going directly from the palace to the terrace and from the terrace directly to the garden. He wants to be close to nature."

"But there have to be cellars," Paul insisted. "Where does he store his wine? And surely the kitchen needs to have a place to store provisions of all kinds? Who ever heard of a large house without a cellar, let alone a palace without one?"

"Well, there's a wine cellar and there are underground storage rooms next to it, but they're in the East Wing, not under the palace itself. Threatening to blow up the cellars is unlikely to scare Frederick into fleeing to Berlin. The relevant area of the East Wing would be thoroughly searched, nothing would be found, and that would be that."

"Is there some other way we can induce Frederick to flee his palace?" Paul asked. "Fire, perhaps?"

"If we arrange to have a message left at the hut in the forest stating that there's going to be a fire at Sanssouci, all that will happen is that additional guards will be put into each room to keep an eye out for arson attempts. No, that's not going to work either."

"So we go back to Vienna?"

"Yes. I mean no. Definitely no," Franz said. "I've had an idea."

"Yes? What is it?" Paul asked.

"The reason we can't kill Frederick is because the security is too tight."

"I agree."

"So why don't we do something about the palace security, first, and then kill Frederick?"

"What exactly are you suggesting?"

"Who's been causing us all these problems? Not King Frederick. I'm sure it wasn't Frederick who moved the cordon at Viereck back to the edge of the large parade ground. It was von Hochenheimer. And the raid on the Taverne zum Schwarzen Adler —that was von Hochenheimer, once more. As for the double agents, Frederick invented the idea, but von Hochenheimer is carrying it out. So," Franz continued, "first, we kill von Hochenheimer. There's no way his successor will be able to initially impose the same high level of security. In fact, I would imagine that everything will be somewhat chaotic for a number of weeks until things settle down. Once von Hochenheimer is dead, we'll move against Frederick."

"But surely the police force will still be in place after we've finished off von Hochenheimer," Paul said, raising an eyebrow. "After all, the police on the streets report to their superior officers, and their superior officers report to the next level of superior officers, and so on. It's not as if every policeman reports personally to von Hochenheimer."

"True, but the Minister is running the show. He's setting policy; his underlings are carrying it out. Also, once we've killed him, everyone is going to be focused on finding the killers, which will reduce the guard on the King. In fact, that's an even stronger reason for killing von Hochenheimer—not only will security at the palace decrease, but the main focus of the huge police apparatus will change."

"But won't Frederick insist that the primary duty of whoever he appoints as von Hochenheimer's successor will be to keep the King safe?" Paul asked.

"No. Frederick is intensely loyal to those who're loyal to him. He'll leave no stone unturned finding the killers. He'll charge von Hochenheimer's successor with avenging von Hochenheimer, not with defending the King with the same zeal."

"And there's something you may have overlooked," Paul added. "What about the informers?"

"The informers?"

"Yes. Prussia is overflowing with informers, far too many of them Austrian double agents. They report to their spymasters, who presumably report to von Hochenheimer. With von Hochenheimer dead, at the very least the efficiency of the spy networks will be impaired. Hopefully, the entire apparatus will be paralyzed by the assassination of von Hochenheimer."

"The first thing we need to find out is where von Hochenheimer lives," Franz said.

"Surely he has two homes, one here in Potsdam for when the King is living in Sanssouci Palace, and one in Berlin when Frederick occupies the Stadtschloss?" Paul suggested.

"Plus a huge home, probably a castle, on his country estate, and a hunting lodge or three, as well, I assume," Franz added. "But remember what Kurt told us. Frederick is spending every available moment with Old Bach here in Potsdam, so I think we can safely concentrate on the home here."

"How do you propose we find out where he lives?" Paul asked.

"Well, the fanciest street in Potsdam is Hohewegstrasse[2]. It's lined with palatial homes. All we have to do is find out which one is von Hochenheimer's."

"And how would you do that?"

"Suppose you put on your stevedore clothes. I'm sure you can find an empty crate in the docks that looks impressive. Go to a food shop near to Hohewegstrasse and say you have a delivery for Baron von Hochenheimer. See if they know where he lives."

Paul sprung into action. Dressed once more as a stevedore, he made for the nearest canal warehouse. There he found an empty wooden crate of just the right size that had been abandoned in a corner. Pretending to stagger under a heavy load, Paul walked into

---

[2] Now Friedrich-Ebert-Strasse.

a butcher's shop near Charlottenstrasse. He walked up to the counter and asked the butcher where he could find the home of His Excellency, Baron von Hochenheimer.

"Get out!" the shop owner screamed. He raised his cleaver above his head. "And don't you ever dare to come into my shop again."

A scared Paul left the shop hurriedly, almost forgetting to pretend that the empty case was filled with horseshoes and lead bars. Two houses down, he found a bakery. Through the open door, he could see a sweet, little old lady behind the counter, smiling at a customer and her daughter. There were no meat cleavers in sight, so Paul tottered into the shop under the "weight" of the crate.

"Excuse me," said Paul, in his most polite voice, "I have to deliver this crate to the home of Baron von Hochenheimer. I understand it's not too far from here. Do you know where it is?"

The woman burst into tears. "Please don't ask me that," she said, covering her face with her apron.

Paul had no choice but to carry the crate all the way back to the room he shared with Franz.

The two of them pondered the strange reactions of the butcher and baker for a long while. Finally, Franz worked it out. "The Baron has put the fear of God into the good citizens of Potsdam. Everyone who needs to know where he lives in order to deliver food or drink has been instructed not to breathe a word of the address. Von Hochenheimer never makes idle threats. His minions have spelled out to the butcher and the baker precisely what will happen to them—and probably to their families, too—if they disclose the address. And von Hochenheimer's terrorization campaign is clearly working."

"So how can we find out where he lives in Potsdam?" asked Paul. "He must travel from Sanssouci Palace to his residence and back, but we dare not follow his coach—that would give the game away at once. Any other ideas?"

"Where do you think he lives?"

"Earlier this morning, I suggested that Hohewegstrasse is the most likely location. If you're right about the strict rule of total silence that the Baron has imposed, then the baker and the butcher know where he lives. That means that his home is near to their shops.

"I'd like to use some of your money," Paul continued, "to buy a footman's outfit—some footman who was summarily dismissed may have left wearing his uniform, which he then pawned. Some grandes dames have designed their own distinctive uniforms for their footmen, but provided I buy a generic outfit, I should be able to pass as the footman of some respectable household."

"No, you wouldn't," Franz said. "You're built like a stevedore. Haven't you noticed that footmen are tall and thin? Rich women choose footmen on the basis of their good looks, especially well-turned legs, which is why footmen are traditionally attired in stockings worn below knee breeches—it shows off their shapely calves to best advantage. After all, footmen don't actually do much; they're mostly just there for show. So, Paul, with all due respect, there's no way you could pass for a footman. By all means, go out and buy a second-hand footman's outfit if you can find one, but I'll have to be the one who wears it."

"Fine with me," Paul responded. "But you're also not tall enough to be a convincing footman. And even your mother is unlikely to describe you as handsome."

"I see your point. It looks like we're going to have to involve Kurt Kluge in this after all. He's tall and quite good-looking. In fact, I'm sure he could pass as a footman. One of us will buy the uniform for him, and then ask him to deliver the parcel for us. My idea is that he'll go from mansion to mansion, bearing a parcel of some kind, and ring the bell. He'll hand over the parcel while saying, 'For His Excellency the Baron von Hochenheimer.' If it's not his house, it'll just seem that the footman got the address wrong. It certainly won't look like he's asking where von Hochenheimer lives. So, at best, whoever answers the door will send Kurt to the correct house. At worst, they'll just say, 'Sorry, wrong house,' and no harm will be done."

"Does a footman with a parcel go to the front door or the back door?"

"I've no idea," replied Franz. "But, at the first house he comes to, they'll certainly put him right if he uses the wrong door. Servants are the biggest snobs imaginable, so whoever answers that first door will implicitly answer your question."

"That's reasonable," Paul said. "Now, what parcel is Kurt going to deliver? And there's got to be a note of some kind. How will we handle that? For example, suppose Kurt goes round with my empty crate, which, if I recall correctly, bears no markings at all. He'll eventually deliver it to the residence of the Minister of Police. When the crate is opened and found to be empty inside and unmarked outside, von Hochenheimer's servants are sure to report the incident to him. That will trigger a full-scale investigation, which is the very last thing we want. So what are we going to give the Baron?" Paul paused. "Wait! I know. His umbrella."

"What?" Franz asked.

"When the door opens, Kurt will say, 'My master has asked me to return his umbrella to His Excellency the Baron von Hochenheimer.' All we have to do is buy a nice, black, men's umbrella when we buy the footman's outfit. People leave their umbrellas behind all the time, especially at this time of the year, when the weather seems to change every few minutes. Having one's umbrella returned by the footman of some kind host is a natural sort of event."

"What if the person opening the door denies that the umbrella in question belongs to von Hochenheimer?" Franz asked. "For example, his umbrellas may all bear the family crest on the handle, or something."

"Then Kurt just apologizes and says that the umbrella must belong to someone else. There's no way that returning a mislaid umbrella to the wrong owner will trigger any sort of negative reaction, let alone a full-scale inquiry."

"Fine, but what if they accept the umbrella, but someone in the house—perhaps von Hochenheimer himself—realizes that the umbrella doesn't actually belong to him?"

"I really don't see a problem there. Being given someone else's umbrella is hardly likely to set alarm-bells ringing," Paul insisted.

Yet again, a pawnshop proved to be the source of their needed materials. Franz purchased a footman's uniform that looked like it would fit Kurt, and the pawnbroker had for sale a wide variety of black umbrellas in good condition.

***

The next step was to contact Kurt and explain the task allotted to him.

When they found him at his lodgings, Kurt put on the footman's uniform, which fit him reasonably well.

Franz was careful to tell Kurt as little as possible, for obvious reasons. "All we want from you is the address of von Hochenheimer. That's all. Start at the corner of Hohewegstrasse and Charlottenstrasse, and then go from house to house until you reach Kurfürstenstrasse. Then cross over and work your way down the other side of the street. As soon as you encounter a person who opens the door and accepts the umbrella, your job is done. Leave right now, and I'll contact you later."

"I understand," Kurt said. "Oh, by the way, do I ring at the front door or the back door?"

"We don't know either," Franz said, "but you'll certainly find out at the first house you come to."

***

Kurt left the lawyer's house in the footman's uniform, hoping that his landlord wouldn't see him. Carrying the umbrella carefully, he walked swiftly to Hohewegstrasse. At the house on the corner of Charlottenstrasse, he climbed the stairs and knocked twice on the door with the ornate doorknocker. A resplendent footman in gaudy livery opened the door. The plethora of gold braid and intricate white lace dazzled Kurt.

"Yes?" said the footman, in a tone of voice that made it unambiguously clear that he wanted Kurt to know that his master was far richer than Kurt's.

"My master asked me to return his umbrella to His Excellency the Baron von Hochenheimer."

"Idiot, it's three houses up." He slammed the door.

Skipping the second and the third mansions, Kurt pulled the bell next to the front door of the fourth mansion on the block. The rope was embedded in an ornate gray and white Silesian marble pillar to the right of the entrance portal; eight marble pillars supported the balcony over the front door. The base of the two-story building was square, with a huge, glass-encased, pretentious cupola on the flat roof, accessible via a staircase on each side. The walls of the mansion were constructed out of red brick.

Through the partially opened door, Kurt could see an entrance hall that would not have been out of place in a royal palace, but the man who opened the door was dressed in a simple black jacket and knee breeches, white shirt, black cravat and black stockings. He seemed to Kurt to be a secret policeman guarding the Minister, rather than a footman in an opulent dwelling.

"Yes?" asked the man at the door.

"My master asked me to return his umbrella to His Excellency the Baron von Hochenheimer."

"Thank you. And who is your master?"

Thinking quickly, Kurt replied, "My master said that the Baron would undoubtedly recall where he left his umbrella."

The secret policeman naturally assumed that there was a good reason for discretion, so he nodded and closed the door.

***

That evening, Franz came to visit Kurt. "Did you find the house?" he asked. "What's the address?"

"I found it, but it doesn't have an address."

"How can that be?"

"The Baron has cleverly renumbered all the houses on the block where his mansion stands, omitting his house. So, as I said, it doesn't have an address. I can tell you that it's the fourth house on the block, I can describe the palatial architecture, and I can tell you about the garden—or at least, the portion of the garden visible from the street. But I cannot give you the address."

"How clever. A mansion that doesn't exist because it has no number."

"By the way," Kurt added, "the man who opened the front door looked to me more like a secret policeman than a footman. I just thought you'd want to know."

"Thank you," said Franz, and left.

***

The next morning, Franz and Paul strolled past von Hochenheimer's mansion. Both were dressed in their import/export merchant clothes. They appeared to be deep in conversation, but they were actually closely observing the house and the surroundings.

"Look at the huge oak tree to the left of the mansion," muttered Franz. "It reminds me of the tree near the hut where we hid. It seems like an excellent place from which to shoot the Baron."

An elegantly dressed woman, accompanied by her maid, walked toward them. Paul kept quiet. When the two women were safely out of earshot, Paul responded, "Look carefully at the white house diagonally across from the one belonging to the Baron. In fact, let's walk to the end of the block, cross the road and walk back past that house."

"No," Franz insisted. "If there are any guards watching us from the cupola on top of the mansion, we might excite suspicion. Let's walk two or three blocks away before we come back."

They continued up the tree-lined street. "When we walk back, take a careful look at the house I pointed out to you. It seems to me that they are doing major building alterations to the first-floor rooms, but the bedrooms on the second floor are apparently untouched, as are the servants' rooms in the attic. See if you agree."

The two "import/export merchants" strolled back on the other side of the street in the direction of the house diagonally across the road from von Hochenheimer's mansion. They studied the white house with sideways glances, and once past, they continued to walk at the same slow pace until they were again out of sight of the Minister of Police's mansion. Then they walked swiftly back to their room.

"What's so important about the white stucco house?" Franz asked.

"Suppose we break into the house after midnight. It'll be easy to get in. Did you see how many first-floor windows have been removed? There'll be a watchman, of course, but he'll surely be asleep or drunk at that time. We'll take with us three days' worth of food and water. When we arrive, we'll sneak up the stairs and hide in an attic room that overlooks the mansion belonging to the Baron. The white house is obviously unoccupied," Paul continued. "No one could possibly live there while such major alterations are in progress. So, the only danger is the possibility of the night watchman detecting us when we arrive or when we leave. The attic rooms are servants' rooms, so they must have beds. For three days, one of us will sleep and the other will watch. That will give us some idea of the routine in von Hochenheimer's mansion."

Midnight found the two Austrian secret agents sneaking through the streets of Potsdam. They were wearing their merchant clothes so that—if they were stopped—they could reasonably claim that they were on their way home from a dinner party. However, it would have been hard for them to explain why they were carrying so much food and water. Luckily for them, they were able to reach the white stucco house without being challenged by policemen or soldiers.

Now, there were other dangers in the form of the night watchman protecting the white house and the guards patrolling the Minister's mansion, possibly observing the street from the glass cupola. The two secret agents walked as confidently as they could toward the entrance of the white house—only to find the gates to the semicircular drive shut. Franz motioned that they should walk into the garden of the house next door. From there, they were able —with some difficulty—to climb to the top of the wall that separated the two properties; fortunately for them, the wall was not topped with pieces of broken glass.

Now came the problem of climbing down from the wall into the garden of the white stucco house without alerting the night watchman. First, they lowered their provisions as silently as they could, but they had to drop their packages the last three feet or so, which produced a noise. Holding their breaths, they paused on the top of the wall. The thuds did not seem to alert the night watchman. Hidden by the canopy of a large tree, both men waited for another two or three minutes before dropping to the ground as quietly as they could.

As Franz neared the central part of the house, he stepped on a dry twig. It snapped, waking the night watchman's dog. From a window, Franz could see that the barking awoke the watchman in the kitchen. The guard whacked the dog on the head, and went back to sleep. In the process, he knocked over a nearby empty glass bottle of raw schnapps. It rolled along the irregular stone floor of the kitchen, making far more noise than the two Austrians had done. Franz and Paul noiselessly opened the back door, walked along the corridor past the kitchen, located a staircase, and went up two flights of stairs.

They found themselves at the attic level. Choosing a room at random, they opened the door. The small room had an iron bed, a wardrobe, a chair and—most important—a window overlooking the square red mansion across the street.

Franz decided to watch first while Paul slept. The uncomfortable chair he pulled to the window would undoubtedly keep him awake, he told his friend, who was already fast asleep.

Franz noticed that guards checked the area around the Baron's house at irregular intervals, roughly once an hour. He carefully logged the times that he saw guards patrolling. Nothing happened until daybreak.

As the sun rose, the mansion seemed to wake, too. Curtains and windows opened. Two gardeners arrived. One worked a flowerbed at the front of the house while the other toiled away at the side hedges. Franz had been up for nearly 24 hours, so he woke Paul and used the log that he had kept to explain what little had happened while Paul was sleeping.

"Now that the sun is shining, you may be able to see into the cupola," he said. "The glass was like a black screen during the night. We need to know if they use the cupola for observational purposes. Fortunately, both cupola staircases are in plain view, so if von Hochenheimer has posted observers up there, we'll be able to see the changing of the guard." Franz threw himself on the bed. "Wake me if anything interesting happens."

***

More workmen arrived at the white stucco house. A foreman unlocked the gates, and craftsmen and laborers trickled in. After a while, Paul could hear someone using a sledgehammer on the first floor. He looked at Franz, asleep on the bed, but it was obvious that the noise—loud though it was—could not penetrate his exhaustion.

At about nine, a large black coach pulled by four powerful brown horses drew up at the front door of von Hochenheimer's mansion. A few minutes later, four hussars rode up, armed with pistols and sabers. Two of the light cavalrymen positioned themselves in front of the leading pair of horses, while the other two waited at the rear of the coach. Nearly half an hour later, the front door opened. The top of the coach obscured the lower half of the front door and the front steps, so Paul could not see everything in detail. Nevertheless, he saw a tall, thin man wearing a black hat and cloak leave the house and enter the coach. The coachman immediately whipped the horses and the armed guards escorted it down the street.

During the day, almost nothing happened. Deliverymen brought food to the back door, and patrols continued at irregular intervals.

***

After the gardeners resumed work following their lengthy lunch break, Paul woke Franz.

"What's been happening?"

"Very little. Someone left the house this morning in a coach with a hussar escort—it must have been von Hochenheimer himself. Other than that, it's been extremely quiet. Two gardeners arrived, but no one else. The guards must live on the premises. It's a huge building with only one permanent occupant, so there must be plenty of room for the guards to live in the mansion. I suppose that every so often they change the guards, and a new batch moves in."

Franz got up and walked to the window.

"Oh," Paul continued, "the cupola seems to be empty. It's impossible to see the grounds from there. The roof of the building blocks the view. So, an observer in the cupola could see us in the attic if we were incautious enough to light a candle, but other than that, the sightlines from the cupola are pretty useless. It must have been built for decoration."

"Or perhaps for romantic purposes," suggested Franz. "The view from there by moonlight is probably rather lovely."

"It's probably no better than the view from this window by moonlight," Paul said. "Anyhow, romance is the last thing on von Hochenheimer's mind."

Not much happened throughout the afternoon and evening. Then, at about eleven, the coach returned. By coincidence, both men were awake at that time, and they crowded the small window to observe what was happening. As before, the coach partially blocked their view of the front door, but they were able to see a tall man in a black cloak and hat emerge from the coach and stride up the stairs. The door was opened from the inside as he approached it, and was then firmly closed again.

"Where are the hussars?" asked Franz. "This makes no sense. Why should he be protected when he travels from home to work during the day, but at night—when the danger is greatest—there are no escorts?"

"I've no idea. Maybe he left earlier or later than usual. Or maybe there was a breakdown in communications, and the hussars weren't at the right place at the right time."

Franz looked at him quizzically. "This is Prussia, Paul, home of *Zucht, Ordnung, und Pflicht* (discipline, order, and duty.) Prussians don't leave earlier or later than usual, and they don't allow for even the possibility of a breakdown in communication. If there was no hussar escort this evening, that was because there wasn't supposed to be a hussar escort this evening. And so, I repeat my previous question: Why not?"

"I have no idea. Let's see what happens tomorrow night."

***

The pattern on the second day seemed to be identical to the first: guards patrolled at irregular intervals, gardeners worked the bushes, the coach left with four hussars, and people delivered food. As on the previous night, the coach arrived around eleven. This time, two figures walked into the entrance hall. The man in the black hat and cloak entered first. A young woman wrapped in a dark cloak, her fair hair uncovered, followed him into the mansion. Paul and Franz continued to watch. After a few minutes, two figures appeared on the roof and entered the cupola via the staircase on the left. The man had his arm draped over the shoulders of the woman. She had removed her cloak. From her appearance, there could be no doubt that she was a streetwalker.

"Well, well, well," said Paul, "you were right. The cupola is for romantic purposes after all. And that also explains why there are no hussars at night. The Baron clearly wants as few people as possible to see whom he brings home at night. There's probably one trusted servant in the entrance hall, and that's it."

"Which means," interrupted Franz, "that von Hochenheimer's arrival at night is the best time to shoot him. In order to keep his habits as secret as possible, he's essentially unguarded when his coach arrives. That's the time we need to assassinate him."

"How do you suggest we do that?"

"The only possible place where we can hide and kill him is that oak tree to the left of the entrance, the one I pointed out to you before when we walked past the mansion—although, the tree is too far from the mansion to shoot a pistol with any hope of hitting the Baron. We'll need to climb the tree with muskets," Paul said. "We'll be hidden in the foliage, and it'll be night, so the patrolling guards are unlikely to spot us."

"After we kill him, how do we get away?"

"That's certainly going to be a problem. Guards will pour out of the mansion when they hear the shots from the two muskets, and the streets of Potsdam are always under surveillance, obviously."

"That's not the real problem, of course," Paul said.

"What's the 'real problem?'"

"Getting two muskets, together with the black powder, the lead shot, and the cloth patch to load them. How do you propose to get those?"

"Easy," replied Franz. "Musketeers carry muskets with all the accessories."

Paul looked at him in total disbelief. "And you're going to walk up to two musketeers and ask them if you can kindly borrow their muskets with all the accouterments needed to shoot their Minister of Police?" he asked.

"Not exactly," Franz said. "You and I are going to find two musketeers patrolling in an isolated area just outside Potsdam, and we're going to ask them if we can kindly borrow their uniforms, muskets and everything else."

"And why should the two musketeers agree to lend us their uniforms, muskets and everything else?"

"It's going to be hard for them to refuse," said Franz, "after we shoot them through the head with our pistols."

"What?"

"Yes, it's the only way we can get what we need. We'll ambush two musketeers, shoot them carefully so that there's no blood on their shakos or anywhere else, and then take their uniforms and equipment."

"And what about our clothes?" Paul asked. "If we leave them there, we could be identified."

"That's not a problem either. We'll empty their knapsacks of everything we don't need and put our clothes inside. Toward evening, we'll march into Potsdam. If stopped, we'll have the papers belonging to the soldiers, so that won't pose a problem. Then we'll march over to the mansion. If we're early, we'll pretend to guard it for a while with our loaded muskets, and at half-past ten, we'll climb the tree. When von Hochenheimer arrives, we'll have only a second or two to shoot him, but that should be long enough. We'll take aim as the coach slows to a halt and fire as he gets out of the carriage. Then we'll jump down the tree shouting 'After him!' and 'Catch that murderous villain!' while pursuing a nonexistent assassin through the streets of Potsdam. As soon as we can, we'll ditch the rifles and uniforms, put on our own clothes, and make a dash for the border. A few days later, we'll return and kill Frederick."

"You make it sound so easy. Don't you think—"

Two figures had just appeared on the roof of the building across the road. Walking down the stairs by which they had reached the cupola earlier, they re-entered the mansion. A few minutes later, the front door opened and the fair-headed young woman left, once more wrapped in her dark cloak.

"Should one of us follow her?" Paul asked.

"Why would we want to do that? She can't give us any information that will help us kill von Hochenheimer, and, if we confront her, she may give us away to the Baron. No, for her sake, let's just hope that she's not there when we kill her patron. Muskets are not that accurate, and there's a good chance that one of us may hit the wrong person by mistake."

"You're quite right. Shouldn't we try and get our hands on two hunting rifles instead of muskets? Hunting rifles have a rifled bore and good sights."

"Yes, but their owners tend to be landowners. We may be able to waylay two musketeers, but successfully disarming even one hunter is going to be a problem. Also, finding two musketeers semi-naked in a field with bullets in their brains isn't going to cause the new Minister of Police to set up a manhunt, but the body of a dead *Junker* would undeniably result in big problems for us. Furthermore, *Junker* generally don't go hunting alone; huntsmen as well as fellow *Junker* accompany them, and they could cause lots of other difficulties for us. I agree with you that using hunting rifles would greatly increase our chances of successfully shooting von Hochenheimer, but procuring that kind of weapon is probably beyond us."

"Couldn't we break into a hunting lodge and steal two hunting rifles?" Paul asked.

"In theory, that's a good idea. In practice, we'd have to find a hunting lodge in which *Junker* leave their weapons. I would think that most people would keep their weapons at home and take them to their hunting lodge only when going hunting. Also, how do you propose to bring two stolen hunting rifles into Potsdam? My plan has the advantage that we'll be dressed as musketeers, and musketeers all carry muskets."

"Agreed," said Paul. "Let's go with your plan. Do we wait here for another 24 hours, or do we go after the muskets?"

"While we're safely here, let's spend another day observing, just to be safe. Who knows what we'll uncover?"

***

The routine on the third day was similar to that of the first two. The only difference was that von Hochenheimer had brought home a young woman with dark brown hair instead. Once the woman had left in the early hours of the morning, Franz and Paul cleaned up their attic room. They stole down the stairs on tiptoe and walked toward the back door. As they passed the kitchen, they saw that the night watchman and his dog were sound asleep. They noiselessly opened the back door, crept out into the night and dumped the remnants of their supplies in a pile of builders' rubble.

They had seen the foreman lock the gate to the street when he and his crew had left that afternoon, so they climbed the same wall as before. On their way back to their room, two secret policemen stopped them. Their papers were in order, but they were asked why they were on the streets so late. Franz trotted out their previous excuse, that is, that they were on their way back home from a dinner party. That satisfied the secret police, who permitted Paul and Franz to continue on their way.

CHAPTER FOURTEEN

"Our next challenge," said Franz, "is acquiring two musketeers' uniforms, their muskets, and everything we need to load and fire those muskets. We're going to have to choose a fine day for the expedition, because moisture prevents a flintlock musket from firing. I know that the Royal Prussian Army has tried putting a leather cover over the firing mechanism, but that doesn't work most of the time. So, if tomorrow is rainy, there's no point in looking for a pair of musketeers to kill. We've got to shoot Frederick before the bodies of the musketeers are found."

"Why? I thought we agreed that the killing of two musketeers isn't going to trigger a major manhunt."

"It won't," Franz said, "but we're going to be using the military identity papers of those musketeers. When they find the bodies of two musketeers stripped of their uniforms and muskets, they'll quickly find out the names of the men we've shot. The authorities will easily guess that the killers—that is, you and me—will be wearing those uniforms and utilizing the musketeers' military identity papers. The authorities will circulate the names of the two dead musketeers all over Prussia. If they find us in musketeer uniforms with those papers, we're finished. That means that we have to choose fine weather for the assassination, kill the soldiers during the day, and be in the oak tree that night in time for von Hochenheimer's arrival home."

"That doesn't sound too hard," said Paul, nodding. "We go north or west of Potsdam, leaving the walled city through the Hunters Gate. We look for a pair of musketeers in the fields beyond Potsdam. Then we come back the same way, wearing their uniforms. That stratagem will probably work, because we can avoid the closely guarded bridges across the Havel."

"It may take more than one day to carry this out," Franz said. "What if we don't find any musketeers in the area, or if there are more than two in a group? On the other hand, if we walk through the Hunters Gate day after day, the secret police are going to get very suspicious."

"Do you want to try a different gate each time?" Paul asked.

"That might be a solution."

"Let's meet that problem when we come to it."

The next day turned out to be clear. Even though it was still early, the sun was already radiating heat, and only a hint of moisture hung in the air. To Franz and Paul, the day appeared perfect for killing the Minister of Police with stolen flintlock muskets.

They left their room early, dressed as import/export merchants, and made their way to the north gate of the city, each with two loaded pistols. Paul had his compass in his pocket, as well as the map of Prussia that Max had given him.

The identity check at the Hunters Gate was cursory. The policeman on duty hardly glanced at their papers, let alone at the lumps in their pockets. They soon reached farmland and looked around for a place to ambush two soldiers.

"We need to kill them where we won't be seen," Franz said. "I think we need to find a forest or, at the very least, a large stretch of woodland. We can march them at gunpoint into the trees, and kill them there. That will have two advantages. First, the trees may at least partially reduce the sound of our pistols firing. Second—as you know—the desertion rate is extremely high, even though they hang deserters. So, if we kill them in a secluded wooded place, they may assume that the soldiers just ran away."

"And if they do find the bodies," Paul said, "we'll make sure that nothing will identify them as soldiers. For example, we can use their bayonets to cut off their pigtails."

"Now that's good thinking. Even better, let's see if we can bury the bodies."

"No," Paul said. "Two freshly dug graves in a forest will invite suspicion. If we strip them and leave them there, it'll look as if they were waylaid by highwaymen."

***

After walking past a few farms, Franz and Paul found themselves on a wide path next to a small forest.

"This seems like a good place to catch soldiers," said Paul. "Let's sit by the side of the road and see what happens."

After about half an hour, they spied two musketeers on patrol walking toward them. Paul took one look and said, "Leave them alone."

"What? Why?"

"Just do it!"

The soldiers approached the two men and asked for their papers. Paul and Franz handed them to the first soldier, while the other kept them covered with his musket. The first soldier handed back the papers, and the two soldiers moved on.

"Why did you insist that we let those soldiers pass?" Franz asked, when they were well out of earshot. "Are you so sure that there'll be another pair later today whom you'd prefer to kill?"

Paul looked at Franz sideways. "Did you look at those soldiers? Both were thin. There was no way I could've fit into either uniform."

Franz had the good grace to apologize. Then he added, "By the way, did you notice anything about those soldiers, at least the one who examined our papers?"

"Nothing special. Why?"

"Well, the one who examined our papers must be illiterate. My papers were upside down and he didn't turn them round. All they do is check that people are carrying a piece of paper, which they pretend to read."

As he spoke, another pair of soldiers approached them from the other side. Size wise, they were both a reasonable match for the Austrian secret agents. Franz nodded to Paul. As they had planned, when the soldiers asked for their papers, Franz handed his papers to one soldier, Paul to the other. Now neither soldier could cover them with a musket—their weapons remained behind their backs, held vertically upward by the musket slings over the soldiers' left shoulders. As both soldiers reached for the papers presented to them, Paul and Franz drew their pistols and held them to the soldiers' heads.

Unasked, the two soldiers put their hands in the air and explained how little money they had. The secret agents moved behind the soldiers and placed their pistols at the back of the musketeers' heads.

"Walk slowly into the forest," Franz ordered.

As they reached the first trees, the secret agents deftly removed the muskets from the soldiers' shoulders and let them fall into the undergrowth, where they were hidden from view—just in case the first set of soldiers came back. The two musketeers struggled a bit, undoubtedly realizing that this wasn't a common robbery. Franz told them to shut up. When they were well inside the trees, Franz nodded to Paul. They knocked the shakos off the heads of the musketeers, and then squeezed their triggers at almost the same moment.

The two secret agents undressed the bodies, taking great care not to get any blood on the uniforms. Then they took off their import/export merchant clothes and dressed themselves as musketeers. The two uniforms fit quite well, other than one shako. The bigger musketeer's head had been slightly larger than Paul's, but he used paper found in one of the knapsacks to line the band.

"It's too early to go back to Potsdam," Franz said. "Let's retrieve the muskets and take it easy here until the late afternoon. We can eat the soldiers' food."

When they went back to fetch the muskets, they realized both were unloaded.

"A fine pair of soldiers we just killed," Paul remarked. "What use is it to go on patrol with an unloaded weapon?"

"I think we should load the muskets now," Franz suggested, "just in case we need to use them against the two soldiers we saw before."

A flintlock firearm has a piece of flint held tightly in the jaws of the hammer or cock. To fire, the soldier pulls back the hammer to the cocked position. When he squeezes the trigger, a spring moves the hammer forward sharply, striking the vertical part of an L-shaped piece of steel called the "frizzen." The impact creates sparks. In addition, when the hammer moves forward against the frizzen, it pushes the vertical part of the frizzen back, thereby causing the horizontal part, which covers a metal pan, the "flash pan," to rise. This action opens the flash pan, which contains fine gunpowder. When the sparks from the frizzen fall into the flash pan, they ignite the gunpowder. The flame burns through a hole that goes from the flash pan to the barrel of the gun, called the "touchhole."

When loading the musket, the main charge of gunpowder must be placed at the bottom of the barrel, followed by the lead ball wrapped in a piece of cloth (the "patch"). The ramrod, which is usually fastened underneath the barrel when not in use, is now used to push the lead shot in the patch paper down to the bottom of the barrel. When the flame burns through the touchhole between the flash pan and the bottom of the barrel, it ignites the main charge of gunpowder, which explodes, causing the lead ball to fly out of the barrel, hopefully hitting the intended target.

The danger is that, while loading the weapon, the user may accidentally trigger the hammer and cause the gun to fire prematurely. If the soldier is using the ramrod when that happens, he may easily lose his hand. So, to be safe, the hammer has a "half-cocked" or "safe" position in which it cannot fire. In this position, the frizzen can be moved back to open the pan so that some fine gunpowder can be placed there. As an added precaution, the gunpowder and lead shot should be put in first and rammed home. Only then is the frizzen pushed back, a small amount of fine gunpowder put in the flash pan, and the flash pan closed by letting the frizzen spring pull the frizzen back to its original position.

Accordingly, Paul and Franz pulled their hammers back to the half-cocked position and then loaded their muskets with a pre-measured amount of gunpowder (which they had found in the dead soldiers' bandoliers) and with lead shot, wrapped in a piece of cloth. Then they primed the flash pans with fine gunpowder from their priming flasks. The two stolen weapons were now loaded and ready. To fire the muskets, all they had to do was shift from the half-cocked position to fully cocked—thereby releasing the safety mechanism—aim the musket and pull the trigger.

The two secret agents sat in the shade of the forest for the rest of that sultry day. They were not bothered by the fact that the plundered bodies of the two soldiers they had killed were a short distance from where they rested. After all, they felt that they, too, were soldiers, albeit soldiers of a different kind. In the heat of the moment, neither of them felt the slightest guilt at having murdered two men in cold blood for their weapons and uniforms, not even Paul, who earlier had shown some reluctance in letting an innocent man fall into the hands of the secret police.

***

As the sun touched the horizon, the two "musketeers" started to march back to Potsdam. So many soldiers were returning from patrol that Paul and Franz weren't even asked for their papers as they passed through the Hunters Gate. They made their way to Hohewegstrasse arriving, as they'd planned, at about half past ten. The mansion seemed deserted, so they quickly made for the oak tree on the left of the building. Again, they looked around meticulously, but found no one around.

Franz handed his musket to Paul, who helped him climb up the tree to a sturdy branch. Paul handed both weapons to Franz, who held them so that Paul could somewhat clumsily clamber up onto a nearby branch. Paul found a position from which he could comfortably fire a musket, and Franz passed one musket to him. Franz settled himself in a similar firing position. They cocked their weapons and waited for the black coach to arrive.

"Paul, I sense that someone else is here," Franz said in a low whisper.

Paul looked around, behind and below him. The whole area was deserted. "Nonsense; it's just nerves," he said.

"No, there's definitely someone about. I can sense it."

Paul scrutinized the entire area once more. "No, we're alone."

Franz shrugged.

***

About half an hour later, they heard the sound of hooves. Within seconds, they saw the black coach pulled by the large brown horses. The coach slowed to a standstill. The door of the coach opened. A black hat emerged first, followed by the head of a tall, thin man wearing a black cloak. Franz and Paul were just about to squeeze the triggers of their flintlock muskets when they heard a gun firing from above them in the oak tree.

The bullet blew off the back of the head of the tall man. Almost simultaneously, the recoil from his weapon caused the assassin above them in the tree to lose his balance. In order to save himself as he fell, he dropped the hunting rifle he had used to kill von Hochenheimer. But he managed to grasp the branch on which Paul was sitting. The agent got a good look at him. He recognized Caspar Hoffmann.

"Run, we'll save you," Paul shouted to Caspar, who must have thought that Paul and Franz were Prussian musketeers about to arrest him on the spot for murder. Caspar dropped to the ground. Paul and Franz let their muskets fall so that they could climb down and follow Caspar.

Three soldiers sped out of the back of the mansion and ran toward the front of the building to find the dead body of the Minister of Police. Caspar sprinted out of the gate and into the street. Paul and Franz picked up their muskets from where they'd fallen onto the ground and followed Caspar into Hohewegstrasse. Hearing the three soldiers running behind them, they instinctively stopped and aimed their weapons at the fleeing figure.

Paul hissed to Franz, "Be careful—don't hit him," and fired deliberately high and wide. Franz did the same. As the pursuing soldiers reached the secret agents, Franz pretended to display his anger at having missed the assassin by swearing and then throwing his musket on the ground. He threw it in such a way that he tripped up the lead soldier, and the other two fell heavily on top of him. Paul dropped his musket, too, acting if he was equally angry at not hitting the killer. Franz continued to curse realistically, joined by the three soldiers who seemed to be in real agony from their fall.

Hoffmann, in the meantime, had turned the corner into Charlottenstrasse. Forgetting that soldiers never leave their weapons behind, Paul and Franz left their muskets on the ground and took off after Hoffmann. They saw him a block ahead on Charlottenstrasse. Despite the fact that he'd just killed the most hated and feared man in all of Prussia, Caspar Hoffmann had sufficient control over his emotions to slow to a walk and pretend to be an honest citizen out for a stroll. The Austrians looked behind them, but there was no sign of the soldiers, who were still trying to gather themselves.

Now Hoffmann turned on to a side street. The two secret agents quickened their pace. Once more, Hoffmann changed direction. Finally, he slipped around to the back of a house on Heilig-Geist-Strasse. The secret agents stopped. They made a note of the house number.

"He's probably employed there as a servant," whispered Paul. "And that's how he found out where von Hochenheimer lived— servants know these things, as Kurt discovered. And I'd guess that he 'borrowed' that hunting rifle from the householder."

"Let's get back to our room and out of these clothes," Franz said.

They strode back with a military air. After all, they were now two soldiers on duty. But as soon as they were safely inside, they tore off their uniforms and put on the merchant's clothes that they'd stowed in the dead soldiers' knapsacks.

"Why didn't you want us to shoot Hoffmann when we had a chance?" Franz asked Paul. "He'd seen us as *Junker*; he saw us in the tree."

"He undoubtedly would never recognize us as the two *Junker*," Paul replied. "And he could hardly have got a good look at our faces as he fell out of the tree. And if we'd shot him as he fled from the scene of the assassination, they would've hailed us as heroes."

"So?"

"So the fact that we aren't Prussian musketeers would soon have come to light. They would have arrested us and hanged us as spies. And the other reason I didn't want us to shoot him is that we were sent here to kill Frederick. That's our mission, and nothing else."

"But why did you insist on following him?" asked Franz. "Surely there was a risk that he might turn round and see us, and perhaps recognize us."

"We may need him. He's clearly a first-class marksman. He probably learned to shoot in the Royal Prussian Army. I don't know for certain how he acquired that hunting rifle, but he clearly knew what weapon he needed to kill von Hochenheimer."

"There's another thing," Franz said. "Actually, two other things. First, why did Hoffmann want to kill von Hochenheimer? And second, he saw two soldiers climb into his tree. He must have thought that we were the genuine article: soldiers assigned to guard duty in that tree to protect the Minister of Police. He must have heard us cocking our muskets, which would certainly have encouraged Hoffmann to believe that we were on guard in the tree. So, why did he go ahead with the killing, knowing that he would almost certainly be caught by the two soldiers stationed below him?"

"My guess," Paul responded, "is that he was caught with our letter to Max, and he was tortured. Von Hochenheimer himself probably supervised the torture, because our note threatened the life of his King. So Hoffmann wanted revenge on his torturer, no matter what the personal cost to him might be. With his outstanding marksmanship skills he knew that—if he could get a clear shot—he had a good chance of killing the Minister of Police."

"Are you saying that he was so driven to settle scores that he just didn't care what might happen to him after he'd killed von Hochenheimer?"

"Precisely," Paul said.

"Enough about Hoffmann," Franz said. "We know where he's currently living, and we can get hold of him if we need a superb marksman. My present concern now is that we were sent here to kill Frederick, not von Hochenheimer. Now would be an excellent time to move against the King, with the whole security situation chaotic."

"Do you really believe that?" asked Paul. "On the contrary, don't you think that, until they find out who killed von Hochenheimer, security will be at its most intense ever? For all they know, the assassination may be part of an Austrian invasion. They may believe that Maria Theresa's army is at the gates of Potsdam right now. As far as I'm concerned, the authorities will impose the tightest surveillance ever here in Potsdam, and at Sanssouci Palace in particular. I wouldn't be surprised if—even as we speak—they are moving at least one regiment to Sanssouci to protect the King. I know that the King is completely fearless, but his advisors and generals aren't going to take any chances. And if I'm right—and I know I am—there's soon going to be a house-to-house search in Potsdam. They'll open every cupboard, and they'll look under every bed. They'll conduct the search assiduously with Prussian efficiency. And when they find us with the uniforms of the two musketeers, even though we no longer have those muskets, the situation will quickly become most unpleasant for us. As you correctly keep saying, we're here to kill Frederick. The only way we can do that is to dump the uniforms as soon as we can, and get out of Potsdam for a while until things cool down."

Franz thought for a moment. "Suppose—just for the sake of argument—that you're right. Do we want to get rid of the uniforms, or do we want to hide them in a safe place for later use?"

"We got rid of the *Junker* outfits because we couldn't safely reuse them. Those uniforms were inextricably tied to the fictional letter. I believe the same thing applies to the musketeer uniforms. They're part of the assassination. Just think about it. Von Hochenheimer is dead. They know by now that a marksman, sitting in that oak tree, shot him using a hunting rifle. After the killing, the marksman jumped out of the tree and was pursued by two musketeers. They know that no musketeers were supposed to be on guard there, so how did the musketeers get in on the act?"

"Maybe they think that the two musketeers were passing by and saw someone shoot the Minister of Police and jump out of the tree," Franz suggested. "So they pursued the assassin."

"No one would believe that story. Prussian soldiers are trained to obey orders implicitly, but if they show initiative of any kind, they're severely punished. If two musketeers were just passing by and they saw someone jumping out of a tree and running away, they'd do absolutely nothing unless ordered to do so by an officer.

And there were no officers around. In fact, no one was around when the coach returned at night, by express instruction of von Hochenheimer himself. So, why would two Prussian musketeers—who had no reason to be there in Hohewegstrasse in the first place—run into the street after the marksman, shoot at him, drop their muskets and then pursue him as before, not to mention immediately thereafter disappear into thin air? And what Prussian musketeer would drop his musket for any reason other than death?"

"You're assuming that the Prussian secret police will work all that out."

"Von Hochenheimer is undoubtedly dead," Paul said. "He's very dead indeed. But he couldn't have turned Prussia into a police state the way he did without excellent subordinates. I've no doubt whatsoever that the people now running the Ministry of Police have worked out that there's something extremely fishy about those two musketeers. And that's why I said that, when they conduct the house-to-house search and find us with those two uniforms, we're going to be in really big trouble."

"So you think we need to get rid of those uniforms right away?"

"If not sooner than that."

"How do you suggest we dispose of them?" Franz asked.

"I have two suggestions, both bad. We can wrap them up and carry them to the river or to a canal, weight them with stones and drop them in, like what we did with the *Junker* outfits in Berlin after we realized that we couldn't use them any more. If we'd been caught with the outfits in our room in Berlin, it's unlikely that anything would have happened; I doubt that Potsdam police headquarters sent a detailed description of the two outfits to every town in Prussia. If we'd been caught in the act of disposing of those outfits, either on the way to the canal or as we threw them in, again probably nothing would have happened, for the same reason. But if we're found here in Potsdam walking toward the Havel or a Potsdam canal carrying the two musketeer uniforms, our lives are going to be considerably shortened in a most unpleasant way. The difference is that I'm sure the authorities here have been alerted to look out for those uniforms.

"My other suggestion," Paul continued, "is that we put on the uniforms for the final time, put our other clothes back in the knapsacks, and march to the nearest canal, change clothes and dump the uniforms there."

"Could we sell them to a second-hand shop and get rid of them that way?" Franz asked.

"No, it's a serious criminal offense to buy or sell military uniforms. No dealer or pawnbroker would touch them."

"Could we burn them?"

"That's going to be a problem, too," Paul replied. "Apart from the complication of starting a fire in the city of Potsdam in summer, the blaze won't consume the metal parts, and when the remaining gunpowder explodes, we'll certainly receive loads of unwanted attention. No, as I see it, what we have to do is to walk in the middle of night to the river, either carrying the uniforms or wearing them."

"Neither choice is particularly attractive," said Franz unhappily. "There's no question that the authorities are going to carefully check all packages and parcels. So if we carry the uniforms and they stop us, which is extremely likely, that will be that. If we wear the uniforms, we're less likely to be stopped and, if we are, the police aren't going to search our knapsacks for our other clothes. But when we do get to the water, it's not going to be easy to change out of our uniforms unobserved. Is there no other alternative?"

"What about our friends at the theatre?" Paul asked.

"What about them?"

"Do we still have that empty wooden crate?"

"Yes, it's in the corner there."

"Fine," Paul said. "So let's write 'Theatre Costumes: Property of Potsdam Theatre' on the crate in big letters, put the uniforms inside, and carry the crate to the theatre. If we're stopped, everyone knows that theatre people are crazy, so the fact that we're transporting costumes in the middle of the night won't seem at all strange."

"That idea is so crazy, it makes theatre people seem sane."

"Do you have a better idea?" asked Paul, drily. "We either need to get rid of these uniforms before they start the house-to-house search, or we need to have a flawless explanation for why we're in possession of the uniforms."

Franz hurriedly gave in. They packed the uniforms into the crate, being careful to put the gunpowder bandoliers and priming flasks at the bottom. They then checked the room carefully to be sure that no component of either uniform had rolled under the furniture.

Satisfied that searchers would find no evidence that the secret agents had ever possessed the musketeer uniforms, they left the room carrying the crate. They had no idea how import/export merchants with an interest in the theatre would walk, so they transported the crate as if they were delivering an important and valuable item.

To their great relief, they reached the theatre without being stopped by a patrol. They left the crate close to the stage door entrance and started strolling back. They had hardly walked a dozen paces when a voice snarled, "Halt! Papers, please."

Two men dressed in black jackets, knee breeches and stockings, white shirts and black cravats stood behind them. Clearly, these two men were members of the secret police. The secret agents cudgeled their brains and asked themselves: Had they been seen depositing the crate next to the theatre? If not, they could get away with the dinner party explanation they had used before. But if they had been observed leaving the wooden crate by the stage door, they would have a lot to explain. Worst of all, the crate would be opened and, if the gunpowder was found, they would both be finished.

Franz and Paul handed over their papers.

"Why are you out so late?" asked the first policemen.

"We've been to a dinner party," Franz said. "We were having a pleasant evening and didn't notice the time."

"What were you doing next to the theatre?"

"We were taking a shortcut back to our lodgings."

"What's that wooden box?"

"What box?" Franz asked.

"The one you were looking at next to the theatre."

"It's a box. It says on the lid, 'Theatre Costumes: Property of Potsdam Theatre.' We were wondering what play the theatre was going to put on next."

"And?"

"And what?" asked Franz.

"And what play are they putting on next?"

"We've no idea. That was what we were talking about. The next play they're putting on at the theatre. But we have no idea what it is."

The secret policemen must have realized that they weren't going to get anywhere with what appeared to be two more-than-slightly drunk merchants, so they let them pass.

***

Once they were back in their room, Franz didn't waste any time in discussing the narrow escape they'd just had. Instead, he cut straight to the chase. "We have to get out of town, and soon. When someone opens that crate and finds what's inside it, there's a good chance that those two secret policemen will put one and one together and get two, meaning you and me. Where should we go: Paris, Berlin, Brandenburg an der Havel?"

"I suggest we go to Paris," said Paul. "The stagecoach leaves around the corner from the Neuer Markt (New Market). We'll wear our merchant clothes and take with us our traveling trunk, as befits import/export merchants. We still have the transverse flute and the recorder that we took with us to Berlin. Again, those items will help to convince anyone searching our trunk of our Prussian loyalty because this time, the trunk will undoubtedly be searched."

"What about our pistols? Will we hide them in the secret panels?"

"I think we're going to need our pistols. It was hard enough getting the ones we have— I had to masquerade as a *Junker*—and getting replacements for these may prove impossible. So we'll hide the pistol cases in the panels once more, and we'll hope for the best. Perhaps our two flutes will distract the searchers."

"We'll need a porter to take our trunk. Will that be a problem?" Franz asked.

"I don't think so. There should be plenty of out-of-work men on the street to carry the trunk to the market square. And we already know what time the Paris coach leaves—we took that coach from Berlin to Potsdam. Let's start packing."

When everything was ready, the pair still had four hours before the coach was due to depart. Paul suggested that they take a quick nap, remarking that they'd now been awake for 24 hours, but Franz was made of sterner stuff.

"If we sleep now, we'll never wake in time," he said. "I think we should leave now and find a porter to take our trunk over to the inn where the coaches leave for Paris and nose around a little."

"Why? We know what time the coach leaves."

"I've just realized that it probably isn't going to leave."

"What? What are you saying?" Paul asked.

"If you were von Hochenheimer's replacement, wouldn't you seal the borders until the assassins had been found?"

"Yes, I suppose so," said Paul. "So the best we can do is take a coach for Berlin or Brandenburg an der Havel. Probably Berlin would be better, being a large city. It would be easier to hide there.

But why did you just say 'assassins,' plural? The killing was the work of one man, Caspar Hoffmann."

"I know that, and you know that, but what the authorities now know is that there were three unknown men close to where the killing took place. Two of them were wearing the uniform of a Prussian musketeer, but they haven't been found. In fact, the Army will soon discover that two musketeers are missing from their company. The third man wore civilian clothes. So, there's clearly a conspiracy involving both civilians and military men."

"You know, you're correct," Paul said. "The last Austrian conspiracy also involved three men—Secret Agents 79, 312 and 85 if my memory serves me right—and two of them were *Junker*. The employees of the Ministry of Police are obviously now looking for another three men. They may or may not find that two of them are dead. If they do, they may or may not realize that the two soldiers were killed before the assassination took place. But what about the third man? Will they find Hoffmann?"

"I doubt it," Franz said. "We saw his face, but no one else did, and it was nighttime, too. What could link him to the murder?"

"What about the hunting rifle? It was probably made especially for its owner—Hoffmann's employer—and can easily be traced to him."

"You're quite right. Should we take Hoffmann with us as our servant? Is there any possibility that he can identify us if he's arrested and tortured?"

"Possibly. Possibly not," Paul said.

"But if we take him with us, won't he eventually realize that we were the *Junker*?"

"I doubt it. We dressed and spoke like *Junker*; we wore facial disguises. Now we're merchants."

"Yes," Franz agreed, "but a single word or one mannerism could give us away. And we'll have to be extremely careful. Under no circumstances should we enter a tavern with him, let alone drink beer. So, which risk is larger, the risk of Hoffmann being arrested and identifying us if we leave him behind, or the risk of Hoffmann recognizing us if we take him along with us?"

"I don't know," Paul said, "but somehow I'll feel safer if we take Hoffmann with us."

"But how will we persuade him to come with us? We can go to the back door of the house in Heilig-Geist-Strasse and ask for him, and they may or may not summon him. It depends what pretext we give. But what inducement do we provide to get him to come with us?"

"I don't know. But the sun is up, so Hoffmann is probably already at work. Let's go to the house. Tired as we are, maybe we'll get an idea en route."

"I think I know how to do it," Franz said as they walked along. "Leave it to me."

***

They reached the house in Heilig-Geist-Strasse and walked round to the back. Franz rang the bell. A footman opened the door.

"We need to talk to Caspar Hoffmann right away," said Franz in his most officious voice. "It's a police matter."

Like the other inhabitants of Potsdam, the footman was certainly terrified of the power of the secret police. So he rushed off to get Hoffmann.

Caspar Hoffmann appeared at the door. His face bore a mixture of fear and defiance. Franz took him by the arm and led him forcefully to the corner of the back garden farthest from the house.

"We're here to save your life," Franz whispered. "The police can trace you through the hunting rifle you used to kill von Hochenheimer last night. Come with us to Berlin right away."

Hoffmann said nothing. So Franz tried a second time.

"We've come here to save your life. Do you want to be tortured again by the police?"

The word "torture" awoke something in Hoffmann. He looked hopefully at Franz, then at Paul.

"Come with us to Berlin right now," repeated Franz, dragging Caspar toward the street. Paul took his other arm. They could see frightened faces peering at them through the basement-level windows of the house. It was too early for the householder and his wife to be awake, but the servants were up and about, and they watched with wide eyes as the two Austrian secret agents "arrested" a fellow servant.

When they were safely out of sight, Paul and Franz let go of Caspar. They weren't clear as to just how much he understood about what was happening. His ordeal—at the hands of von Hochenheimer, they suspected—had robbed him of some of his reason.

"Walk with us as if we're friends," ordered Franz. Hoffmann seemed to understand, and tagged along with the other two until they all arrived at the secret agents' room.

As the three men entered, Franz took Paul aside. "We'd better leave a month's rent for your landlord. You never know when we might need the room again."

"Good thinking. I'll write a brief note for him."

Having ensured that the room would be available when they next required it, the two secret agents returned to Caspar, who had been standing motionless in a corner of the room.

"We're going to take a coach to Berlin," said Franz, trying to use short words and brief sentences. "You will pretend to be our servant. You will carry our trunk for us."

Caspar Hoffmann went to the bed and hoisted the trunk onto his shoulders. He continued to say nothing.

"Do you have your papers?"

Hoffmann nodded.

"Fine. Just follow us. If you're asked any questions, we'll answer for you."

This time Caspar did not even offer a nod. The two Austrians led the way, and he followed silently until they arrived at the Berlin coach. Police and soldiers surrounded it on all sides. Anyone who wanted to leave Potsdam the day after the killing had to undergo a detailed interrogation first. The three of them handed over their papers to the secret policeman who appeared to be in charge.

"Why are you traveling to Berlin?" the policeman asked Franz.

"We're import/export merchants on our way to France," he replied. "We'll be purchasing Prussian-made goods in Berlin to sell in Paris."

"The borders are closed."

"We know that, but by the time we'll have bought everything we need, the borders will surely be open."

"How do you know that?"

"We don't, of course. We've been import/export merchants for several years, and we've frequently encountered closed borders, but after a day or two the borders always seem to reopen so that trade can continue. France was Prussia's ally in our war with Austria, so it seems likely that the border with France will reopen soon, and we'll be able to go on our way."

The answer seemed to satisfy the official, but he suddenly pointed at Hoffmann. "Who's this man?"

"He's our servant. He's worked for us for two years, and he knows the business well."

Franz suddenly realized that their taking Hoffmann along with them was not the cleverest of moves, because the police were looking for a group of three men. Had he and Paul traveled alone, there might have been considerably less suspicion on the part of the official.

Caspar was just about to load the trunk onto the roof of the coach when the policeman suddenly ordered, "Open the trunk!"

Paul reached into his pocket, drew out a set of keys, and proceeded to unlock the trunk. The policeman threw open the lid, then pointed to an underling, who handed him a measuring rod. Just as Fritz Apfelkern—the trunk repairer in Berlin—had predicted, the official carefully compared the inside height of the trunk with the outside height. Satisfied that there was not a false bottom, he signaled to Paul that he could close and relock the trunk. Hoffmann then picked up the trunk and placed it carefully on the roof of the coach, where the coachman tied it down with rope. The policeman returned their papers, and the three men entered the coach and sat down.

They did not speak the whole way to Berlin. Franz and Paul were seriously concerned that something they said or, more particularly, the way that they might say it, would trigger a memory in Hoffmann's otherwise slightly befuddled brain. So, for their own safety, they slept for most of the journey and kept absolutely silent when they were awake. Fortunately for them, the other passengers were equally silent. No one tried to strike up a conversation. Franz thought that the detailed interrogation they had all undergone at the hands of the secret police before they were allowed to enter the coach and leave Potsdam might have had something to do with everyone's reluctance to speak.

The coach arrived late in Berlin, having been thoroughly searched at three roadblocks. Each time the Austrians had unlocked and opened their trunk so a team of officials could carefully examine the contents. Fortunately for Franz and Paul, none of the searchers found the secret compartments containing the pistol cases.

Arriving at Viereck in the early evening, Franz instructed Hoffmann to take the trunk and follow them. The news of the assassination had quickly spread, and a stranger looking for accommodation would certainly be looked at askance. Worse, three strangers arriving together might be reported to the secret police.

But the two Austrians had spent a month in Frau Deitel's dining room, so their arrival there would be unlikely to trigger any suspicion.

As they walked toward Frau Deitel's house, Franz whispered to Paul, "What are we going to do about Hoffmann?"

"I don't know," he said. "If we send him away, he may talk. If we keep him with us, he may recognize us. We're in the same quandary as before."

They walked on in silence. "I have an idea," Franz whispered as they approached Frau Deitel's house. He knocked on the door.

Frau Deitel was home and welcomed them back. "The dining room is still unoccupied," she said. "I would be happy to let you have it again for the same rental."

"That would be wonderful," Franz said. "Let me pay you right now for the first week. We have our servant with us this time. Do you have a servant's room for him?"

"Yes, there are two empty attic rooms, and he can certainly have one."

"Excellent." He paid her for Caspar's lodgings, as well.

Hoffmann carried their trunk into the dining room, and then went up to his room.

"Hoffmann has only the clothes he's wearing," said Paul after they'd entered the dining room. "I think we need to give him some money to buy what he needs to survive here in Berlin."

"Are we going to pay him wages? After all, we took him away from his job in Potsdam, and he's our servant now."

"I think we should. Let's find out how much he was earning and pay him that amount."

"But we don't need a servant," Franz said. "What on earth are we going to do with him all day?"

"I think that we should keep him on until it's safe for us to return to Potsdam. At that time, we can pay him some sort of lump sum and give him a letter of reference he can use to get a job here in Berlin. You know the sort of thing: 'Caspar Hoffmann is strong and hardworking, honest and willing,' and so on. Ensuring that he's safely here in Berlin will reduce the risks—albeit ever so slightly—when we kill Frederick in Potsdam."

Hardly had he finished speaking when they heard a peremptory knock on the door. Before either of them could say, "Enter," three secret policemen in their usual black suits forced open the door and marched in.

"Papers, please." The "please" was clearly from force of habit as the word was entirely superfluous.

The Austrians handed over their forged Prussian identity papers. Yet again, they passed muster.

"We know that you just arrived in the coach from Potsdam. Where were you last night?"

"In our room in Potsdam," Franz said.

"Can anyone support that?"

"Probably not. We had no visitors."

"And where were you during the day?"

"In our room deciding what goods to buy to take with us to Paris. We're import/export merchants," Franz explained.

"Did anyone see you there?"

"No. We were working alone all day."

"When were you last northwest of the city?"

"I don't think I've ever been northwest of the city," replied Franz, pretending to consider the question thoughtfully. "What about you, Paul?"

"No, I've never been there either."

"Strange, because two soldiers have reported seeing two men yesterday near Golm who look like the two of you and who were wearing clothes like yours."

"I'm sure that there are lots of men who look like us, and our clothes are similar to those of other merchants," Paul said.

"Why are your clothes so creased?" the policeman asked.

"We've just slept in our clothes in the coach from Potsdam."

"Your clothes look as if they were folded up and crammed into a trunk."

"We stored our clothes in this trunk here when we were in Potsdam. We just haven't had them ironed recently."

"Do you have two military uniforms in your trunk?"

"Obviously not. It's illegal to buy or sell uniforms. Here, see for yourself."

Paul opened the chest. Two of the policemen pawed through the contents, which had already been searched three times that day.

The secret policeman in charge didn't seem satisfied. "You will stay in Berlin until I tell you that you have permission to travel," he said. Then the three policemen marched out of the room.

The two Austrian secret agents sat in silence until they heard the front door slam.

"Thank heavens they didn't interrogate poor Hoffmann. Who knows what he might have told them," Paul said.

"We have to get out of Berlin, and quickly. They may arrest us and take us back to Potsdam to see if the two soldiers who saw us can identify us."

"On the other hand, if they really thought that we were the men who killed the two musketeers and stole their uniforms, they would've arrested us on the spot. In fact, I wonder why they didn't."

"Perhaps because they've been told to look for three men, two of whom have been described by the soldiers who saw them northwest of the city, near Golm. If Hoffmann had been in the room, that would've been fatal for us. As I just said, we have to get out of Berlin and fast. Where should we go?"

"I think we need to leave Prussia until they stop looking for us," Paul said.

"But the borders have been closed. Who knows when they'll reopen them?"

"Borders are porous," Paul added. "Thanks to Kurt, we've got money, so we can bribe our way out, or pay a smuggler to take us across.

"But where can we go?"

"How about Saxony?" Paul suggested. "The peace treaty of December 25, 1745 was signed in Dresden, the capital of the Electorate of Saxony."

"The whole Saxony issue is so bizarre," said Franz, pausing to think for a minute. "Just after Prussia started the war against Austria at the end of 1740, Saxony was an ally. Then Saxony changed sides and fought against Prussia. But you're right; the Electorate of Saxony made peace with Prussia a couple of years back. Yes, that has to be the situation, because Old Bach came to Potsdam from Leipzig in Saxony. If Saxony were still at war with Prussia, the border guards would never have let his coach enter Prussia. So, let's make for Saxony quickly before the situation changes once more."

"Where in Saxony should we go?" Paul asked. "Old Bach's Leipzig? Dresden, the capital? Somewhere else?"

"Here, take a look at my map," said Franz, handing Paul the crumpled paper he had pulled from his pocket. "If we travel south from Berlin, keeping away from the main roads, we should arrive in Dresden. It's a long walk, about 100 miles. Let's head for Dresden along back roads and then decide what to do. We'll leave everything in our trunk here in Berlin except for the bare essentials we have to take with us, which include our pistol cases and my compass. Of course, we can't walk to Saxony dressed as merchants. The three of us have to be laborers, looking for work in Saxony."

"You said 'the three of us,'" Franz said. "Do you really think that Hoffmann should come with us?"

"We can't leave him behind. When that secret policeman comes back to arrest us and finds that his two birds have flown the coop, he'll ask Frau Deitel a few pertinent questions, and Hoffmann will soon be under arrest. I'm pretty sure that he's already been tortured quite badly, so it won't be at all hard for them to get the whole story from him. Then everyone in Prussia will be on the lookout for us. No, we'll have to take Hoffmann with us. And we have to leave right now."

The two of them found Frau Deitel and explained that the next day they would have to go out of town for a few weeks. Franz asked her if they could pay her to keep their trunk while they were gone. She readily agreed, suggesting that her cellar would be a safe place to store it. Then Paul asked her if she had a spare knapsack she could lend them. Frau Deitel said that she had a whole collection of knapsacks and other bags that previous travelers had left behind, and she would be only too delighted to let them take whatever they wanted.

They chose three strong knapsacks with a well-worn appearance, returned to the dining room, and changed into appropriate clothes for the long hike to Dresden. They transferred only what they needed to take with them into two of the knapsacks, summoned Hoffmann, and told him to put the trunk into the cellar. As soon as they heard Frau Deitel go upstairs to bed, they stole out of the house and headed south.

Their first stop was a food shop that—luckily for them—was still open. Paul bought provisions for the first part of their journey, while Franz waited outside with Hoffmann in silence. Paul loaded the food into the third knapsack, which he instructed Hoffmann to carry.

They walked briskly through the dark streets of Berlin. When they reached Charlottenstrasse, Paul whispered to Franz, "Whether we're in Potsdam or Berlin, we seem to find ourselves walking down Charlottenstrasse."

Franz gave him a withering stare, and looked meaningfully toward Caspar Hoffmann. Hoffmann walked on, apparently unaware that anything had been said.

When they reached Lindenstrasse, a patrol stopped them. Two musketeers determined that the three travelers' papers were in order. The soldiers didn't ask them the purpose of their journey, and—most importantly—they did not search their knapsacks.

Avoiding the highway, they walked south along byways for about three hours, until they were well and truly clear of Berlin. The route outside the town was mostly forested, but later on they came upon clearings and farms. Paul spotted a haystack on their left. They decided to spend the night there. They weren't too worried that the farmer might find them sheltering in his haystack. After all, they had their own food, and many farmers just turned a blind eye to travelers who made use of their haystacks as rural inns.

CHAPTER FIFTEEN

"Come with me," Paul called to Franz the next morning. "Let's find a stream for us to wash in." As soon as they were out of earshot, Paul said, "We've got four big problems."

Franz looked at his fellow secret agent and nodded for him to continue.

"Problem one, Potsdam is approximately due west of us. Once we walk south for another mile or two, we're going to look like three men walking away from Potsdam. And we know that the whole country is looking for three men doing precisely that. Problem two is that they say that Prussia isn't a country, it's an army. And the army is run by the *Junker*, supplied by the merchants, and manned by the peasants."

"So?"

"So the three of us are dressed like peasants," Paul continued. "Impressment is part of the way of life here. Military press gangs roam the countryside, and able-bodied men whom they find are immediately pressed into service. And there's no way out of the army. The penalties for desertion are draconian, usually hanging, or running the gauntlet if you're lucky. Once we're in the Royal Prussian Army, there's no way we'll be able to kill Frederick.

"Problem three is the money in your pocket, more than a thousand reichsthaler in gold pieces. Peasants with that amount of money are hanged for theft. And I can assure you there won't be a trial. Finding you in possession of even a small fraction of all that money would be proof enough. And problem four is the pistols in our bags. Remember what that pawnbroker on the Judengasse said to you. So, if schoolmasters aren't supposed to have firearms, then peasants certainly aren't."

"What are you suggesting?"

"We have to keep our pistols in our pockets. If we're stopped, we're probably going to have to kill or be killed. And we've got to get rid of Hoffmann."

"And when you say 'get rid of,'" asked Franz, "what exactly do you mean?"

"I mean exactly what you think I mean."

"And how do you propose to kill him?"

"We can't shoot him," Paul said. "The noise will alert the farmer. We can't strangle him because he's a lot stronger than both of us. So, you use your stiletto."

"Now?"

"Now."

The two secret agents walked back to the side of the haystack away from the road. Paul called to Caspar. "Hoffmann, come over here. There's something important we need to discuss with you."

Caspar Hoffmann stood up and approached Paul. As he did so, Franz slipped behind him.

"Hoffmann, show me your wrists."

Suspecting nothing, Hoffmann held up his arms with the wrists vertical. Paul grabbed a wrist in each hand. And as he did so, Franz plunged his stiletto into Caspar's back, piercing his heart. Max Hirsch had trained his secret agents well.

Caspar's body slumped to the ground. The two Austrian assassins waited for the blood to finish flowing onto the layer of hay Paul had chosen. Then they removed as much of the evidence as they could.

First, they stripped the body. As Franz removed Hoffmann's shirt, he let out a whistle. "Look at all these fresh whip marks on his back. And there are so many older scars, too. No wonder he wanted to kill von Hochenheimer."

They burrowed deeply into the hay from one side, and buried the body of their former companion. They stuffed the bloodstained straw into a hole on the other side.

Franz tied Hoffmann's clothes into a bundle, and they both meticulously searched the area for any possible evidence of the murder that they had committed. Finding none, Paul picked up two of their backpacks, while Franz carried the third backpack and the bundle of clothing. They walked swiftly back to the road that ran next to the farm.

"Hopefully, they're not going to find the body until late autumn or even winter, when the farmer needs the hay to feed his cattle," said Franz. "Even if they do find the body today, there's nothing to tie us to the crime. All they'll have is a body with a stiletto wound in its back.

"More precisely," he continued, "what they'll find is the naked body of someone who's recently been horrifically flogged. After a few seconds, they'll realize that the police tortured the murder victim. And then they'll bury the body as quickly as possible without alerting the authorities. No sane person wants to get involved unnecessarily with the Prussian police. So we're safe—no matter how soon they find the body."

***

They walked briskly on and soon found what they were looking for: a bridge over a tree-lined stream. They climbed down the side of the bridge and walked downstream on the bank of the swiftly flowing water until they were about a half a mile away from the road. It was hard to make their way through the leafy trees and the thick undergrowth, but they persisted. They untied the bundle of clothing and gathered a few heavy river rocks. Then they weighted each piece of clothing separately with a rock and sank the remaining evidence of their crime.

"We loaded our pistols on the day of the parade," Franz said. "We fired two of them in the forest, but we haven't had a chance to reload them, let alone clean them. And the other two are still loaded. The powder is possibly damp. While we're here where no one can see us, let's unload the two loaded pistols and reload them with fresh powder."

"Are you crazy? Unloading a flintlock pistol is a dangerous undertaking," Paul said. "If I were to push the steel rod down the barrel to clear it, there's a danger of a spark, and that would mean that I'd lose my hand. We need a brass rod with a screw on the end to twist into the ball and pull it out, but we don't have one of those in either of the cases. And I don't see how we could possibly lay our hands on a brass rod out here. Let's take a chance and fire the two pistols into a dead tree, then clean and reload them. We're in the middle of nowhere; I'm sure that no one could possibly hear the noise."

"No, the risk is too great. If the noise of the firing alerts someone, we could be in big trouble. Hoffmann's body isn't that far away from here."

"Well, let's compromise," Paul said. "Let's clean the gunpowder out of each flash pan, and use a small, sharp piece of wood to clean the touchhole. Then we can reload the flash pan with fresh gunpowder from a flask."

"Agreed."

The two men each took their loaded pistol out of its case and meticulously checked that the firearm was half-cocked. Then they moved the frizzen back to open the pan, carefully removed every last trace of old gunpowder, cleaned the touchhole, and reloaded the flash pan using fresh powder from the flask in their respective cases. Next, they cleaned the pistols they'd used to kill the musketeers outside Potsdam and reloaded them. They inserted the correct quantity of gunpowder into the barrel using the measure, placed a patch on the top of the barrel, put a lead ball on the patch, and rammed it home with the ramrod. As with the other two pistols, they put a small amount of fine gunpowder in the flash pans.

Finally, they put a loaded pistol in each of their pockets. They closed the pistol cases and replaced them in their backpacks. After checking to see that there was no evidence of their visit to that part of the stream, they retraced their steps through the wooded undergrowth to the road, where they resumed their walk toward Saxony.

***

The rest of the day was uneventful. They passed a farmer on a trap, a minister and his wife on a dogcart, and a few pedestrians, mostly tramps. Every so often, Paul checked that they were still moving south, either by looking at the sun or glancing at his compass. The road was lined with farms, interspersed with woodland. At one stage, they walked for more than half an hour through a forest. Then the route along which they were traveling became more of a footpath than a road. Toward evening, they came to a farm with a large barn.

"Why don't we ask the farmer if we can stay in his barn overnight?" Franz asked. "We can even offer to pay for food and accommodation."

"We'll get a good night's sleep, if nothing else," Paul said. "But wouldn't it be safer if we were invisible? Suppose the police go from farm to farm, asking about us?"

"I see your point, but the police are looking for three men escaping from Potsdam after killing von Hochenheimer, not two peasants looking for work."

"Fine, let's ask the farmer."

They went through the wooden gate and to the back door of the prosperous-looking wooden farmhouse.

The farmer's wife opened the door. "Yes?" Her plump red face wrinkled when she spoke.

"We're on our way south to look for work," Franz said, "and we were wondering if we could stay in your barn overnight. We'll pay if you insist, but we don't have much money."

"You may certainly sleep there overnight. Do you have food?"

"Yes, we do, but if you have milk and bread for sale we'd be most grateful."

She fetched two large earthenware cups and filled them with milk from a bucket in the corner. "Here, we have plenty." She handed them to the two secret agents.

They thanked her. While they drank the milk, she went to a cupboard and took out a loaf of bread and gave it them. They returned the cups to her and went to the barn, where they settled down for the night.

***

The next morning, they went to the farmhouse to thank the farmer's wife. She insisted that they drink another cup of fresh milk before leaving. And she insisted that they take another loaf of bread with them for their journey.

They resumed their walk in a southerly direction. Paul walked in silence. But every so often he sighed deeply.

Franz finally turned to him. "What's on your mind?"

"Yesterday we murdered a man."

"No, yesterday we executed a murderer, an assassin."

"The reason that Hoffmann shot von Hochenheimer is because we agreed to pay him to deliver a letter to the hut near Brandenburg an der Havel. As a result of our action, that swine von Hochenheimer mercilessly flogged him. And we killed Hoffmann to protect ourselves, and not in retribution for the assassination, which we were responsible for in the first place. And not only that, we didn't even pay him the 10 reichsthaler we promised him. But what kept me awake last night and is bothering me so much this morning is not that we killed Hofmann, but that our reward for what we did to him was free accommodation, bread, and milk. That woman wouldn't take a pfennig from us. She did it all out of the kindness of her heart. She didn't ask us any questions. She just saw that we were in need, and she responded to it. I feel like a worm. I feel lower than a worm."

***

For the rest of the day, they walked without speaking. Even during their midday meal, they exchanged only the bare minimum of words.

Franz grew concerned about the success of their mission. Would Paul be able to work with him toward their goal, the killing of Frederick? In his current state of mind, Franz thought, Paul was essentially useless. Franz even considered the idea of disposing of Paul the way they'd disposed of Caspar Hoffmann, but he quickly suppressed the thought.

Finally, as the sun was nearing the western horizon, Franz spoke. "We must be getting close to the border."

Paul continued to say nothing.

"We'd better try and find out just how far away from Saxony we are."

Again, no response.

"I suggest we stop for a beer at the next inn we find. We can ask the innkeeper how close we are."

This time Franz did not expect a response.

A few minutes later, the rural track they had been following joined the main road. The route entered a forest. They saw a hamlet in a clearing in the woods: a small church, a cluster of cottages, a village store, a smithy and an inn. Franz led Paul into the inn.

"Good day, innkeeper. Two beers, please!"

Other than the large, redheaded, freckle-faced man behind the bar, the room was empty. Franz paid for the beer, which looked thin and watery, and took their pints to a table in the corner.

After a few more minutes of silence, Franz finished his beer, got up and walked to the counter.

"Innkeeper, where exactly are we?" he asked.

"Falkendorf."

"We're on our way to Saxony to look for work."

"Plenty of work here in Prussia."

"Yes, but we're not particularly keen to serve in the army. We're looking for a different line of work."

"Nothing wrong with serving in the Royal Prussian Army."

"No, nothing wrong at all. But my friend and I aren't terribly comfortable with military discipline. We prefer a more relaxed way of life. For example, I feel like another beer. And please, take one for yourself."

The innkeeper poured the two beers. Franz paid, adding a small tip. The innkeeper thanked him and raised his own tankard in a toast.

"Innkeeper, how far is Falkendorf from the border?"

"It'll take you another 30 minutes or so to get there. You could easily sleep tonight in Saxony instead of here in Prussia. Except for one thing."

"What's that?"

"They've sealed the border."

"Sealed the border? Why?"

"They say they are looking for three men who killed the Minister of Police."

"Won't they let us through?"

"No. No one leaves Prussia until the three men are found."

Franz took a gulp and let the tepid beer wash down his throat. He set the tankard down before speaking. "Would you happen to know of any other way of getting from here to Saxony?"

This time it was the innkeeper who waited before replying. Both men were obviously aware that their conversation could lead to serious, possibly fatal, consequences. "Just what did you have in mind?"

Franz realized that he had no choice. In order to complete their mission, they had to get out of Prussia. So he spoke more openly than he would otherwise have liked. "We're rather keen to get to Saxony. If there's a route, through the forest, say, that bypasses the border post, we'd like to know about it."

"I've heard there's a route of that kind. I've never used it myself, mind you. But it's a rather complicated path. Was it your idea to hire a guide?"

The innkeeper's use of the word "hire" was the signal for Franz to take some money out of his pocket and lay the coins on the counter, being extremely careful to keep all his gold pieces out of sight.

"I'll send for my brother-in-law," said the innkeeper, pocketing the money. "He's a forester and knows the path. If he can, he'll take you across to Saxony tonight."

The innkeeper left. Franz returned to the table. He smiled at Paul, but there was no response.

"The innkeeper has sent for his brother-in-law. Hopefully we'll cross the border through the forest tonight."

As before, Paul said nothing. Franz had long since realized that Paul wasn't being rude and deliberately ignoring him. Paul was suffering a reaction to the previous day's murder.

A few minutes later, the innkeeper returned and walked over to their table. "I've sent one of my children to fetch their uncle. He should be here in an hour or so."

The two Austrian secret agents sat in silence as the sky slowly darkened. A few villagers entered the inn and bought beer. No one greeted the two strangers. Eventually the door opened and in walked a redhaired freckle-faced boy of about 10—the spitting image of the innkeeper—followed by a burly forester. The innkeeper pointed to the two men in the corner.

The forester looked at the Austrians and then jerked his head to the right—in the direction of the doorway—to indicate that they should talk outside. Paul and Franz followed him out the door as he led them to a large tree behind the inn.

"Now, what's all this about?" asked the forester.

"My friend and I are looking for work in Saxony. We understand that the border is closed, so we were hoping to hire a guide to take us through the forest. Can you help us?"

"Maybe I can; maybe I can't. Tell me again why you want to go to Saxony."

"We're looking for work. If we stay here in Prussia, we'll soon find ourselves back in the army for another five years, and neither of us likes military life at all. We've heard that, since the peace, there's plenty of work of all kinds in Saxony."

"Maybe there is; maybe there isn't. But there's one thing I don't understand. You say that you two are out of work, yet you've got money to pay for a guide to take you across the border."

"We're down to our last few coins," said Franz. "If we pay you to take us across, we have a good chance of earning more money. So it's an investment in our future."

The expression on the forester's face led Franz to discern that the man did not believe him. But the guide's body language suggested he was keen to make money out of them.

"How much money were you thinking of paying?" he asked.

Franz took the last of the coins out of his pocket and showed that it was now empty. He kept his gold coins safely hidden in a pouch around his neck. "Here," he said. "Take everything we have."

The forester took the money. He sighed a little, giving the impression he'd been hoping for a larger fee. On the other hand, he wasn't going to turn down the proffered cash.

"Follow me." He led them into the trees behind the hamlet.

***

"What's your name?" asked Franz, addressing the forester's back.

"No names," replied the forester, sharply. "It's better that way."

As they entered a thick glade, he stepped up the pace. Franz had difficulty keeping up, but his pride prevented him from asking the forester to slow down. They walked for just over an hour, the path twisting and turning.

"Forester, stop!" Paul yelled suddenly.

The guide came to a halt, waiting for Paul to catch up with him.

"Forester, why are we traveling north?"

"What nonsense is this?" the forester blustered. "We're heading for the border. We'll be across in a few minutes."

"No, we won't," Paul said. "For the past 15 minutes we've been walking north, presumably into some trap that you've set for us."

"North? What do you mean, north? I've lived in this forest all my life. I know every path, every route, and I'm telling you we're heading for the border."

"No, this path heads north, away from the border."

"And just how do you know that?"

"I've been looking at my compass every few minutes ever since we left the inn. You took us due east, deep into the forest, then south toward the border. But then you led us in a wide loop to the north, and we've been walking north ever since. I think you're taking us in a huge circle back to the area of the inn, where you, the innkeeper and your friends plan to rob us."

"Nonsense!"

There was a click as Franz took the pistol out of his pocket and cocked it. A second click closely followed when Paul did the same.

The forester raised his arms. "Gentlemen, maybe I made a slight mistake. I'm sorry. I'll take you across the border right now."

"You have exactly 30 minutes to get us into Saxony," Paul said. "If we aren't safely across the border by then, we're going to kill you. Don't try any more tricks. And if we encounter any friends of yours in this forest, we'll kill you first, and then your friends. Is that clear?"

"I understand."

"And don't walk quite so fast," Paul added. "If you get too far ahead, I'll shoot."

After about 25 minutes, the frightened forester claimed that they were now in Saxony. Paul wasn't convinced. "Keep going," he said. "Take us to a village or some other place."

"But I'll be arrested if they find me in Saxony."

"That's part of the risk of being paid to smuggle people across a border. Keep going."

***

They soon found themselves on the outskirts of a village as tiny as Falkendorf. Even though it was after midnight, there was a light on in one of the cottages.

"You two can go there and they'll tell you that this is Saxony."

"Not so fast. You're probably up to more of your tricks," Paul said. "You wait here with my friend. I'll go inside and find out where we are. If I'm not out in a few minutes, my friend will kill you. This had better not be a trap."

Franz and the forester stayed at the edge of the wood. Franz kept his cocked pistol firmly pointed at their guide.

Paul carefully entered the village, fearing an ambush behind every tree. He knocked softly on the door of the cottage.

An old man opened the door. He had a lamp in his one hand and the book he had obviously been reading in the other.

"I'm so sorry to disturb you," said Paul in his most apologetic voice, "but we were wondering if we're still in Prussia."

"No," replied the wrinkled reader, "this is the village of Kleinbrock, in Saxony. You and your friends are safe here; you're beyond the reach of the Prussian police. Anyone who has fled Prussia is welcome here. Please come inside."

"You're most kind," replied Paul, "but I must first fetch my friend. We'll be back in a few minutes."

"That's fine; just let yourselves in when you get back. The door will be unlocked."

Somewhat reassured, Paul returned to Franz and the forester. Approaching Franz, he muttered softly, "We're in Saxony, and we have a place to sleep."

Then glancing at the forester, he added, "Do we need to do another Hoffmann?"

"I don't think so," Franz said softly. "His brother-in-law has also seen us, and it's far too late to do anything about the innkeeper now." Turning to the forester, he said, "I strongly suggest that you —and everyone else involved in your little game—keep your mouths firmly shut. If not, my friend and I will come back and do what I am strongly tempted to do, which is shoot you through the head right now."

The forester turned and fled toward the trees, zigzagging from side to side, just in case Franz shot at him.

CHAPTER SIXTEEN

When Paul returned to the cottage with Franz, they found the door unlocked as promised, and the elderly man setting the table for the evening meal.

"Sit, sit. You must be famished." He seemed delighted to see them. His furrowed face held a new glow.

"But it's the middle of the night," Paul said. "We're keeping you up."

"Nonsense, nonsense, my boy. I'm an old man, I can't sleep. I read until dawn. Sit, sit, and eat."

"We are most grateful to you," Franz said.

"Nonsense, nonsense, my boy. Anyone fleeing Prussia is a friend of mine."

"Do you dislike the Prussians, then?" Paul asked.

"I abhor them." The joy in his face vanished instantaneously, to be replaced by a look of intense hatred. So extreme was his revulsion that neither man dared raise the obvious question. However, there was no need to ask; the old man was only too willing to explain.

"When the war started, eight years ago, the Prussians poured across the frontier. They came to the nearby town of Grossbrock, which, despite its name, isn't that much bigger than Kleinbrock here. I was the schoolmaster at Grossbrock.

"It seemed that a number of the local inhabitants were engaging in ambushes, sabotage, and raids against the invaders. The Prussians decided to put a stop to such activities, not just in Grossbrock but also in the whole of Saxony. So, a company of soldiers marched into the town, ordered everyone into the town square, and proceeded to burn down the school." The old man stopped, incapable of continuing.

Paul and Franz attempted sympathetic remarks.

"No, no," the schoolmaster suddenly continued, "it's not the loss of the school building. The Prussians first herded all the children into the school, screwed the wooden door shut, and *then* burnt down the school."

Paul and Franz recoiled in horror.

"The idea," the schoolmaster continued, "was that the Prussians would publicize their slaughter of the innocents to deter any Saxons from daring to oppose them. But a senior officer arrived on the scene and quickly realized that, if the story got out, the whole of Saxony would rise against the Prussians with unparalleled fury. So, to try to defuse the magnitude of the atrocity, they ascribed the whole incident to Saxon propaganda. But I was there; I witnessed the massacre. I will never, never forget the screams of the children as they burned to death at the hands of those Prussian monsters."

The schoolmaster lapsed into silence. He sat, totally immobile, clearly replaying the incident in his mind. The two Austrians quickly cleared the table as best they could. Then they found comfortable spots on the floor of the cottage to sleep.

Hardly had they dropped off when the elderly schoolmaster shook them awake.

"Quick, quick, Prussian soldiers have entered the village. Run! Run for the forest."

He had extinguished the light. He took them over to the window, where they could see a troop of about 10 soldiers marching toward the hamlet. Their former guide, the forester, was in the lead.

"Quick, quick, take your things and get out the back door."

Paul and Franz grabbed their possessions and ran out. Fortunately for them, the tramping feet of the soldiers masked what little noise the secret agents made as they raced to the trees. By carefully keeping the cottage between them and the Prussian soldiers, they were able to reach the forest unobserved.

From the shelter of the trees, they saw the soldiers knock down the door of the schoolmaster's cottage and march in. They heard the sergeant scream, "Where are the two men?"

Next, they heard the ransacking of the small cottage. The schoolmaster couldn't deny that the secret agents had been there.

The remnants of a recent meal for three remained in the kitchen. But he insisted that the men had left and were headed for Dresden.

After a few minutes of slaps and screams, there was silence. The elderly schoolmaster was unconscious. They could hear the sound of his body being dragged outside, followed by a single pistol shot. A few seconds later, the sky lit up as the soldiers set fire to the schoolmaster's cottage. The Prussians stood around for only a few seconds—just to be sure that the cottage would burn to the ground—before they continued south, guided by the forester. The courageous schoolmaster, despite knowing for certain that he was facing imminent death, had managed to convince the Prussian troops that the two men were already on the road, headed for Dresden.

***

Franz realized that Paul was once more in a state of shock. As a result of their decision not to shoot the villainous forester, the kindly schoolmaster had been murdered. This time, Franz tried to engage Paul in discussion in order to assuage him of the guilt.

"How do think that the forester persuaded the Prussians to come after us without getting arrested for taking us across the border?" he asked.

The trick worked. By posing the question, Franz had distracted Paul's attention from the horror of what he had just witnessed.

"My guess," said Paul slowly, "is that the forester rushed to the border post and told the soldiers there that two desperadoes had held pistols to his head and forced him to take them through the forest into Saxony."

"Why do you think the soldiers were so keen to find us?" he continued, hoping to keep Paul engaged in the discussion.

"I have no idea whether the forester told them that we were part of the plot to kill von Hochenheimer, or whether they came after us because they had orders to let no one across the border."

"Do you think that the innkeeper had anything to do with it?" Franz asked.

"Now there's an idea," said Paul. "It's highly likely that he would've found out about the assassination from soldiers who came to his inn to drink his watery, tasteless beer. I strongly suspect that he told his brother-in-law that you and I were probably involved in the von Hochenheimer killing. So, when the forester escaped from us, he ran to the border post, told them that the assassins were in Kleinbrock, and led them to the house he'd seen me enter. If the soldiers had thought that we were just illegal border-crossers, I doubt they would've beaten up and killed the schoolmaster to get information about us—let alone leave their border post and march into a friendly country. They must have thought that—thanks to the forester—they were about to do their country a great service by getting their hands on the von Hochenheimer assassins. Do you know, I'm greatly tempted to go back to Prussia and kill that forester and his brother-in-law."

"Well," said Franz, gently, "we were sent to Prussia by Max Hirsch to kill Frederick. Don't you think that revenge should wait until after we've achieved our mission? And more important than revenge is getting past those Prussian soldiers to Dresden."

Hardly had he made that remark when they heard the Prussian troops returning. Franz and then Paul inched forward from where they had hid, taking the greatest care to stay under cover. The soldiers seemed to stomp angrily through the clearing. Furthermore, instead of the forester leading the column—as he had before—he was now the last man in line. His hands were tied behind his back, and a Prussian soldier pulled him forward by tugging on a rope around his neck.

"It looks like the Prussians are extremely angry with the forester," Franz whispered.

"I wonder if they think he sent them into Saxony on some sort of false alarm."

"That can't be it," Franz replied, taking care to keep his voice low. "They saw the plates in the kitchen at the schoolmaster's cottage. They must have realized that the forester was telling the truth when he said that two men forced him to take them across the border."

"Perhaps they're just angry that they couldn't find us, and they've finally realized that they're going to be severely punished for crossing the border without permission. Initiative of any kind is not exactly highly prized in the lower ranks of the Prussian army. And while the illegal crossing of a national boundary during peacetime may or may not result in the death penalty, murdering an innocent Saxon civilian certainly will. So they're taking out their frustrations on the forester."

CHAPTER SEVENTEEN

Franz and Paul reached the Elbe River the next afternoon at a point downstream from Dresden. They walked toward the city until they reached Coswig. There they found a ferryman who took them across the wide river to Wörlitz on the south side of the Elbe. Franz and Paul continued walking until they came to the fortified city of Dresden, where they crossed the moat and entered the city through the Wilsdruffer Gate[3]. Franz turned to a soldier standing guard.

"Could you please tell us how to get to the Frauenkirsche (Church of our Lady)?"

The soldier, assuming that the two travel-worn peasants were on some sort of religious pilgrimage, readily obliged.

Once they were well past the gate, Paul turned to Franz. "I assume that there's a good reason why we're going to church?"

"We're not going to church. We're trying to find the Austrian Embassy, and it's located in the vicinity of the church."

"Is there a reason why you didn't ask the soldier where the embassy is?" Paul asked.

"We're dressed as peasants, and peasants don't go to embassies, unless they're up to no good. If I'd asked the soldier to direct us to the embassy, he'd have assumed that we wanted to burn down it, and reacted accordingly. Instead, he eagerly directed us to one of the most beautiful Protestant churches, with a huge sandstone dome. And inside is an organ that King Frederick's fortepiano maker, Gottfried Silbermann, made. And guess who gave a recital on the organ just one week after it was dedicated? Yes, Frederick's good friend, Johann Sebastian Bach.

---

[3] The site of the Wilsdruffer Gate is now the Postplatz (Post Office Square).

"But, as I said, we're not here to pray, admire beautiful churches or even listen to the organ. We're looking for the Austrian Embassy. Hopefully it'll be easy to find, with the Imperial Banner of the Holy Roman Empire flying—a black double-headed eagle with red claws and beak, on a yellow background, in case you've forgotten. And in front, we should find Austrian grenadiers in their white uniforms and bearskin caps. Let's start walking and looking."

"But why are we going to our Embassy?" Paul asked.

"You'll see. Come on. It'll be closed before we get there if we don't hurry."

They walked swiftly in the direction indicated by the soldier at the Wilsdruffer Gate. As Paul sighted the dome of the Frauenkirche, Franz exclaimed, "See, on the left, there's the embassy."

They walked toward the lavishly decorated building. Two imposing grenadiers stopped them.

"What do you want here?" snarled the first guard at the two exceedingly scruffy peasants.

"I need to see the ambassador, Baron Octavian von Bruno-Bader. I was sent here by Max Hirsch in Vienna."

The first guard was about to push the two men away from the embassy with the butt of his rifle when the second, more senior guard intervened.

"Did you say Max Hirsch sent you?"

"Yes, Max Hirsch in Vienna."

"Wait here."

The second guard pressed a bell, and an immaculately turned-out officer emerged from the building and walked up to them. Before the lieutenant could say anything, the second guard went up to him and whispered in his ear.

"You are here from Max Hirsch?" the lieutenant asked Franz.

"I am." Franz nodded.

"You say you wish to meet with His Excellency?"

"I do."

"Is he with you?" asked the lieutenant, pointing at Paul.

"Yes."

"What is your name?" he asked, looking back at Franz.

"Franz Braun."

"Do you have any identity documents?"

"Only in the name of Franz Braun."

"You will wait here."

Clearly, the lieutenant was exceedingly reluctant to let the two bedraggled men into the embassy building. He nodded meaningfully to the guards to indicate that they were to keep a careful eye on the two secret agents, and went inside.

A few minutes later, the lieutenant returned and spoke to Franz.

"Please come with me."

"What about my friend?"

"He must wait outside for now."

The lieutenant then ushered Franz through an elaborate entranceway and into the embassy building. Franz found himself in the foyer. The room contained a magnificent wooden inlaid Austrian Rococo escritoire, a French Rococo chair, and two more burly grenadiers, both of whom glowered at Franz. The escritoire was furnished with paper, ink, two quill pens, and a sander. There was also sealing wax and a seal, and a lighted candle burned in a bronze candlestick. The officer indicated, with some disdain, that Franz was to sit on the chair, filthy clothes and all.

"His Excellency wishes you to write your real name on a piece of paper. Underneath that, you are to write the code word you were given by Herr Hirsch. Then fold the paper closed, seal it, and give it to me to take to His Excellency."

The chair in front of the escritoire was positioned with its back to the center of the room, so Franz's body could shield prying eyes from seeing what he was writing. Franz wrote his name and his personal code word. He sprinkled sand from the sander onto the paper to dry the ink. He folded the paper in thirds, and then folded the two short sides so that they overlapped. Finally, he used the burning candle to melt the sealing wax and dripped it across the open edge. He carefully embedded the seal in the soft red wax for two seconds. The lieutenant took the sealed document and carried it up the curving staircase. The officer returned surprisingly soon.

"His Excellency wishes to meet with you and your colleague."

One of the grenadiers fetched Paul from outside, and he and Franz were escorted upstairs into the ambassador's office. Baron Octavian von Bruno-Bader was a portly man dressed in court clothing for a formal dinner. His dark, turquoise-blue jacket was embossed with gold brocade and draped with a variety of medals and decorations. Over his jacket, he wore a light turquoise-blue sash bearing the large insignia of yet another order. His ruddy face and pop-eyes added a comic aspect to his otherwise dignified mien.

"Please sit down," he rumbled, waving a large, fat hand in the direction of the two secret agents.

"Herr 'Braun,' I presume," said the Baron to Franz.

"Yes, Your Excellency."

"And you are?"

"Herr 'Müller,' Your Excellency," Paul said.

"And what can I do for you?"

Franz spoke. "As you obviously know, Max Hirsch sent us to kill King Frederick."

The ambassador kept a totally neutral expression on his face.

"Frederick was most effectively guarded by his Minister of Police, the Baron Manfred von Hochenheimer, who thwarted our first attempt at assassinating the King. We felt that, if we killed von Hochenheimer, the King would be considerably more vulnerable."

The ambassador continued to hold his poker face. The diplomat was undoubtedly an excellent card player.

"We were present when a young Prussian ex-soldier, whom we'd previously employed, shot and killed von Hochenheimer outside his home in Potsdam. At the time, we were disguised as Prussian musketeers. Three Prussian soldiers saw us in the vicinity of the assassin. The two of us followed the assassin after the killing, pretending to be chasing him, and all three of us managed to get away. We decided that we could increase our chances of successfully killing Frederick by leaving Prussia while the hunt for the killers was underway, and returning and resuming our mission when a new—presumably much less effective—Minister of Police was in office."

"And where is the assassin now?"

"He's dead, Your Excellency. The risk of his being able to identify us was too great. The assassination can no longer be tied to Austria in any way," replied Franz, being careful to say the absolute bare minimum regarding their murder of Caspar Hoffmann.

"Can it be tied to this Prussian?"

"Perhaps, Your Excellency."

"How?"

"The Minister was killed with a hunting rifle. We believe that the assassin stole the rifle from his employer. If the Prussians can identify the owner of the rifle, it seems very likely that they can find out the identity of the killer."

"Why did the Prussian kill von Hochenheimer? Was he bribed? Was a woman involved?"

"Not at all, Your Excellency. The Minister of Police had tortured the young man. This was just a revenge killing, nothing more. The problem is that the marks of what the minions of the Minister of Police did to the young man are on his dead body, which is unlikely to be found in the near future. Furthermore, even if the body is eventually discovered, it's almost inconceivable that it would ever be identified, let alone as the body of the assassin. So, the sole evidence against the killer is the hunting rifle."

"Do you know where the body is?"

"Yes, Your Excellency."

"If required, could you bring it back to Potsdam so that the evidence of von Hochenheimer's actions can be made public?"

"I suppose so, Your Excellency."

The ambassador changed topics.

"Herr Braun, I have a letter in my safe for you from Herr Hirsch. Please excuse me."

The ambassador rose from his chair, and walked to a large safe on one side of the room. He took a key from his chain and unlocked the safe. It took him a few minutes to locate the letter. He closed the safe and carefully locked it. Then he walked over to Franz and handed him the letter.

Franz observed that the letter had been sealed, but he was absolutely certain that the letter had been carefully opened, shown to the ambassador, and resealed without leaving any evidence of the deed. Franz broke the seal and read the instructions sent to him from Vienna. When he'd finished, he told the ambassador that his instructions were to burn the letter after reading it. The ambassador gesticulated in the direction of the candles on his desk; a bronze candlestick stood on a bronze tray. Franz got up, walked to the desk, and solemnly ignited the letter, dropping the burning piece of paper onto the tray. When the flames had entirely consumed the letter, Franz sat down again.

"Do you have any questions?" asked the ambassador.

"Your Excellency, do you have any information regarding the current border situation?"

"As far as I know, the Prussians are not allowing anyone to leave the country at present, but there are no restrictions on entering Prussia. So, if someone were to take the coach from here to Berlin, it's unlikely that he would encounter any problems."

"And have you heard whether Frederick has appointed a new Minister of Police yet?" asked Paul, speaking for the first time.

"I haven't received any information about that. There is no question that the country is being turned upside down to find the assassins, but it's not clear to me who is in charge of the investigation. It may even be Frederick himself. Any other questions?"

Franz and Paul remained silent.

"I have to go to dinner now at the Russian Embassy," the ambassador continued, "but before I leave you, is there anything I can do for you?"

"Tomorrow morning, we need to return to Vienna. But we'd greatly appreciate a bath, clean clothing, and a bed for the night."

"Of course. You'll stay in the residence. I'll instruct Lieutenant Schulz von Schulzenheim to look after you. Please do not hesitate to ask him for anything you may need."

Baron von Bruno-Bader rose from his chair and escorted the two secret agents to the door. Outside, the lieutenant was waiting. The ambassador exchanged a few words with him, then bid farewell to Franz and Paul.

***

After a bath, a delicious dinner, and a good night's sleep in a comfortable bed, both of the Austrians were looking forward to seeing their beloved Vienna once more. But as they sat down to breakfast, Lieutenant Schulz von Schulzenheim entered the room and told them that the ambassador wished to see them.

"Good morning," said Baron Octavian von Bruno-Bader, smiling broadly. "I trust you both slept well."

"Yes, indeed, Your Excellency," Franz said.

"And I'm sure that Lieutenant Schulz von Schulzenheim has been looking after you."

"Yes, we are most grateful to the lieutenant, and to you, naturally, for arranging everything."

The Baron stopped smiling, to indicate that the pleasantries were over. "I'm sorry to interrupt your breakfasts, but I've received information that may be of interest to you, and may even change your plans. As I was returning from dinner last night, an Austrian secret agent arrived from Berlin. He gave me this poster, headed *Belohnung* (reward) in huge letters. Berlin has been plastered with the posters, and copies are being handed out to passersby. I assume that they're being distributed all over Prussia, but the secret agent didn't say anything about that.

"Underneath the heading," Baron Octavian von Bruno-Bader continued, "is this crude line drawing of a face, and, below that, the name Caspar Hoffmann. Is that the name of the Prussian whom you saw shoot von Hochenheimer?"

"Yes, that's the man," Franz said. "The drawing is not a particularly good likeness, but it was obviously done from a description of Hoffmann, not from life."

"As you can see," the ambassador added, "the poster says that he's wanted for the murder of Baron von Hochenheimer, Minister of Police. And there's no mention here of two other people being in the vicinity of the assassination. Furthermore, the secret agent told me that he had no trouble riding from Prussia to Saxony. Now that they know who killed von Hochenheimer, they've reopened the borders."

"That's extremely helpful information, Your Excellency," said Paul.

"Well, I'm glad to have been of some service. I suggest that you resume your breakfasts."

Paul and Franz returned to the residency dining room. They were alone there, so Paul turned to Franz. "Do you think that this is some sort of trap?"

"What exactly do you mean?"

"The authorities know that Caspar Hoffmann killed von Hochenheimer. The poster is proof of that. They also know that there were two men in musketeer uniforms who chased after the assassin, shot at him (but missed), dropped their muskets, and ran after the assassin. From what the secret policeman had said when he raided our room in Frau Deitel's house, it's almost certain that they've found the two dead musketeers whom we'd stripped of their muskets and uniforms. So, it's reasonable to believe that the authorities have put two and two together, and concluded that the two men in musketeer uniforms at von Hochenheimer's mansion were the people who killed the two true musketeers. Surely they must also have found the uniforms in the wooden crate next to the theater by now. Two people who look like us were seen on the day of the murder of the musketeers in the vicinity of that killing. We know that the Prussian police authorities are highly intelligent and efficient. There's no question whatsoever in my mind that the Prussian police know or strongly suspect several things. First, two men who look like you and me killed the two musketeers and took their uniforms and equipment. Second, those two men were near Hoffmann when he shot von Hochenheimer. Third, the two men deliberately prevented the three soldiers from running after Hoffmann. Fourth, those two men and Hoffmann traveled to Berlin the day after the killing and stayed at Frau Deitel's house."

"Yes," said Franz, "I agree with all four of your items. But why does that mean that they've set a trap for us?"

"They know that Hoffmann stole the rifle and, in all probability, fired the shot that killed von Hochenheimer. They know that you and I were right next to him at the time, and that we protected him after the assassination. Yet the 'Wanted' poster is all about Hoffmann, and doesn't even mention that two other men are also being sought. Why? The only reason I can come up with is that they want you and me to think that we're off the hook. It's the sort of trap that I would have expected from von Hochenheimer, and it's probably Frederick's idea. Whatever else you may think about him, you have to admit that he's a great general."

"So what do we do now?" Franz asked.

"I don't know. You told the ambassador that we need to return to Vienna. Presumably, you decided this on the basis of the contents of the letter from Max that you burned. Now you have additional information—namely, the wanted poster that studiously avoids any mention of you or me. Are we still going to Vienna, or are we heading back to Potsdam?"

"We're only two days away from Vienna by post coach. I think I need to consult with Max and then, depending what he says, we can return to Prussia."

CHAPTER EIGHTEEN

Their journey to Vienna had been uneventful, even boring at times. Prague proved the only point of interest on the route. But the half-hour stop there was far too short to enjoy the beauty of that cosmopolitan city. On their arrival in the Austrian capital around noon the next day, they ate a hasty meal, then made straight for the building from which Max Hirsch conducted his spy network. On the outside, it looked like an ordinary office complex, perhaps a government building of some kind. Inside, however, the entire edifice was dedicated to the training and management of spies.

One of the guards on duty at the front entrance led them to Max's austere office. The walls were bare, as was his modest wooden desk. The major feature of the room was the set of three identical, heavy metal doors in the wall behind the desk that led to walk-in safes. For additional security, every important document stored in any of the safes had been encrypted in a code known only to Hirsch and his secretary, Herr Faschbinder.

Hirsch warmly welcomed Franz and Paul. He was a short, fat, jolly man, with a halo of extremely curly, light brown hair, like the tonsure of a monk. His eyes twinkled. He was almost always smiling, and when he smiled, his smile was genuine.

"I've heard rumors—just rumors—about what you two have achieved. Tell me everything, and in the greatest detail."

Franz described what had happened, beginning with police raid of the back room at the Taverne zum Schwarzen Adler. He was careful to explain not only what he and Paul had done, but also the reasons why they had acted the way they had.

Max listened attentively. He did not make any notes, relying instead on his perfect memory to store away the information he was being given. Once the interview was over, Max would write a summary of the key points, encode it and burn the plaintext original. He'd file just the encrypted version in the appropriate dossier.

The only time he interrupted was when Franz described the killings of the poacher, the two soldiers, and Caspar Hoffmann. Max wanted an exhaustive description to ensure that, when new recruits were taught the art of killing, the information they were given would be totally accurate in every way.

Franz finally described the help the Austrian ambassador in Saxony had given them. He stated that the reason that he and Paul were now in Vienna was because of the letter from Max that Baron Octavian von Bruno-Bader had given him, instructing him to return to Vienna for further instructions.

Max groaned. "If it weren't for the fact that my letters to my secret agents sent to Dresden are routinely opened by the embassy there, I could've saved you a trip to Vienna. However, what I have to say to you is too secret for the Baron and his fellow snoopers to know. In my opinion, this may be our last chance to kill Frederick. I'll tell you about it when you two are about to leave Vienna.

"In the meantime, I have another task for you," he continued. "When Kurt Kluge was back here, he told me that he was certain that Gerhard Schuster was the double agent who had betrayed you and your group to the Prussian police in Brandenburg an der Havel. When I asked him for evidence to support his statement, he told me he had none. When I asked him for his reasons for his suspicions, again he said he had none. What I want to know is: Why does an otherwise levelheaded secret agent make accusations against another secret agent without the slightest evidence of any kind? Why should allegations of this sort be made on intuitive grounds, rather than based on facts? The reason I raise these questions with you today is that Schuster is back in Vienna with his Prussian wife, Wilhelmina."

"He's married?" Franz asked.

"Yes, he recently married a Prussian woman. And that's the whole point. Obviously, there's no way I could possibly send a double agent back to Potsdam. But if he's not a double agent—contrary to what Kluge suspects—then I can understand why he married a Prussian. If he's still a loyal Austrian, then Wilhelmina would provide marvelous cover for him. Using her as his entrée, he could get into Prussian circles that wouldn't dream of admitting you and your colleague."

"But we're Prussians. We talk with a Prussian accent, we carry Prussian papers, we wear Prussian clothes. We're more Prussian than the Prussians," Paul said.

"Well, yes and no," Max said. "You may think of yourselves as Prussians, and there's certainly no logical reason why other people wouldn't think of you as Prussians. And yet, you'll never be fully accepted as Prussians. There's something subtle about an adopted nationality that precludes total acceptance. There's no rational reason for it. It's exactly like Kluge's impregnably held belief that Schuster is a double agent."

"How on earth am I supposed to find out about Schuster?" Franz protested. "I assume that you've spoken to him, interrogated him, tested him, and done everything in your power to determine where his true loyalty lies. The fact that you're asking me to investigate him tells me that you've failed. As far as I'm concerned —knowing you as I do—if you can't determine whether Schuster is a double agent, then I certainly can't. In fact, it would probably be equally true to state that if you can't find out, then no one can."

"That's very flattering of you, Franz, but I do have to admit that I've failed. I've listened carefully to everything that Schuster has told me, and I've thought about it for hours. The end result is that I just don't know whether he's loyal or not. I want you and Paul to find out."

"But why should he tell us anything? He and I have never been more than professional colleagues, so there's no reason for me to take up with him socially. And the same applies to Paul. He saw Paul only at our monthly meetings. We weren't even trained at the same time as he was here in Vienna, so we don't have that sort of connection, either. And we don't have the power to interrogate him the way you can. If you tell him to cooperate with us and answer all our questions, he'll realize that he's under suspicion, which is the last thing we'd want. So surely there's no point in our even trying to find out where his loyalties lie?"

"Franz, I'm truly desperate. Despite my sending streams of competent secret agents to Potsdam and Berlin, Frederick is very much alive. Yes, you've killed von Hochenheimer, and I'm most grateful to the two of you for accomplishing that. I am sorry to have to say that the Baron was a most successful adversary. I've lost far too many secret agents to him. By removing him, you've unquestionably done your country a great service in the long term. In the short term, however, the situation is, paradoxically, worse than it was. As you may've heard, Frederick is acting as his own Minister of Police until he finds an acceptable replacement for von Hochenheimer. The problem, of course, is that Frederick is an outstanding tactician. He's an infinitely more cunning opponent than von Hochenheimer ever was, and that's saying something. Until things settle down, killing Frederick has become even harder than it ever was, which is also saying something."

"What exactly do you want us to do?" Paul asked.

"I'm going to give you a month to determine whether Schuster is a double agent. At the end of that time, I'm sending you both back to Potsdam to make one final attempt on Frederick's life.

"Regarding Schuster," Max continued, "If you fail to come up with a definitive answer one way or the other, then I'll have to restructure the entire organization in Prussia. For everyone's safety, if you can't determine whether he's a double agent, I'll have to assume that he is. If you find that Schuster is an honest man, I'll send him back to Prussia with his wife. But if you discover that he's dishonest...

"Come back in two days' time to tell me how you intend to proceed. In the meantime, you'll obviously live in this building. Herr Faschbinder will assign a room to you. The food is as excellent as ever, the coffee is still strong, and I'm sure you'll both make good use of the gymnasium. Walking from Berlin to Dresden isn't real exercise. And talking about exercise, I want you both to practice daily in the shooting range in the basement. You'll probably get the opportunity to fire only one shot at Frederick, so it'd better be a good one. Once again, my congratulations on a job well done, and I look forward to another successful mission." He ushered them out of his office with a cheery smile.

The two secret agents, however, were anything but cheerful.

***

After arranging with Herr Faschbinder a room in the dormitory area, they went to drink coffee in the refectory. Neither of them could think of a way to proceed.

Finally, Franz had an idea. "You're not going to like this plan. In fact, you're not going to like it at all. In a word: deception."

"Not again," said Paul with a loud sigh. "Look what happened the first time you tried that approach. We had no idea what von Hochenheimer was doing in response to the fictional letter that we gave Hoffmann to put in the hut. The outcome was catastrophic. We were unable to shoot Frederick because the cordon had been moved back, Hoffmann was tortured, and then we had to kill him."

"Actually, the outcome was a triumph. Von Hochenheimer is dead."

"And cunning Frederick himself is running the Prussian police. As I said, the outcome was catastrophic."

"Maybe for now, but when we go back to Prussia in a month's time, there'll surely be a new Minister of Police in place, and we'll have a chance to kill Frederick."

Paul sighed a second time. "We're not going to agree on this issue, no matter how long we sit here and drink Max's truly excellent coffee. However, I'm going to have to agree to your plan, for the simple reason that I can't come up with *any* idea, let alone one that's better than yours. How do you propose to deceive Gerhard?"

"I'm not sure yet. The four of us (you, me, and the Schusters) need to be together somewhere outside of Vienna, a place where, if Gerhard tries to contact Prussia, Max will undoubtedly find out about it."

"Why don't we ask Max to send the four of us on holiday to an inn out in the countryside?" Paul suggested. "If the inn is in the middle of nowhere, Schuster won't be able to send any message to anyone."

"No, no, you're missing the point. The idea is that Gerhard Schuster must receive a fictional letter while we're with him and his wife. In that way, no suspicion will rest on us. Most importantly," Franz continued, "he has to receive the letter in a place with a postal service, so that he can reply to the letter if he so chooses. The letter will appear to have been sent to Schuster by a Prussian secret agent. We have to make sure that the letter is delivered in such a way that we'll know that Gerhard has actually received it. That was one of the many problems we had with the letter for von Hochenheimer. Until the anti-bribery posters appeared on the walls of Potsdam, we had no way of knowing whether the letter had reached him. And even then, we couldn't be completely sure. Something else could have sparked those anti-bribery posters."

Franz paused to make sure Paul understood. "Then we wait to see how Schuster reacts," he continued. "He may ignore the letter, he may report it to us or to Max, or he may respond by returning a message to Prussia. If he reports the letter to someone in the Austrian secret police, you or me or Max, say, then he's either an honest Austrian or he's an incredibly clever double agent. And I don't think he's that clever. If he ignores the letter, then he's a double agent in all probability. A loyal Austrian would certainly report the message to someone. And if he sends a reply to Prussia, then we'll be certain he's a double agent."

"Unless he's a loyal Austrian pretending to be a double agent," Paul said.

"No, this time you're wrong. If Gerhard receives a letter from Prussia that implies that he's a double agent, and he responds to it, then there's no doubt that he's a double agent. Is it likely that you or I would receive a letter from Prussia couched in terms that make it clear that we're double agents? Of course not. And if we did receive such a letter, we'd know that it was probably a trap of some sort, and report it to Max without delay. The last thing that we'd do is to respond to the letter as if we really were double agents. The risk of being labeled a double agent would be far too great."

"So, what you're saying," Paul said, "is that, if we know that Gerhard received the fictional letter and if we know for certain that he did nothing, didn't report it, and didn't reply to it, we'd gain some information regarding his loyalty."

"Precisely!"

***

Two days later, they were back in Max's office.

"Max, we have a plan," Franz said. "We want you to send the Schusters on holiday to Glockmannstein."

"I've never heard of it."

"That's not surprising," Franz said, "even for someone with your encyclopedic knowledge. It's a tiny village in the Alps. There's a small inn there, where the Schusters will stay. The village—if you can use the use word *village* for a settlement that nowadays consists of just an inn—is at the end of a long, narrow valley with high mountains on three sides. Many years ago, the town held a number of holiday houses, but they're all deserted and ruined now. The place is just too isolated. Anything or anyone who comes into or goes out of Glockmannstein has to pass through the village of Sankt Johann am Waldeck, which is situated right at the entrance to the valley. The idea is that you send the Schusters to that inn, then put a police post just outside Sankt Johann am Waldeck, on the only road to Glockmannstein. If anyone travels from Glockmannstein, they'll be searched at the post. So you'll have full control over everything leaving the village."

"And why would I want full control over everything leaving Glockmannstein?"

"Because," Franz continued, "you're going to send a fictional letter to Gerhard purporting to come from his new controller in Prussia. It'll be addressed to where he's staying in Vienna—if he's a Prussian double agent, he certainly would've sent a message to his controller telling him his new address—and it'll be forwarded to the inn in Glockmannstein. The letter will explain that, due to the assassination of von Hochenheimer, the whole Ministry of Police is undergoing reorganization. In particular, Gerhard has been given a new controller. The letter will contain instructions for sending a reply to that controller, namely, an address in Graz. The letter will instruct Gerhard to tell his new controller what your reaction was to learning that he (Gerhard) is now married, to a Prussian no less."

"And why do I want to send that letter to Gerhard?"

"If he ignores the letter," Franz explained, "he's probably a double agent. If he reports the letter to you, he's either honest, or an incredibly smart double agent. And if he sends a reply to Graz, then he's definitely a double agent."

"There's something you've overlooked," Max said after a long pause. "What if Gerhard takes a walk over the mountains into the next valley and posts his letter there?"

"Ah, yes, Franz said, "I was coming to that. That's why you'll arrange for Paul and me also to stay at the inn in Glockmannstein. We can keep an eye on Gerhard and his wife."

"His wife?"

"If he's a Prussian double agent, she may well be a Prussian secret agent herself. He may give a letter to her, and she may try to somehow smuggle it out of Glockmannstein. The two of us are needed to keep a watch on the two of them," Franz added.

"So, you want me to send the Schusters to the inn. Once they've settled down there, the two of you arrive. Correct?"

"Correct."

"I assume that you want me to arrange that there are no other guests at the inn."

"We didn't think of that," Paul said. "That's a really good idea. If there are no other guests, then there's no way the Schusters can give a letter to another guest to smuggle out of Glockmannstein."

"And the inn staff must be told not to leave Glockmannstein under any circumstances," Franz added. "If you pay them some sort of bonus for the month, they'll probably cooperate."

"Just how many people work at the inn?" Max asked.

"I've no idea," Franz said. "I'd imagine that a small inn like that could manage with no more than three people: the innkeeper, his wife (who would double as cook and waitress), and a maid."

"Fine, let's assume that there are three people involved." Max paused to think. He pursed his lips and continued. "When do I send my letter to Gerhard?"

"After we've arrived at the inn." Paul explained. "That way, the Schusters won't think of tying us to the arrival of your letter. But we have to know when the letter has been delivered to Gerhard.

"How can we do that?" Max asked.

"Suppose you instruct the staff at the inn that all letters addressed to the Schusters are to be given to me," Franz suggested. "I can then hand the letter to Gerhard and tell him the maid had made a mistake."

"Yes, that would work," Max said. "In fact, that's an excellent idea, because there's something that I don't think any of us have considered. What if a real letter from Prussia arrives for the Schusters? For example, suppose a letter comes, purportedly from Wilhelmina's family, but in actuality it's from her controller? The staff must be told to give to you all letters addressed to the Schusters, and to do so without the Schusters knowing about it. You'll then give my fictional letter to Gerhard, but make sure that I receive all other letters sent to the Schusters."

"How would I do that?" Franz asked.

"What do you mean?" Max questioned.

"Well, the staff will have been told not to leave the vicinity of the inn. If Paul or I were to hike over to the police post just outside Sankt Johann am Waldeck, there's always a chance that one or both of the Schusters will insist on accompanying us, or worse, they may say nothing but follow us surreptitiously. So, how am I to get letters to you or, for that matter, reports or any other materials?"

"There must be a cart of some sort that delivers provisions to the inn on a regular basis," Paul said. "You'll have to arrange with the carter to act as a courier, taking letters and reports from us to the police post."

Max looked a little startled. "This is starting to get out of hand," he said. "I've got the two of you watching the Schusters at the inn, the three staff members, the carter, and there are also the teams of policemen that have to be on duty at the post outside Sankt Johann am Waldeck 24 hours a day. Isn't there a way of doing this without involving a whole army?"

"The short answer is *no*," Paul said. "The plan is for you to send a fictional letter to Gerhard Schuster and then retrieve his answer. You need the whole crew to make sure that he and his wife don't smuggle any letters out."

"And why not?" Max asked.

"What do you mean, 'and why not'?" Paul asked.

"Why should I care if they smuggle a letter out? They'll be told to send their reply to a certain address in Graz. Why does it matter how the letter gets there?"

There was a long silence. Then Paul and Franz looked at one another and started laughing. Max joined in. The three of them laughed uncontrollably as they all realized just how complex their plan had become.

When they finally stopped laughing, Max spoke. "All we need to do is get the fictional letter to Gerhard at his current lodgings, and have someone retrieve his reply, if any, from the address in Graz and bring it to me in Vienna. We don't need the inn. We don't need you staying at the inn. In fact, we don't need the two of you at all. You've come up with a great plan, and I can take over from here. I am most grateful to you, as always."

The two secret agents got up to go. As Paul was shaking hands with Max, he suddenly said, "And what if Gerhard sends a reply to his previous controller at the previously agreed address?"

All three men sat down, suddenly sobered.

"Please repeat what you just said," Max ordered, "and be as precise as possible. I want to be quite sure that you meant exactly what I thought you meant."

Paul cleared his throat, reflected for a few seconds, and then began. "Suppose that Gerhard is indeed a Prussian double agent. Let's say that his controller in Berlin is Herr A, and communications are to be sent to an address in Salzburg for forwarding to Berlin. Now you send Gerhard a fictional letter, telling him that his controller is now Herr B, and all letters must go to Graz. One possibility is that Gerhard will obey you and send a letter to Graz. But another possibility is that Gerhard will be suspicious of your letter for some reason. He would then send a letter to Herr A, via Salzburg, to say he received a letter from someone purporting to be Herr B, his new controller, and asking Herr A if the letter is genuine."

"Yes," said Max. "That's what I thought you meant. But he won't report the letter to me, so I'll have grounds to strongly suspect him."

"Not necessarily," Paul said. "If someone gets a message that reads something like, 'Meet me under the second purple pumpkin tree on the left in the orchard of the hairy milkmaid on the 49th day of the month of Ibalory,' he'd just toss it away."

"But that wouldn't be the case if he were a secret agent," Max said. "If someone in your profession were to receive a message like that, at the very least he'd pass it on to me. Gerhard is an Austrian secret agent. Yes, he may also be a Prussian double agent, but he's been trained as an Austrian secret agent. So, if he were to receive a strange message of some sort, he'd definitely bring it to me—unless he's a double agent and his primary loyalty is now to Prussia.

"So the answer is this," he continued. "I send Gerhard a message telling him that he has a new controller, Herr B; all communications from now on are to go to a certain address in Graz; and Gerhard is to immediately acknowledge receipt of the message. If he doesn't report the letter to me, he's definitely a double agent. If he reports it to me, either he's not a double agent, or he's an exceedingly clever double agent. And if he replies to the message, we arrest him at once for treason. It's not perfect, it's not foolproof, but it's reasonable. Yes, there's always the risk that he reports the message to me and then communicates with his old controller, Herr A, as well. But I think that's too Byzantine for our friend Gerhard. This way is cheap, quick, and about as accurate as we'll get when dealing with deception."

"Does that mean that the two of us are not going to get a month-long, all-expenses-paid holiday in the mountains?" Paul asked. "Look how much money we've saved you. You don't have to pay for the Schusters to stay at the inn; you don't have to bribe the three members of the inn staff or that chap with the cart who brings the provisions two or three times a week. There's no need to man a police post just outside Sankt Johann am Waldeck 24 hours a day for a whole month. We've saved you a small fortune. I know you're most grateful to us for coming up with our brilliant suggestion, and I think you should show your gratitude in concrete form."

Max laughed so hard that the two secret agents started to get worried he might do himself a serious injury. Wiping the tears of mirth from his eyes, he eventually downgraded his laughter to chortling, and then finally a smile. "That's surely the funniest suggestion I've heard this month. All I asked you to do was come up with a way of determining if Schuster is a double agent, which is part of your job. I don't give all-expenses-paid holidays to my secret agents for doing their jobs. On the other hand," his voice softened, "you've come up with a good solution to a problem that I couldn't solve myself. I'm prepared to be generous. I'll pay for two weeks at a most comfortable inn here in Vienna."

Paul smiled his appreciation, but Franz caught on quickly. "You're looking for something else for us to do before you send us back to Potsdam. So this is a job, not a holiday. There's someone staying at the inn you want us to check out. Who is it?"

"Franz, Franz, always so suspicious. Am I so heartless that I wouldn't give two of my finest secret agents a two-week stay at a comfortable inn to thank them for their wonderful work?"

"Max, you wouldn't give a copper coin to a dying beggar unless there was something in it for you or, more accurately, unless there was a lot in it for you."

"Franz, how can you make such a vile accusation? You're absolutely correct, of course, but you really mustn't say such terrible things."

"So who are we to check out at the inn?" Franz asked.

"There's a Prussian *Junker* staying there. He calls himself the Viscount von Waldstein zu Eckelberg. My secret agents suspect that he's a Prussian secret agent. The Prussians have been clever, but perhaps not clever enough. Regrettably, no one has yet come up with a book that contains a list of all European nobility that we can consult and see if there really is such a viscountship[4]. However, I've sent secret agents to the offices of the *Vossische Zeitung* in Berlin. They looked through years of old newspapers for reports of court receptions, and they found a reference to a Viscount von Waldstein zu Eckelberg in an article published three years ago. Unfortunately for the Prussians, the article mentions that his grandson, Oskar von Waldstein zu Eckelberg, accompanied the Viscount at court. Oskar had just graduated from the Liegnitz Ritter-Akademie, which would presumably have made him about 18 years of age. So the Viscount must have been around 60 years old then."

---

[4] The first edition of the *Almanach de Gotha* was published only in 1763.

"So?" Franz said.

"The Viscount staying at Im weissen Rössl (White Horse Inn) is no more than 30 years old."

"So the Viscount died and was succeeded by his son," Franz guessed.

"Not quite. The father of his grandson must be at least 40 by now."

Franz tried again. "So that son died, and a younger son succeeded in the title."

"Not exactly. If the oldest son is dead, the Viscount would be succeeded by the oldest son of the oldest son, possibly the grandson in the newspaper article."

"Maybe the grandson is dead, too," Franz persisted.

"I'll admit that Prussian casualties during the Silesian War were higher than expected," Max said, "but it seems unlikely that, in the past three years, the old Viscount died, and was preceded in death by his oldest son and at least one grandson."

"Possibly they had an outbreak of bubonic plague in Schloss Waldstein or whatever the family castle is called."

"The last outbreak was the Great Plague of Marseilles in 1720, nearly 30 years ago."

"You're not making this easy for me, are you?" Franz said. "Fine, I give up. The man staying at Im weissen Rössl is an imposter."

Max nodded. "I gathered from our conversation two days ago that you've recently successfully masqueraded as *Junker*."

"Yes and no," replied Paul. "Yes, we've fooled an obsequious theatre manager, a frightened tavern keeper, and an out-of-work, slightly drunk ex-soldier. No, we haven't fooled a real-life *Junker*."

"I hear what you're saying, but you have to remember that the 'Viscount von Waldstein zu Eckelberg' is no more of a real-life *Junker* than the 'Earl von Schloss Müller' and the 'Marquis zu Braun und Weissburg,' if I recall your names correctly."

"Your perfect memory is in excellent working order," Franz said.

"Two other things. In Prussia, when you were pretending to be *Junker*, the stakes were high. If you were found out, you might well have been executed as spies. But here in Austria, you're at home and pretending to be *Junker* at my behest. So the worst that can happen is that the Viscount von Waldstein zu Eckelberg will call your bluff and that would be that—there wouldn't be any sort of negative consequences for either of you.

"Second," Max continued, "the Viscount doesn't have access to the *Vossische Zeitung* or to any other Prussian newspaper, for that matter. You'd have to do something that would make him suspicious. Then he'd have to send a message to his Viennese contact, who, in turn, would have to send a message to Prussia. Swarms of their secret agents would have to try to find out whether or not the 'Earl von Schloss Müller' and the 'Marquis zu Braun und Weissburg' are genuine *Junker* nobles. That information would have to be sent back here. That's why I'm giving you two weeks to unmask the *Junker*—longer than that, and he can possibly unmask you."

"If you're so certain that he's an imposter," Paul said, "why are you asking us to do this? Why don't you just deport him?"

"That would provoke an international incident, which is the last thing we need now. The man is ostensibly a Prussian nobleman, a Viscount. Packing him off home to Prussia will lead to all manner of complications."

"Well, in that case," Paul said, "why not just have him followed day and night while making him fully aware of the watchers? That will make it impossible for him to achieve anything here."

"I want him to go back to Prussia totally humiliated," Max said. "That should discourage his masters from sending other secret agents to Vienna. If he goes back in triumph as the Viscount von Waldstein zu Eckelberg, the Prussians will get the idea that we Viennese are country bumpkins who're easy to fool. But if he goes back exposed as a charlatan and a mountebank—like a frightened dog with his tail between his legs—the Prussians will be less likely to send us more secret agents in disguise. Come back and see me in two days' time," Max instructed. "Obviously you'll need clothes that befit two *Junker* staying in a suite at Im weissen Rössl. At that time, let me know what else you'll need. Naturally, by then I expect you to tell me how you'll succeed in unmasking the Viscount."

CHAPTER NINETEEN

When Paul and Franz were ushered into Max's office two days later, he smiled even more broadly than usual. "Congratulations. Your plan worked like a dream."

"You mean—"

"Yes, both Schusters are now sitting in jail charged as Prussian spies."

"What happened?"

"As soon as you left me, I drafted a letter along the lines we'd agreed. I identified myself as Heinrich von Mombauer. I informed Gerhard that I was his new controller, and I told him that all future messages from him to me were to be sent care of Frau Möwe at 15 Pomeranzengasse in Graz. I was a little worried that Gerhard might recognize my handwriting, so I gave my draft to a new recruit to write out. I told him to address it to Schuster at the apartment where he and his wife have been living for the past few days. Then I asked him to take the letter to a courier service for urgent delivery.

"An hour after the letter was delivered to him," Max continued, "Gerhard turned up at the Imperial Postal Service with a reply addressed to Frau Möwe at 15 Pomeranzengasse in Graz. I had two men waiting at the postal service to arrest Gerhard on the spot. We arrested Wilhelmina in their apartment a few minutes later.

"I was surprised at how stupid Gerhard had been. He made two mistakes, one extremely serious. We learned from him that his previous controller was none other than the late unlamented Baron von Hochenheimer himself. If I'd known that, I'd have made some reference to the Baron in my letter. The omission of any reference at all to his previous controller should have alerted him.

"His second and much bigger mistake was that, in his excitement in getting new instructions from Berlin, Gerhard forgot that he hadn't given his address in Vienna to the Prussians. And the reason I'm certain that they didn't know his address is that I had him and his wife followed day and night from the moment he made contact with me on his return from Prussia.

"So, when the courier arrived, Gerard Schuster should've been extremely suspicious. After all, just about the only person who knew where he and his wife were staying was yours truly. Anyhow, thanks to you, the Schusters are safely locked up where they cannot possibly do any more harm to Austria. And kudos to Kurt Kluge and his intuition. I just wonder what made him so certain that Gerhard Schuster was a double agent and that he was the person who tipped off the police raid on the Taverne zum Schwarzen Adler. Now tell me how you intend to unmask Viscount von Waldstein zu Eckelberg."

"I'm going to ask Paul to tell you about the plan," Franz said. "It's his idea, and he deserves the credit for it."

"Thank you, Franz. Max, in devising a plan, my biggest concern was that I'm not a Prussian, let alone a *Junker*. The problem I had pondered was how to convince the Viscount (who isn't a *Junker* himself, of course) that Franz and I are unquestionably, 100 percent genuine *Junker*. I realized that we possess some special knowledge. We were the two *Junker* who tricked Hoffmann into taking the letter to the hut near Brandenburg an der Havel. Furthermore, the Viscount is actually a member of the Prussian secret service, so he knows all about those two *Junker*. In particular, he knows full well that the two *Junker* were involved in the assassination of von Hochenheimer.

"My strategy is simple: We'll talk to the Viscount, and then we'll turn the conversation in the direction of the two *Junker*. We'll tell him that we were sent to Vienna to track down the two *Junker* who were there when the Minister of Police was killed. In view of the fact that only confidants of the Prussian Police even know about the existence of the two *Junker*, let alone the role they played in the killing, I'm pretty certain that he'll let something slip that will give him away."

"That sounds like a good strategy," Max said. "Actually, I'd like to be a fly on the wall when the two of you go to work. Two

Austrian secret agents pretending to be *Junker* trying to trap a Prussian secret agent who's also pretending to be a *Junker* should be something to witness. In addition to clothing and money, is there anything else you two will need for your masquerade?"

"We still have our pistols," replied Franz, "and we'll certainly be taking them along. It may prove necessary to dispatch the Viscount. Other than that, I think we have everything."

"Has it occurred to you," Max asked, "that, if he finds out that you two were involved in any way at all in the assassination of the Minister of Police, he'll try to dispatch both of you? And don't think that it's going to be two against one. He has a valet, who's probably a secret agent, too."

"Surely we also need a valet?" asked Paul. "After all, we're also *Junker*. That new recruit who wrote your letter and took it to the courier service—why don't you send him along with us as our valet? Not only will our having a valet add credibility, but he can assist if the two Prussians get violent."

"Now that's a good idea," said Max. "I'll tell him. His name is Hermann Stricker, by the way. I'll arrange a valet's uniform for him, and also pistols. I'm sure that the Viscount von Waldstein zu Eckelberg's valet is armed."

"Oh, I've just thought of something," added Paul. "We're going to need visiting cards. The etiquette is quite straightforward. Our valet will present our cards to his valet. If he wishes to receive us—and I'm certain that he will—his valet will present two of his cards to our valet. We can then call on him in his rooms."

"It's going to take an extra day to organize the valet and your cards, but I agree with you; both are essential," Max said. "This fellow has to believe that the two of you are dyed-in-the-wool *Junker*, and visiting cards and a valet will certainly help with the illusion."

"What address will you print on the cards?" asked Franz. "We don't want any slip-ups there."

"No, that's not how it's done," Paul said. "This isn't a business card. A visiting card has just a name and title on it, nothing more. That will be enough to pique his interest. Nobility are always interested in other nobility. Clearly, when he sees our mannerisms and hears us talking, he'll realize that we're not just nobles, but fellow Prussian *Junker*. From then on, it's going to be very, very interesting."

***

Two days later, the two Austrian secret agents knocked on the door of the Prussian secret agent's room. They'd arrived at the inn the previous day with their valet in tow, and without delay, they had dispatched Stricker with their visiting cards. The Prussian's valet had accepted them. An hour later, he came to the Austrians' rooms with two of his master's cards.

Franz and Paul decided to wait until the following afternoon at five before visiting the Viscount von Waldstein zu Eckelberg. The valet opened the door. Franz gave their names. The valet disappeared for a few seconds, and then invited the Austrians to enter his master's room.

"Welcome, Earl. Welcome, Marquis. I'm delighted to make your acquaintance," said the Prussian secret agent. "Schottky, fetch us some champagne."

Turning to the Austrians, he invited them to sit in the comfortable armchairs with which the sitting room had been furnished. When they were seated, he asked them where they were from. On hearing that he was entertaining fellow Prussian *Junker*, he exclaimed that he couldn't possibly be more delighted.

"I'm here because I love Vienna. Wonderful women, wonderful food, wonderful music. And what brings you to Austria?"

As they'd previously agreed, Franz gave a partial answer. "We've been sent here by His Majesty, King Frederick II, in his capacity as Acting Minister of Police."

"Really? And what's the purpose of your mission?"

"I'm afraid that's confidential, of course. All that we can tell you is that we are visiting all our fellow *Junker* here in Vienna."

"Including me?"

"Including you, of course."

The three secret agents engaged in superficial conversation. The Austrians took the greatest care to ensure that nothing that they said about Frederick could possibly be interpreted as criticism of any kind. The Prussian, in turn, was careful not to say too much about his life as a *Junker* for fear that the two actual Junker in his sitting room might expose his lies—or so he believed. The Austrians were less worried about being found out, because they knew that their host was no more *Junker* than they were, but they nevertheless were extremely careful, just in case the Prussian had been coached in detail and therefore knew certain facts that every *Junker* should know. The three of them drank champagne and chatted about Potsdam and Berlin and steered away from any topic that could possibly lead to an unmasking.

***

Franz and Paul left after about 45 minutes, but not before inviting their host to join them for a dinner in their room in two days' time. They used the intervening 48 hours to arrange with the inn to send up a gourmet meal. In addition, they ordered bottles of the finest French white wine, as well as bottles filled with colored water. Then they gave detailed instructions to Stricker, their valet.

"Hermann," said Franz, "We're going to give the impression of drinking far too much wine at dinner. More precisely, you're going to have to switch bottles behind the Prussian's back so that you fill his glass with wine, but you fill our glasses with colored water. Max's people have sworn to us that the colored water that they've supplied has the identical hue as the genuine wine. I cannot impress on you how important it is not to confuse the bottles. If you give him colored water or if you give us wine, the whole plan will be ruined. The labels on the bottles are identical, obviously, so you're going to have to find some way of distinguishing between the bottles. Don't tell us what it is, or we may study the bottles too intently while you're pouring, and give the game away. So, the success or demise of the whole scheme is in your hands."

"You can rely on me totally," Hermann said.

"Good. In addition, you need to have a loaded pistol in your pocket. We're going to use the meal to try to expose the Viscount."

The Viscount von Waldstein zu Eckelberg arrived promptly. Stricker invited him in.

"Welcome, Viscount," said Franz, slightly slurring his consonants. "We've been drinking Montrachet all day—care to join us in a glass?"

"I never turn down Montrachet," the Prussian said. "What have I done to deserve the finest white wine in the world?"

"What you've done is to honor us by joining us," said Paul in a smarmy voice, also starting to slur his consonants.

Over the next half hour, the Prussian secret agent drank almost a whole bottle of Montrachet. The Austrians, however, drank only the colored water, while appearing to have imbibed even more Montrachet than their guest. They sat down to dine on the first course, smoked salmon and pickled herring.

"Viscount," said Franz, his voice slurring to the extreme. "I trust you, so I'm going to tell you why we're here in Vienna."

"I am honored that you are taking me into your confidence."

"No, the honor is all ours," Paul interjected, "all ours, all ours." It seemed as though Paul had also put back considerably more Montrachet than he could comfortably handle.

"Yes, it's our honor," echoed Franz. "It's our honor because we're here to look for the two *Junker* who were involved in the assassination of the Baron Manfred von Hochenheimer."

"Yes, I know all about that," the Prussian said.

"You do?" Paul asked, hoping for their guest to go on.

"Yes, I know that there were two *Junker* who organized the killing."

"And just how do you know that?" asked Franz in a steely voice with all trace of drunkenness gone. "Stricker!"

The valet, who was standing behind the Prussian, drew his pistol, quickly cocked it and placed it against the back of the Prussian's head.

"What's this? What's this?"

"Answer my question: How do you know that there were two *Junker* who organized the assassination of von Hochenheimer?"

"I'm not sure what this is all about," he replied in a shaky voice, "and I think this behavior is in really bad taste but, in answer to your question, everyone knows that."

"No, not everyone knows that," Paul responded. "The existence of the two *Junker* has not been made public. In fact, the only people who know about it are the Prussian secret police, which makes you a secret agent."

"Nonsense, every *Junker* knows about it."

"First, that's not true," Paul said. "And second, if it were true, it wouldn't explain why you know it, because you are no *Junker*."

"I certainly am. I'm the Viscount von Waldstein zu Eckelberg."

"No, you're not," Franz said. "The Viscount is a man of about 65, with a grandson who is now about 21 years of age. And keep your hands on the table." Franz had just noticed that the Prussian's hands were starting to slide slowly into his lap, presumably to access a pistol he had hidden in his pocket.

"Paul, disarm him."

Paul got up from his chair, moved to the Prussian's right side and carefully took a pistol out of his pocket.

"While on the subject of bad taste, Viscount, coming to a dinner with a loaded pistol is considered to be extremely gauche behavior in the best circles. Paul, see if he has another pistol on the other side."

Paul walked behind Hermann and approached the Prussian from the left. He reached into his other pocket and found another pistol. "Two pistols at dinner, Viscount? Two? That's even more gauche."

"Now, as I was saying," Franz continued, "the real Viscount is a man of roughly 65, with a grandson of about 21. You're not even 30."

"My father died two years ago. I inherited the viscountship."

"Really?" asked Franz. "And why you and not your older brother?"

"I don't have an older brother."

"You have a nephew who is 21 years old," Franz said, "but you aren't even 30 yet."

"I have a much older sister. My nephew is her child."

"I see. And what's his name?"

"Er, Felix."

"Family name?"

"Um, von Blumenstein."

"Then who is Oskar von Waldstein zu Eckelberg, who accompanied your father to court three years ago?"

"I've never heard of him."

"Now," said Franz, "isn't it interesting that you've never heard of him? You'll no doubt be most surprised to learn that the *Vossische Zeitung* knows all about him. The Berlin newspaper of record described him as your father's grandson, which would make him your nephew. And his family name is von Waldstein zu Eckelberg, which would make him the son of your nonexistent older brother, not your older sister."

There was silence.

"Who are you?"

More silence.

"I've been authorized to give you a choice," Franz said. "If you admit who you are and write a full confession, you'll be deported to Prussia. If not, you'll be jailed for fraud for a long, long time. As you know, pretending to be a nobleman is a serious crime, both in Prussia and in Austria."

There was no response from the erstwhile Viscount.

"Get up!"

The Prussian slowly rose from the table. Hermann Stricker kept him covered with the pistol.

"Walk slowly to the door."

The Prussian secret agent started walking. When he was halfway across the room, he stopped. He turned to Franz and said, "I've just realized who you two are. You're the two *Junker* who killed von Hochenheimer."

As he spoke, he reached for the small pistol hidden behind his back in the waistband of his knee breeches. Hermann fired at the secret agent's hand as it touched the pistol. The shot missed the hand, hit the pistol instead, and ricocheted into the secret agent's left hip. The pistol fell to the ground. The Prussian secret agent collapsed, writhing in pain.

"Hermann, go and get some help," ordered Paul as he picked up the small pistol. "We're going to need a stretcher to get him to jail, and he'll certainly need medical attention when he gets there."

Ninety minutes later, the two Austrian secret agents were once more sitting in Max's Spartan office.

"Yet again, congratulations on a job well done," Max said.

"Thank you," replied Franz, "but we have a problem. As I'm sure you've already heard, the Prussian secret agent decided that Paul and I were the two *Junker* who were involved in the assassination of von Hochenheimer. I've no idea why he arrived at that conclusion, but there it is. If you deport him to Berlin, as I think you were intending to do, he'll describe us to his colleagues. That will make it extremely difficult for Paul and me when we return to Prussia."

"Don't worry about that," Max said. "He's currently in the prison hospital, in isolation. When he recovers from the surgery to extract the bullet, we'll make sure he stays in isolation until the two of you get safely back from Prussia. In any event, he's going to stay in prison until he signs a full confession."

"Now that we've sorted out the Viscount von Waldstein zu Eckelberg for you," Franz said, "can we please go back to Prussia now?"

"Not quite yet. For my plan to work, I need the level of security around Frederick to be somewhat lowered. So you'll have to stay in Austria for at least another three weeks."

"Doing what?"

"At the moment, nothing. If your inestimable services are needed, I'll certainly let you know. But for now, I suggest you take it easy and enjoy life in beautiful Vienna. Just come to my secretary's office once a day. Herr Faschbinder will tell you if I need you."

CHAPTER TWENTY

"Big news, gentlemen, big news," Max said.

The two secret agents had been ushered into his office Monday morning.

"There's been a huge breakthrough with Gerhard and Wilhelmina Schuster. Sit down, and I'll tell you all about it." He waited for the men to get settled before continuing. "Immediately after we arrested the two of them, I interrogated them—separately, as was necessary—but neither said a word. I assumed that each of them was trying not to implicate his or her spouse. After a fruitless 15 minutes or so, I sent them back to their cells. The next day I decided to use the standard trick: I told each of them that the other had confessed, and started reading them the 'confession' I'd made up. Gerhard—being a secret agent that I had trained—didn't fall for it, but Wilhelmina did, and she told me everything. I then had Gerhard brought into the interrogation room and made his wife repeat the key parts of her confession in front of him. Gerhard then came clean, and he told me everything that I wanted to know.

"I tell my secret agents over and over," said Max, shaking his head, "don't get involved with women, particularly not women from the country in which you're gathering information, but Gerhard obviously didn't listen. After he'd met Wilhelmina, a Prussian woman, he'd moved in with her. It seems that he talks in his sleep, and night after night he spoke in an Austrian accent about spies, Vienna and King Frederick. Wilhelmina was torn between her love for Gerhard and her love for her King and her country. As a dutiful daughter of Royal Prussia, however, she eventually went to the authorities.

"Gerhard was given the choice between death by hanging or changing his allegiance and becoming a double agent. He chose to be a double agent, partly because it would give him the opportunity to be with Wilhelmina. As you know—with his bald head, huge red nose, and big red ears—Gerhard isn't exactly handsome. Wilhelmina had been the first woman to ever look at him, and he fell for her in the manner of an adolescent schoolboy. So it was easy for him to forget his loyalty to Austria and become a double agent.

"When the Schusters arrived here in Austria from Prussia, and Gerhard came to see me," Max continued, "he was extremely convincing. Were it not for Kurt Kluge's allegation that Gerhard Schuster was the double agent who betrayed you and your group to the Prussian police, the possibility of Schuster's disloyalty would never have crossed my mind. As we've discussed, Kluge had no evidence whatsoever against Gerhard, and no grounds of any kind for his unshakeable belief that Schuster was the traitor. Nevertheless, Kurt's insistence made me suspicious. One of my credos is 'better safe than sorry,' so I'd arranged an apartment for the Schusters to live in not far from here, and I also arranged to have them both watched night and day. The reports I received from the watchers were consistent. The Schusters' behavior was exemplary in the extreme. In particular, I learned that neither of them had attempted to communicate in any way with Prussian secret agents.

"Let me remind you that I told you last week how stupid Schuster had been to reply to the letter I'd sent to his apartment, considering that he hadn't given his new address to the Prussians. Well, now it turns out that he wasn't quite so stupid after all. In his confession, he told me about a bakery around the corner from their apartment. It seems that the baker's wife is hard of hearing, so the customers are asked to write their names and what they want to buy on a piece of paper. Next to each item she writes down the price, adds up the amounts, and shows the total to the customer, who then pays her. She assembles the order and hands it to the customer, all without saying a word. In reality, her hearing is as good as yours and mine; it's all a clever trick.

"The baker is the leader of the Prussian spy ring here in Vienna," Max went on. "When one of his secret agents wants to communicate with the baker, the Prussian secret agent sends his wife or his servant to the bakery with an order that looks like every other bakery order. You know, bread, rolls, torte, that sort of thing. On the other side of the page, however, is an invisible message written in lemon juice. When the shop is closed for the day, the baker heats an iron, applies it to the back of the secret agent's order, and reads the message, now visible in brown letters. And communication in the other direction is as equally straightforward. The message is written in lemon juice on the paper in which the secret agent's bread is wrapped. Obviously, when a message is to be sent to a secret agent, his bread is pre-wrapped and set aside in the back room of the bakery, but then many regular orders are also handled that way."

Franz and Paul continued to listen to their esteemed spymaster with interest.

"The scheme is devilishly simple," Max said. "Once a customer has paid for an order, the baker's wife puts the paper, on which the order was written, in one of two neat piles in the back room of the bakery. The baker's wife knows the names used on the bakery orders from the secret agents, so she knows which notes to put in a separate pile to pass on to her husband at the end of the day. When a new secret agent is about to arrive in Vienna, the baker is told the name that the secret agent will use on his orders, and the baker tells his wife. She keeps a lookout for the name, and memorizes the face of the new go-between so that she can quickly pass messages to him or her.

"No customer can possibly see that a message is being passed in either direction," Max explained. "Dried lemon juice is colorless. Every customer presents a written order to the baker's 'deaf' wife, and every customer's order is wrapped in paper, so nothing is done differently when a message is passed. Finally, no secret agent ever needs to visit the bakery. Instead, he sends an intermediary—his wife, a servant, a neighbor, a friend. I learned from our Prussian friend, the Viscount von Waldstein zu Eckelberg, that he sent his valet Schottky there, but Schottky had no idea at all that he was involved in message passing. Wilhelmina went to the bakery every day to buy bread, and she also didn't realize that on one occasion she was passing a message, namely, their address in Vienna.

"And that's why my secret agents didn't know that Gerhard Schuster had in fact told the Prussians exactly where he was staying, and that's why he replied to my message without wondering how they knew where he and his wife were living. He told me that, when the courier arrived at his apartment with my message, ostensibly from 'Heinrich von Mombauer,' he assumed that there was some problem with the bakery, and that was why my message was sent to his home, and why he was told to write to Frau Möwe at 15 Pomeranzengasse in Graz. Just so you know, that's the address of a tobacco shop run by a retired Austrian secret agent, who forwards all mail addressed to Frau Möwe to me without delay.

"The only stupid person in the piece was me," Max went on. "Having been informed that Gerhard hadn't told the Austrians where he and Wilhelmina were staying, I nevertheless sent a message to him there. But all's well that ends well, except for the Schusters, of course."

"What'll happen to them?" Franz asked.

"Their hope is that, if they continue to cooperate with me, they'll receive a long jail term, not the death sentence."

"And?"

"And we'll have to see."

"If they're so keen to cooperate," said Franz, "there's some information I need to know.

"Go on."

"It's about the raid at the Taverne zum Schwarzen Adler and, more generally, the group of 12 secret agents I led in Brandenburg an der Havel. It seems clear that information provided by Gerhard —once he'd become a double agent—had triggered the raid. But more than one of the other 11 Austrians could be a double agent. If there is a double agent still at large in Potsdam, encountering him would endanger our mission when we return.

"I fully realize that, under ordinary circumstances, von Hochenheimer would never have dreamed of telling one double agent about another double agent. The risk of losing both double agents would've been too great. That's why confidential information is always given out on a need-to-know basis. But there might just have been a reason why Schuster needed to know about another double agent. Have you asked him about other double agents in the service of the Prussians?"

"Yes, naturally. He claims that his spymaster, von Hochenheimer, took every precaution to ensure that no double agent ever knew about another double agent. I'm inclined to believe him. That's the sort of thing that even a halfway intelligent spymaster would undoubtedly do—let alone an evil genius like the Baron. But I'll certainly ask Schuster a second time. He may well be holding back information as a bargaining chip."

"Can I ask him myself?"

Max thought for a moment. "It can't do any harm, I suppose. I'll have him brought here under guard."

A few minutes later, a shamefaced Gerhard Schuster stood in front of them with his hands cuffed behind his back. Two jailers stood just outside the room.

Franz cut right to the chase. "Gerhard, you were one of 11 secret agents who met with me at 10 o'clock on the first Saturday night of every month in the Taverne zum Schwarzen Adler in Brandenburg an der Havel."

"Yes, I was."

"By your own admission, you were a Prussian double agent."

"Yes."

"I have two questions to ask you. First, did you tip off the Prussians? That is, were you responsible for the raid?"

"I told Baron von Hochenheimer about our monthly meetings."

"Second, and more importantly, think hard: Did you ever suspect that any of the other 11 secret agents in the group were also double agents?"

Schuster thought for a moment and then shook his head. "No, I can't say that I did."

Max spoke up. "And in your dealings with von Hochenheimer and his minions, did you ever encounter anyone who you thought was a double agent?"

This time Schuster shook his head immediately. "No. Never."

Franz looked at Max and nodded. Max ordered the two jailers to take Schuster back to his cell.

When the prisoner had left, Max turned to his two secret agents. "Well, what do you think?"

Paul answered. "I believe he's telling the truth when he says that he doesn't know of any other double agents in our group. But he's obviously trying hard to conceal his knowledge of other double agents. He's lying, and he knows that we know he's lying. I assume that that's the bargaining chip he wants to use to save his life, as well as Wilhelmina's."

"I agree," added Franz.

"We're all in agreement then," Max said. "I'll let him stew for a few days and then offer him their lives in return for verifiable information about other double agents. In fact, bearing in mind your recent successes, both with Schuster and with von Waldstein zu Eckelberg—I still haven't found out his real name—we may need you two to work on any double agents Schuster names."

"How much does his wife know?" Franz asked.

"I'm not sure. She's told us all she thinks we want to know. Is she holding something back? Maybe. On the other hand, unlike her husband, she's in no way devious, so it's quite possible that we've nothing more at all to learn from her. And I don't think she's a secret agent, just a loving wife who's more loyal to her country than to her husband."

"And what's happened with the bakery?"

"We've obviously arrested the baker and his wife, and we've installed our own people there—a new baker, a new 'deaf' shop assistant, and two or three of our agents pretending to be customers, plus two more hidden in the back room. When a customer has paid for an order, the new shop assistant takes the paper to the back room of the bakery, where one of our people instantly irons it. If any brown writing appears, our men in the shop grab the intermediary right away, and tell him or her to take us directly to the person who gave them the order. So far, we've arrested two Prussian secret agents, but we expect to catch all of them eventually."

"Could I make a suggestion?" Paul asked.

"Certainly!" replied Max. "You and Franz are proven experts at this sort of stratagem."

"Take every piece of unused wrapping paper in the shop, and write on it in lemon juice something like 'When you read this, go straight to such-and-such an address.' Then have your men waiting there to arrest everyone who goes to that address."

The habitual grin on Max's face widened into a beatific smile.

"What a marvelous idea," he said. "I'll instruct my men to do that right away. In fact, I'm starting to have second thoughts about sending you back to Potsdam to kill Frederick. You're both far too useful to me here.

"Don't worry," he quickly added, seeing the looks of total disappointment on their faces, "assassinating Frederick is the number one goal that our Empress Maria Theresa has set for me. You'll leave for Potsdam just as soon as I consider the time to be appropriate."

***

Before getting ready to take a walk in the Vienna Woods the next day, Paul turned to Franz. "We'd better go to Herr Faschbinder and find out whether Max needs us again."

He did. "Good morning, gentlemen." Max smiled broadly at them. "Please sit down and make yourselves comfortable. You'll be delighted to hear that Klaus Jürgens is singing like a canary."

"Klaus who?" Franz asked.

"The former Viscount von Waldstein zu Eckelberg. After you left my office yesterday, I was told that your fellow *Junker* wanted to talk to me. He was brought here from the prison hospital, and he told me a few interesting items. It seems that he was a protégé of Baron von Hochenheimer, and not just as a spy. It appears that he worked as one of the Baron's private secretaries for a period of eight years. In view of the fact that Klaus had spent so much time in the presence of a genuine *Junker*, the Baron felt that Klaus would have no problem passing himself off as a Prussian nobleman. As a matter of interest, how good an imitation did he do when you met with him in his rooms and in yours at Im weissen Rössl?"

"He was good, very good," Paul said. "The first time he was somewhat nervous. After all, unlike Franz and me, he'd had no previous experience of playing the role. Also, we'd not only pretended to be *Junker*, but we'd been extremely successful in the part—if I say so myself—so we were a lot more confident than he was. Finally, we'd had an excellent teacher—you, Max—who taught us that we had to *be* the part, not just *act* the part. But given all that, his first effort was very good. The second time, when he came to our rooms at the inn for dinner, he started off excellently, and the bottle of Montrachet that he downed, probably on an empty stomach, helped him to relax. Also, once he was convinced that Franz and I were drunk—and getting drunker by the minute—he was even more at his ease, and his performance began approaching perfection. It's a great pity that the three greatest *Junker* impersonators in the world are now permanently out of work."

"Ah, but there you're wrong," Max said. "Two of them may still get the opportunity to reprise their most notorious roles, the Earl von Schloss Müller and his distinguished colleague, the Marquis zu Braun und Weissburg. And the third may also yet again grace the stage of history as the Viscount von Waldstein zu Eckelberg."

"Are you serious?" Paul interrupted. "Isn't he locked up, and isn't he going to stay locked up until we return from Potsdam?"

"In reply to your three questions: yes and yes and yes, but please be patient. A lot has happened in the past 24 hours. As I was saying, Klaus Jürgens said he wanted to talk to me. He'd apparently been thinking hard. I'd given him two choices: Say nothing and sit in jail for fraud for a very long time, or confess everything and be deported back to Prussia in disgrace. Well, in his role of Viscount von Waldstein zu Eckelberg, he had the unutterable cheek to tell me that he'd selected a third choice."

"And that was—"

"Turning double agent."

There was a gasp of admiration from Franz; from Paul, a shocked silence.

"Yes, you heard correctly. He was sitting right there, handcuffed, a man faced with two alternatives, namely, a lengthy period of imprisonment or a humiliating return to Prussia. And he told me, with all the insolence of a Prussian *Junker* born and bred, that he had chosen a third alternative.

"And that's why I asked you how well you thought he played the role at Im weissen Rössl. I thought he was superb yesterday, truly superb. And that's why I intend to accede to his suggestion, with one obvious proviso—he stays in jail here incommunicado until you two come safely back from Prussia. Naturally, in the meantime I intend to make full use of his services. He'll write regular fictional reports, which will be sent to Prussia. The problem is how to ensure that they get there.

"As I told you yesterday," Max continued, "Jürgens had been instructed to communicate with Berlin by sending his valet, Schottky, to the bakery. Schottky is now in jail, obviously. Jürgens claims–and I'm going to believe him for now—that Schottky is a genuine valet, who has no ties whatsoever with the Prussian secret police. I'll interrogate Schottky further, of course, but for now I'm prepared to accept, as a working hypothesis, that he was simply the wrong person in the wrong place at the wrong time. Fortunately, the valet has no idea why he's in jail or that we've arrested and imprisoned his master, so when I release our Viscount, I'll release Schottky, too, and he can continue to act as Jürgens' valet. It'll be up to Jürgens to come up with a convincing story to account for his valet's imprisonment and subsequent release. Mistaken identity should do the trick."

"But how is Jürgens going to send his fictional reports to Berlin?" asked Franz. "How did the baker forward the information he received?"

"That's undoubtedly the problem. At this stage, we don't know who the next link in the chain of communication is. The baker isn't talking—so far. Of course, he realizes that he and his wife are potentially facing the rope, so he may change his mind. His wife doesn't know too much—as far as I can tell. She knew the names used by all the secret agents, of course, so that she could separate their orders for subsequent ironing by her husband. She also needed to know their names in order to pass communications from Berlin on to them. Each message was written in lemon juice on that secret agent's bread wrapper. But she doesn't seem to know much beyond the names used by the secret agents. As I told you, her husband, Herr Mössbauer the baker, is the leader of the Prussian secret agents here in Vienna, and he may be in charge of all their secret agents in Austria. A few more days in his cell should soften him up—unless you two have another one of your creative ideas?"

"Have you asked Frau Mössbauer to give you a list of the names of all the secret agents or, more correctly, the names used by all the secret agents?" Paul asked. "That would help you to know when all the secret agents have been arrested. Conversely, if you find a secret agent who's not on the list, that will tell you that she's lying."

"Excellent!" boomed Max. "Actually, we've already obtained such a list from her, and we also have a description from her of the intermediaries who usually act for the secret agents, bringing their orders to the bakery and taking their bread back to them."

"How did the messages from Berlin get to the baker?" Franz asked.

This time there was a long silence.

"That's a really good question," said Max. "I don't know. I'll tell our people at the bakery to be on the lookout for messengers bearing messages from Prussia."

"I think it's simpler than that," Paul said. "They had a great system going: incoming messages from secret agents written on bakery orders, outgoing messages to secret agents written on bread wrappers. Surely the same scheme was used with messages from Berlin? So, all you need to do is keep looking for brown writing on ironed orders. That will lead you not only to the secret agents here in Vienna, but also to the couriers who are transporting messages to and from Berlin."

Once more there was a long silence. Then Max spoke. "Yesterday I made a joke. I said that I was starting to have second thoughts about sending you back to Potsdam to kill Frederick, because you're far too useful to me here. Yes, it really was a joke—all three of us know how essential it is for you to return to Potsdam. But in the meantime, I intend to make full use of your inestimable skills. Furthermore, don't even think of going to the Vienna Woods tomorrow. I intend to meet with you every day from now until we've milked Jürgens the *Junker*, the Schuster couple, and Mössbauer the baker and his wife of every iota of information they possess."

***

The next morning, when they reported to his office, Franz and Paul again received an effusive welcome from Max. "I have good news to share with you," he began. "I spent yesterday afternoon talking to Klaus Jürgens, and I—" Max paused when Herr Faschbinder entered the room. "Yes, what is it?"

Herr Faschbinder approached and whispered in Max's ear.

"Gentlemen, please stay here. I'll come back as soon as I can."

About 15 minutes later, Max returned, smiling. "I said earlier that I have good news to share with you. But now I have even better news, as well. First, let me tell you what I learned from Jürgens yesterday. He and I have come to an understanding. I told him that I've decided to accept his offer of acting as a double agent. He will continue to be the Viscount von Waldstein zu Eckelberg, and Schottky will continue to be his valet. I have made it absolutely clear to him that if he tries any trickery at all, and in particular if he tries to reveal to Prussia that he's now a double agent, I will immediately have him executed. He completely understands every aspect of the situation, and he promises to cooperate fully.

"He told me that, as we all know, Frederick is fully aware that our Empress is trying to have him assassinated. Frederick, it seems, is a true gentleman. He believes that it would be inappropriate to retaliate by trying to have Maria Theresa killed. Accordingly, the primary purpose of his espionage efforts here in Austria is to find out exactly what we're doing to try to assassinate him and then to frustrate our plans. A secondary goal, however, is to discover the names of the two *Junker* who killed von Hochenheimer and have them killed.

"Jürgens was quite clear on that point. The Austrian authorities are fully aware that Hoffmann was not acting on his own when he shot the Baron. They believe that three people were involved:

Secret Agent 79, Secret Agent 312 and Secret Agent 85. They're convinced that two of the secret agents are *Junker* who have fled to Austria, and that the third is Hoffmann, who seems to have disappeared. So, Jürgens was sent here to track down the two *Junker* and have them killed.

"The bad news, as you both know very well, is that Jürgens believes that the two of you are the two *Junker* he was sent here to find," Max continued. "The good news is that he's going to sit in jail, in isolation, until you two return to Vienna. That's one less thing for you to worry about when you arrive in Potsdam."

Paul turned to Franz. "Isn't it amazing how our fictional letter has returned to haunt us? The Prussians are utterly convinced of the existence of Secret Agent 79, Secret Agent 312 and Secret Agent 85."

"And another of our deceptions—our dressing up as *Junker* to persuade poor Hoffmann to deliver our letter to the hut in the forest—also has a life of its own," Franz added. "When we were in the tree outside von Hochenheimer's mansion, we were dressed as grenadiers. When we fled Prussia, we were laborers. Most of the time that we were in Berlin, we were import/export merchants. But the Prussians will never forget our brief performances as *Junker*. In fact, our hour with Hoffmann in that bar on the Judengasse may ultimately cost us our lives."

"Yes, indeed," Max said. "Contrary to what I said yesterday, I think that you should never again portray the role of *Junker*. That way you'll be perfectly safe.

"And now I'll tell you the news I received when I left the room," Max added. "My secret agents at the Mössbauer Bakery have just discovered how messages are sent between Berlin and Vienna. If von Hochenheimer wanted to send a message to a secret agent in Vienna, he would arrange for a woman in Berlin to write a perfectly innocent letter to her friend in Vienna. On the back of the letter, the Baron wrote the real message in lemon juice. The 'friend in Vienna' turns out to be Frau Baumfelder, a dressmaker who was born in Berlin. She married an Austrian tailor and came to live with him here in Vienna. Her husband died several years ago. When a letter from her 'friend in Berlin' arrives, Frau Baumfelder irons the paper, thereby revealing the hidden message. Next, she prepares her order for the bakery. On the top of the page, she writes the name that she uses for her bakery orders, and under that she lists the various items she wants from the bakery that day. On the back of her order, she transcribes the hidden message, as always in lemon juice. She then gives the order to her assistant to take to the bakery—she never sets foot in the Mössbauer Bakery herself. And that's the way that the baker receives messages from Berlin."

"And, I suppose," Franz said, "if a secret agent wants to send a message to Berlin, he writes it on the back of a bakery order, which is handed to Frau Mössbauer. She puts it in the special pile in the back room for her husband. After the shop is closed for the day, he irons the back of the order, and the message to be taken to Berlin appears. Herr Mössbauer transcribes the message onto a bread wrapper, obviously in lemon juice. When the dressmaker's assistant comes in to buy bread, she's given a previously wrapped loaf that's been set aside. The assistant comes back to Frau Baumfelder and hands her the bread. That evening, the dressmaker irons the bread wrapper, then transcribes the message in lemon juice on the back of a perfectly innocent letter that she sends to her 'friend in Berlin.'"

Max applauded. "Bravo! It's as simple as that. Paul, you were quite right. They're definitely using the same means of communication throughout their operation. So, we've now arrested the baker, his wife, the two secret agents I told you about yesterday, plus the dressmaker and three more secret agents. And if Frau Mössbauer is telling the truth, there's only one more Prussian secret agent at large in Austria."

"Are you going to start sending fictional reports to Berlin from all the secret agents you have in custody, or just from the Viscount?" Paul asked.

"Well, the whole situation has changed now, hasn't it?" Max said. "We've just learned that all the Prussian secret agents send their reports to Herr Mössbauer. He copies their reports, verbatim, and sends them on to the dressmaker. She copies their reports, verbatim, and sends them on to Berlin. Consequently, the only person whose co-operation I need is the dressmaker's. I'm delighted to report that Frau Baumfelder is willing to help us. So, from now on, when I write a fictional report purporting to come from a Prussian secret agent, Frau Baumfelder will write an innocent letter to her friend in Berlin, and on the back she'll transcribe my report in lemon juice. The new Minister of Police will receive reports from all his secret agents here in Vienna, exactly the way it used to be done in the days of his predecessor, the Baron von Hochenheimer."

"Just a minute," Franz interrupted. "I think you've forgotten one thing. How will you ensure that your fictional reports are consistent in style and content with the previous actual reports? Von Hochenheimer surely filed away all the reports he received via the baker and Frau Baumfelder. If you're the author of a fictional report, the new Minister will see right away that someone other than the secret agent wrote it, because your style will be different than that of the secret agent. Also, suppose that a secret agent has been told to report on, say, troop movements. How will you know this? If you send a fictional report, purportedly from that secret agent, that deals with banking, the secret agent's controller will immediately smell a rat."

Max's smile was so broad that it seemed to fill not just the room but also the whole of Vienna. "Actually," he began, "there's no problem. It seems that no one bothered to instruct Frau Baumfelder to burn all the messages to and from the baker after transcribing them. No Prussian would dare to destroy an official document without a specific written instruction to do so. Accordingly, our Prussian dressmaker has methodically filed away every single message she has received from Herr Mössbauer, in chronological order, of course, as well as every message sent from Berlin to the secret agents, as before in the precise order that she received them. I can simply read through her meticulously maintained records and learn each secret agent's writing style, as well as his activities. So, I see no problem in running a stable of fictional secret agents and filling the minds of their Prussian spymasters with false information."

"Actually, Max, you may have missed two things," said Paul. "If I may return to Franz's example, suppose that a secret agent has been here for a while and that he's sent seven reports via the baker, all dealing with troop movements. Furthermore, his instructions from Berlin all state that his primary task is to find out about troop movements. It would then be reasonable for you to send fictional reports to Berlin about troop movements, purporting to come from that secret agent. And that leads to two possible problems. First, as I understand it, the only report sent to Berlin by Gerhard and Wilhelmina Schuster was their new address. So, how are you going to copy their style?"

"That's easy," Max said. "I won't. If they receive no further reports from the Schusters, the Prussians will just assume that Gerhard had second thoughts and is once again working for Austria, and that he persuaded his loving wife Wilhelmina to change her allegiance, too. So, I see no difficulty there. And what's the second problem I missed?"

"The Viscount von Waldstein zu Eckelberg has been here in Vienna for only a short time. How many reports from Berlin do you have regarding his instructions? How many reports do you have that he's sent to Berlin?"

"I understand that there have been no instructions sent from Berlin, and only one report from him sent to Berlin."

"Well, how are you going to write appropriate reports when you don't know precisely what he's been instructed to do? And how are you going to copy his style after you've seen just one thing that he's written? Are you prepared to rely on his word regarding his instructions? Will you trust him enough to ask him to write a few more reports so that you can learn his writing style?"

As almost always, Max was one step ahead. "Actually it's worse than that," he said. "Using the information in the dressmaker's files, I've no doubt whatsoever that I can write fictional reports purporting to come from the other secret agents that will fool everyone in Berlin. No one in Prussia would dream of even suggesting that my reports are fictional. I'll ensure that they'll be consistent in every way with the earlier reports filed by Frau Baumfelder. But if—as a consequence of my relying on false information from Jürgens—my reports (supposedly from the Viscount) should appear to be suspicious in any way at all, then every single report from Vienna to Berlin will be treated as suspect. In other words, unless I can totally depend on what Jürgens chooses to tell me, there's a grave risk that the entire operation will quickly become a waste of time and money."

"Do you agree?"

Both secret agents nodded.

"Can I rely on what Jürgens tells me?"

Both secret agents shook their heads.

"So what am I to do about the Viscount?" Max asked.

"The same thing that I strongly suspect that you're soon going to do with all the other secret agents, with the exception of the dressmaker, Frau Baumfelder," Paul said. A grim expression formed on his face. "But it's the only way to be certain that Berlin never finds out that all the reports they're going to receive from Frau Baumfelder will be fictional."

"But what's going to happen when someone in Berlin realizes that all the other secret agents are doing their jobs perfectly and sending in regular reports, but the Viscount seems to have disappeared?" Franz asked.

"Don't you worry about that," Max said. The broad grin returned to his face. "I've got everything under control."

CHAPTER TWENTY-ONE

"Your Majesty," said von Kunersdorf, bowing as low as he could while entering the King's study in the Palace of Sanssouci, "you instructed me to come to you as soon as I had definite information about Klaus Jürgens and his pursuit of the two *Junker* who assassinated the late Baron von Hochenheimer."

"Yes, yes, sit down and tell me everything you know," King Frederick said.

"I've received a message from Jürgens himself, as well as a message regarding Jürgens from Mössbauer via Frau Baumfelder," von Kunersdorf continued.

"Remind me who Mössbauer and Frau Baumfelder are."

"Mössbauer is the baker who leads our group in Vienna. All communications from our secret agents in Vienna are sent to him. He forwards them to Frau Baumfelder, a dressmaker, and she then forwards them to us in Berlin."

"Ah, yes, I remember now. I never cease to be amazed how the late Baron von Hochenheimer was able to recall every detail regarding all his secret agents both here and abroad. He was an amazing man, von Kunersdorf, a truly astonishing man. As you know, I haven't yet found anyone to replace him as Minister of Police. Maybe I'm setting the bar too high."

Von Kunersdorf, who desperately wanted to be the new Minister of Police, didn't say a word and made sure that his face betrayed nothing. But he wanted to scream at the top of his voice,

"Appoint *me* to the position, you miserable bastard. I'd do a much better job than that old fool von Hochenheimer."

"So, Kunersdorf, what have you found out about Jürgens?"

"As I said, I've received two messages. The first was a report from Jürgens himself, transcribed in turn by Mössbauer and Frau Baumfelder. He wrote that he'd taken rooms at an inn in Vienna called Im weissen Rössl. Two other *Junker* were also staying there, the Earl von Schloss Müller and the Marquis zu Braun und Weissburg. Two days before he wrote the report, they'd paid a short social visit to him, and he was about to have dinner with them in their rooms. As soon as I received that message, I had my secret agents here investigate the two *Junker*. No one could find the slightest information about either the Earl von Schloss Müller or the Marquis zu Braun und Weissburg. Then I had an idea. I had Otto Lendler, the stage manager of the Potsdam theatre, brought back for questioning. I asked him a question he'd been asked a number of times before, focusing on the names of the two *Junker* who'd come to his theatre and taken that false facial hair and the black eye patch. As before, he couldn't remember. All that he could recall was both names had been amusing. His inability to remember the names wasn't surprising. After all, he'd heard each name only once, and he'd been overwhelmed by the sudden visit to the theatre of two such high-ranking noblemen.

"Then I asked him: Were the two *Junker* by any chance the Earl von Schloss Müller and the Marquis zu Braun und Weissburg? His face lit up. 'Yes, that's it,' he said. And he suddenly remembered why he thought that both names were funny. First, *Schloss Müller* means 'the miller's castle,' but according to him, millers live in mills, not in castles. And *Braun und Weissburg* means 'brown and white castle.' However, Lendler said that made him picture a cow.

"My conclusion," he continued, "is that the Earl von Schloss Müller and the Marquis zu Braun und Weissburg are no more *Junker* than Jürgens himself is the Viscount von Waldstein zu Eckelberg. In other words, for weeks we've been searching high and low for two traitorous *Junker* who don't exist."

"But von Hochenheimer was absolutely adamant that the two men who told Hoffmann to go to the hut in the forest had been *Junker*," the King said. "Not only couldn't he shake Hoffmann on this point, but there were two other independent witnesses who were equally dogmatic that the two men were *Junker*."

"With the greatest of respect, Your Majesty," said von Kunersdorf, "if the late Baron von Hochenheimer had encountered the two *Junker* himself, there's no question that he would've seen through their disguises in an instant. But his three witnesses were: Hoffmann, a slightly drunk, 25-year-old ex-soldier; a tavern keeper, who had interacted only briefly and superficially with the two men; and an elderly ex-soldier who comes to the tavern every afternoon for a beer and had seen them only at a distance."

"But what about Jürgens? Was he fooled too?"

"Your Majesty, Jürgens believed that the two men were indeed *Junker*. Because he'd never played that role before, I have no doubt that—during their short social meeting—he was extremely nervous about being unmasked by them. Also, I believe that the thought that his guests were no more *Junker* than he was hadn't crossed his mind. To be fair to Jürgens, the two men are consummate actors. Not only did they fool Hoffmann, the tavern keeper and the old soldier, they also fooled Otto Lendler, a theatre professional. And one of them even fooled a pawnbroker; in order to survive in that cutthroat business, a pawnbroker needs to be extremely quick-witted. I suppose that if Jürgens had been suspicious of the two *Junker* in his rooms at the inn, he might've seen through them. But nothing in his report reveals that he harbored the slighted disbelief of any kind."

"Go on."

"Well, we'd sent Jürgens to Vienna to find the two *Junker* who shot the Baron. And Jürgens had succeeded within a day or so, only he didn't know it. So I immediately dispatched a message to him informing him he'd found the murderous *Junker*, but to be extremely careful. Under no circumstances was he to be alone with them—there were to be no more visits, no more dinners. And he was to arrange to avenge the killing of Baron von Hochenheimer immediately. But it seems that I was too late."

"Too late, Kunersdorf?"

"Yes, Your Majesty. As I said before, the message from Jürgens himself had been written just before he was to have dinner with the two assassins. Six days later, I received a message from Mössbauer. Jürgens had instructed his valet to buy fresh bread every day at Mössbauer's bakery so that Jürgens could receive our messages as soon as they arrived in Vienna. Mössbauer wrote that the valet—his name is Schottky—hadn't been to the bakery for four days, so Mössbauer made discreet inquiries at the inn. He learned that the Earl von Schloss Müller and the Marquis zu Braun und Weissburg had paid their bill and left the inn directly after the dinner, on their way to Dresden. The porter at the inn confirmed that he took their trunks to the Dresden coach. But Jürgens and Schottky had disappeared into thin air."

"Disappeared?"

"Yes. The innkeeper was angry. Jürgens had racked up a large bill, including numerous bottles of the finest French champagne. All his possessions were still in his rooms, and Schottky's clothes and trunk were in the garret, but both men had vanished. Mössbauer discovered that the innkeeper was about to call in the police, but the baker was greatly concerned that they might find incriminating documents of some kind. So he told the innkeeper that he would arrange for the bill to be paid at once. He went back to his baker's shop, took the emergency funds he'd been given by the Baron, and he paid their bill in full. He then went to their rooms to pack up their possessions and have them sent to the bakery.

"And did he find any compromising items?" the King asked.

"Apparently not, Your Majesty. But he immediately noticed that their rooms had been thoroughly searched—ransacked would be a more accurate description. He pointed this out to the innkeeper and asked if the police had done it. The innkeeper was emphatic that the police hadn't been involved in any way. Also, Mössbauer made diligent inquiries using his many contacts, but the two missing Prussians are definitely not in prison. From this, Mössbauer has come to three conclusions: First, the two men who've been masquerading as *Junker* did the ransacking. Second, Jürgens and Schottky are both dead, killed by the two assassins, and Mössbauer is extremely doubtful that their bodies will ever be found. Third, whoever the Earl von Schloss Müller and the Marquis zu Braun und Weissburg really are, they're not Austrian secret agents, otherwise the Austrian police would've been involved at the inn from the very beginning. In view of the fact that the two men left Vienna for Dresden, it seems likely that they're actually Saxons. Some Saxons are still furious about the schoolchildren in Grossbrock, who were burnt alive in their schoolhouse. It's possible that the two men came to Prussia to exact revenge; perhaps they're related to some of the dead children."

"But if they're Saxons, why did they write to Max Hirsch for instructions?"

"As you know, the Electorate of Saxony has only the most rudimentary secret police system, so much so that the men were in all probability acting on their own, and not on behalf of Saxony. In order to get some assistance in carrying out their revenge killing, they probably had approached Hirsch in Vienna."

"But I thought that the intention of the *Junker* was to kill me, not von Hochenheimer. That's what their letter to Hirsch had stated. And while we're on the subject of the shooting, why was Hoffmann involved in the assassination?"

Von Kunersdorf was now in a quandary. Having spoken to Sergeant Winterfeldt, he knew every detail of the reason why Hoffmann shot von Hochenheimer, but he didn't know just how far he should go in telling his King the truth. After all, he wanted von Hochenheimer's job, but he knew that Frederick had liked and greatly admired his Minister of Police. So, how should he reply?

He began to speak hesitantly. "Your Majesty, you'll remember that we intercepted the letter that Hoffmann had been carrying. It outlined a plot to kill Your Majesty during your birthday parade. The late Minister was desperate to ensure that nothing would happen to you. In order to uncover every last detail of the plot, it's possible that he went a little too far when he extracted information from Hoffmann."

"You mean that von Hochenheimer tortured Hoffmann far more brutally than necessary to get the information he needed, and Hoffmann took his revenge?"

Von Kunersdorf wisely said nothing at all.

"And another thing," King Fredrick continued. "The two Saxons came to Prussia to kill me, not von Hochenheimer. Hoffmann wanted to kill von Hochenheimer, not me. So how did the three of them get involved?"

"Your Majesty, here's how I see it. The two Saxons came here to try to kill you. To do this, they enlisted the help of Hirsch in Vienna. He agreed, provided they were willing to submit their plan for his approval before they carried it out. So they dressed up as *Junker* and persuaded Hoffmann to take their letter to the hut in the forest for forwarding to Hirsch. Hoffmann was arrested with the letter and viciously tortured. The Saxons were unable to assassinate you—the Lord be praised! Their plan having failed, they contacted Hoffmann again before returning to Saxony. He told them what had happened to him. Realizing that they'd been the cause of his misfortunes, they agreed to help him kill von Hochenheimer."

"Your explanation fits all the facts as we know them. Most impressive. So what do we do next?"

"With the greatest respect, Your Majesty, I humbly suggest that we do nothing."

"Nothing?"

"Yes, Your Majesty, nothing. Unfortunately, there's nothing we can do and nothing we should do. First, consider Hoffmann. Three days ago a farmer found a naked, dead body in one of his haystacks. The farm is located about midway between Potsdam and the Electorate of Saxony."

"Saxony yet another time."

"Yes, Your Majesty, Saxony yet another time. There's probably no way to identify the body, which is now partially decomposed. But this we do know: The man was stabbed with a stiletto, and, you'll recall, the poacher in the hut was also stabbed with a stiletto. The body bore signs of torture identical to what we know was inflicted on Hoffmann. So it seems likely that Hoffmann is dead, killed by his former co-conspirators, the two Saxons. What we don't know is why they stabbed him. My best guess is that they wanted to be certain that he could never identify them, but I cannot be sure that that's the actual reason, of course.

"We have several descriptions of the Saxons dressed as *Junker*. Those descriptions are essentially useless. The two Saxons seem extremely clever, so I'm certain that they'll never masquerade as *Junker* again.

"We also have descriptions of the two Saxons in ordinary clothes from two musketeers who saw them in a forest near Golm, on the north side of Potsdam. In addition, we have descriptions from three half-witted secret policemen who interviewed the two of them in their rented room in Berlin, but let them go. All five descriptions are vague and unspecific, and essentially useless. So, Your Majesty, with Hoffmann dead we have no way of identifying the two Saxons. Furthermore—bearing in mind that the two men came to Prussia as individuals to take private vengeance and not on behalf of the Electorate of Saxony—I most respectfully suggest that it might be inappropriate to take action against Saxony. Finally, as I said, the two Saxons seem exceptionally clever, so I'm certain that they'll never return to Prussia in the future."

King Frederick II thought long and hard. His eyes, usually piercing, stared blankly up at one corner of the room. His lips occasionally moved, but only for a second or two each time. Finally, he turned to von Kunersdorf. "As I said before, I accept your explanation for what has happened. It fits all the facts. I can find no contradictions or loose ends.

"I also accept your recommendation. As far as I'm concerned, the murder of my friend the Baron von Hochenheimer has been solved. One of the perpetrators is dead; the other two have fled Prussia and will never be found. Update the files to reflect everything we now know, and seal them. The matter is closed.

"Oh, one other thing, Kunersdorf. You'll no doubt be interested to know that, now that the murder investigation is over, I'm about to appoint a new Minister of Police. I believe that you'll be quite pleased with my choice."

CHAPTER TWENTY-TWO

"I know that you two have been here in Vienna for less than three weeks," said Max Hirsch, "but I've had some news from Prussia that indicates that the time has come for you to go back there for a final attempt on the life of Frederick. Hubertus von Kunersdorf is the new Minister of Police. I've also received more than one report that the level of security around Frederick is roughly where it had been before the assassination took place. So it seems that it's now or never. But before you leave for Prussia tomorrow, there's one final task I need you to do for me. I want you to suggest how I can teach our ambassador in Dresden, the Baron Octavian von Bruno-Bader, to stop opening letters that aren't addressed to him."

"That's easy," Franz responded. "Lemon juice."

"Lemon juice?" Max asked. "Meaning what exactly?"

"Well, suppose you send him three letters by courier today, and tell the courier that the Ambassador has to sign a receipt for each of the three letters. In the first letter, you describe the communications protocol of the Prussian spy ring here in Vienna. In particular, you need to tell the ambassador that, if he intercepts an otherwise blank piece of paper from Prussia, he should iron it carefully and a hidden message will appear. You should also mention that Paul and I are due to arrive the next day on the coach from Vienna, and we're to be given our letters on arrival at his embassy."

"Go on."

"Then you must also give two other letters to the courier, one addressed to each of us. Each of our letters must be identical—a totally blank piece of paper."

"But the blank letters will contain a message in lemon juice, won't they?" Max asked.

"Yes, certainly," Franz replied. "And the messages in lemon juice should read something like: 'If you can read this letter, it means that it's been opened by some unauthorized person and heated.'

"What's going to happen," Franz continued, "is that the Baron or one of his aides is going to open our two letters as carefully as possible, so that they can be resealed without showing that they were opened. He'll see that our letters are blank, but he'll certainly remember that he's just received a message regarding blank pieces of paper. So, he'll summon a maid with an iron, and the messages will appear in brown letters. *But they won't fade.* In other words, there'll be proof that the Baron received your letters—the signature he has to give to the courier—and there'll be proof that he opened the letters addressed to us and heated them. That should teach him a lesson."

"But there's one problem," Paul said. "The Ambassador is going to be extremely embarrassed—his honor is at stake. What if he takes a pistol and shoots himself? Enough blood has been shed already."

Max laughed. "The man's an ambassador, and a successful one at that. Diplomats don't shoot themselves out of a sense of embarrassment; if they did, there wouldn't be a diplomat alive today. No, they're trained to lie themselves out of trouble. What he'll tell you is that, while he was attending to the mail, the candle he uses for melting sealing wax fell over, and the incoming mail was burned. Wait a minute, I think there's a more likely excuse: He's going to blame it on the lowest ranking officer assigned to the embassy. Did you encounter a lieutenant when you were there?"

"Yes," Paul said. "We were assisted by Lieutenant Schulz von Schulzenheim."

"Well, when you find that your letters have been opened, the Ambassador will summon the lieutenant, who will shamefacedly admit that he opened your letters 'by mistake, thinking they were addressed to the ambassador.' And that will be that. But the Ambassador will in all probability have been cured of his bad habit. He'll know that there may well be another booby trap in his mail, the next one more public and more embarrassing," Max added.

"If you want to send the courier by coach," Franz said, "today's post coach leaves in three hours. Should we leave you now so that you can bait the trap?"

***

The next day, Paul and Franz took the coach for Dresden. When they arrived outside the Austrian embassy, they noticed wisps of smoke seeping out of the windows of one of the rooms. The sentries at the door recognized them from their previous visit, but, because they had not been given orders regarding the two secret agents, they did not let them in. The senior guard pressed the bell for Lieutenant Schulz von Schulzenheim, who took a considerable amount of time to arrive.

Franz and Paul immediately noticed that his uniform—impeccable on the previous visit—now had smoke and water stains. The lieutenant apologized profusely. "I was meeting with the Baron when I accidentally knocked over the candle he uses for melting sealing wax. The papers on the desk caught fire, and there's been some damage to the desk." He pointed upward at the smoke creeping out of the window. "Fortunately, there was a bucket of water in the next room, and I was able to douse the blaze."

"And were the papers on the desk all destroyed?" asked Franz, in a simulated sympathetic tone.

"Regrettably, yes."

"And did the papers that were burned to a cinder include yesterday's mail from Vienna?"

"Yes, indeed. How on earth did you know that?"

"Don't worry, we understand," Paul said. "In fact, we understand everything. Please give the Ambassador our best wishes, and tell him we'll come and see him some other time when he doesn't need to attend to burning issues."

The lieutenant had the good manners to blush. As they left the embassy, Paul turned to Franz, "Trust Max to come up with two altogether different predictions of how the opening of our letters might be explained away, and have both of them turn out to be correct."

On to Potsdam. They knew that the coaches that ran from Dresden to Prussia went to Berlin, bypassing Potsdam. Convinced that the secret police in Berlin were still looking for them, they were extremely hesitant to travel to the Prussian capital. So they decided to take the coach from Dresden to Berlin, but to leave it at

Verasdorf, when it stopped there to change horses. They would then walk from Verasdorf to Potsdam. By not revealing their plan to leave the coach until they actually reached Verasdorf, they would minimize suspicions.

Both men carried worn-looking leather valises, carefully constructed by Viennese master craftsmen to conceal pistols. They wore clothes that bore the ingrained road dust that often coated coach passengers.

The coach to Berlin departed on time. Just after leaving Dresden in the late afternoon, the passengers noticed a squeaking noise coming from the front left wheel. The noise grew louder and louder, and after a few hours it became clear that the wheel bearing needed repair. In the middle of the night, the coach came to a halt at the border post between the Electorate of Saxony and the Kingdom of Prussia. The passengers all got out to have their papers inspected. The customs officials seemed extremely relaxed. On the other hand, the soldiers manning the border were clearly uneasy. Paul muttered to Franz that he wondered if the soldiers had only just been posted there. Left unspoken was the implication that the current soldiers had replaced the soldiers who had previously been on duty and, without authorization to do so, had raced after them into the Electorate of Saxony. The inexperience of a new squad would account for their unease.

As they were about to get back into the coach, Franz overheard one of the customs officials talking to the coachman. "The only blacksmith in the vicinity who can fix that bearing is in Falkendorf," he said. "I suggest that you drive your coach to the inn there. Your passengers can then savor the insipid, watery beer while waiting for the blacksmith to repair your bearing."

Franz pulled Paul aside.

"When the coach stops at Falkendorf, grab your valise and head for the forest surrounding the inn. And make sure that that villainous, redheaded, freckle-faced innkeeper doesn't spot us."

The noise from the bearing grew even louder as they slowly covered the short distance to Falkendorf, but the highly experienced coachman managed to bring his vehicle to a halt in front of the inn. The passengers opened the doors and clambered out. The Austrian secret agents were careful to exit through the street-side door, away from the building. Feigning a carefree attitude, they strolled to the forest that ringed the inn.

As they reached the trees, the innkeeper—not pleased to be losing two customers—shouted after them. "Hey, you two, where do you think you're going?"

"Just taking a quick stroll," Paul yelled back, "to build up a thirst for your beer."

The innkeeper recalled that the last time that two Prussian travelers had entered the forest, it had resulted in the hanging of his brother-in-law. This memory increased his rage even further.

"Dieter, Asmus, two strangers in the forest. After them, quick!" yelled the innkeeper.

"Run, Franz," shouted Paul, "and get your pistols out of your valise as soon as you can."

The two secret agents sprinted as fast as they could, but soon they could hear the thudding of heavy footsteps behind them.

"They're catching up with us; we're going to have to shoot them."

"Let's stop behind that big tree just around the bend."

"It's too close. They'll hear the shots at the inn."

"Can't help it," wheezed Paul.

They crouched behind the tree, dropping their valises to the ground. As the burly foresters rounded the bend and spotted them, Paul and Franz had time to extract only one pistol each. The secret agents drew their weapons and pointed them at the foresters' chests.

They foresters halted at once, raising their hands high above their heads. "Don't worry, we'll go right back. No harm done," said the first forester, backing up.

"Stay right where you are," snarled Franz.

"Do we have to do a Hoffmann here?" asked Paul, a definite note of reluctance in his voice.

"Yes. We need a clear head start in getting back to Saxony."

Paul was a little surprised that Franz had mentioned Saxony, but he said nothing.

"Turn around," Franz ordered. With the greatest of reluctance, the two men slowly turned until they faced back in the direction of the inn from which they had run.

Franz pointed his pistol at the head of the first forester, and pulled the trigger. There was a click as the flint in the hammer hit the frizzen, but the resulting sparks failed to ignite the gunpowder in the flash pan.

The two secret agents immediately realized that, if Paul now used his pistol to kill the second forester, they would be unarmed, and the first forester would—in all probability—kill them both in revenge. So Franz signaled to Paul to keep both foresters covered so that he could take his second pistol out of his valise. The foresters couldn't see what was happening behind them but, being keen of hearing, realized that the situation had somehow changed. Instinctively, the second forester started running toward the inn, and the first one joined him. Paul dared not fire his pistol until he knew that Franz was once more armed, but by the time he looked behind him and saw his friend had successfully retrieved his second pistol, both foresters had run back around the bend.

"Take out your second pistol, grab your valise, and let's find the first path that leads northward," Franz said.

"Northward? I thought you said we were heading back to Saxony."

"That was deception," Franz said. "I was thinking ahead. If for some reason we couldn't kill them, I wanted them to spread the story that we were headed for Saxony."

"I have no problem in principle with our heading northward into Prussia," said Paul, "but in practice it's going to be a little hard."

"Why?"

"Because I forgot to ask Max to provide me with a compass. We're going to have to rely on the stars, which is a real problem in a thick forest on a dark, cloudy night."

"We'll just have to do our best."

The two Austrians followed the path. Whenever they came to a fork, they chose the route that they thought led north. They continued in that way for about an hour. "We should be out of the forest by now," Franz said. "Remember when the innkeeper's evil brother-in-law led us out at gunpoint? It took no more than half an hour."

"We're probably going around in circles. I suggest we take shelter as best we can and try and get some sleep until the sun rises. Then we can head north."

"Wait, I hear something."

"Yes, you're right. There's someone coming in our direction. No, it's a whole group of people. Are they the soldiers from the border post? Are they foresters?"

"Let's get off the path, climb a tree, and hope that they move past us. We must be close to Saxony, thanks to my brilliant deception."

"Franz, you've got to stop with this deception. It just causes us problems."

"As I said, move away from the path and climb a big tree. It's so dark here that I'm hopeful that they'll miss us."

"Did you hear what I said about deception?"

There was no response.

Yet again Paul and Franz found themselves in a large tree, hiding from pursuers. And yet again, the thick, leafy canopy provided adequate cover. Through the foliage, they saw glimpses of their hunters, about 20 uniformed soldiers and foresters, passing below them. Either it never occurred to the Prussians that the two secret agents might hide in a tree, or else they realized that it would be a hopeless task to find them there in the pitch dark, so they concentrated on the paths.

After a short while, Franz and Paul could no longer hear the hunters. They cautiously climbed down, moving slowly from branch to branch, clutching their valises, until they reached the ground. All seemed quiet.

"What now?" Paul asked. "We've no idea where we are. The men approached from that direction, so I assume that that's where the border is. If I'm right, they're moving north, into Prussia. We certainly don't want to bump into them on our way to Potsdam. Also, we can't see a thing. Come daylight tomorrow, we'll be able see, but they'll also be able to see us. So what do we do?"

"It's probably best if we stay where we are. They've already combed this area, so they surely won't come back. When the sun rises, we'll know where east is, and we can then carefully walk northward until we get out of this forest."

"But what if they do come back? Or, what if another group of searchers arrives?"

"I see what you mean," Franz said. "One of us will have to stand guard while the other sleeps. Then we'll change over. That way we'll both get some rest, and hopefully we'll both stay alive."

"There's one other possibility," Paul said. "What if the border with Saxony isn't too far? Why don't we walk for 10 minutes in the direction from which the men came? If we get into Saxony, fine. If not, we'll spend the night where we find ourselves."

Franz agreed. They tried to keep as straight a path as they could in the direction from which the searchers had come.

"Five minutes more," begged Paul.

"But what if we're walking toward the soldiers and foresters?" Franz asked.

"Just five minutes more. I promise."

Just two minutes later, the trees suddenly thinned, and they found themselves in a meadow. They climbed a grassy hillock. Below them appeared a darkened village.

"Where are we?" Franz asked.

"Prussia or Saxony. Either way, we're probably safe now. Or maybe not.

CHAPTER TWENTY-THREE

"It's in the middle of the night. It would be a really bad idea to knock on a door and ask the householder whether we're in Prussia or Saxony."

"I agree," said Paul. "But maybe there's a sign somewhere in the village that will tell us where we are, or even just the name of the village."

"Walking around a sleeping village at night will get the dogs barking and wake everyone. Another really bad idea."

"I think that's a farm over there on the left. Let's see if there's an unlocked barn where we can sleep without fear of the hunters finding us."

The two secret agents walked as quietly as they could toward the farm. The first building they encountered was an empty grain silo. They ducked inside, settled down and fell into a deep sleep.

***

A few hours later the sun roused them. They grabbed their valises and headed for the houses in the village. One house in particular seemed larger than the others, so Franz knocked on the wooden door. A tall, old woman opened it. There was no question that she'd been strong and athletic in her day, but now her back was badly bent and her unkempt, wispy gray hair revealed a distinct lack of interest in her personal appearance.

"Yes?" she asked in a deep voice.

"Good morning. My friend and I are lost. Can you please tell us where we are?"

"Müllwalde."

"Are we in Prussia or Saxony?"

"You're in Müllwalde," said the old woman firmly. "I just told you. Come inside. We're about to have breakfast."

She led them to a table set for three, piled with bread, butter, jam, marmalade, cheese, ham, and a dish of hard-boiled eggs. Paul was about to make a joke about her having prepared the breakfast for them when he realized that there was something not quite right about the woman. She seemed to be confused. He decided to say as little as possible.

Franz was equally curious as to why the table had been set for three. He, too, realized that she seemed to be befuddled. "Who else is coming to breakfast?" he asked.

"My two sons, Erasmus and Dietrich, will soon be here."

"Your sons are foresters, are they not?" Franz asked.

"Yes," she replied. "How did you know?"

Without replying, Franz yelled to Paul to take his valise. "Keep running. Head for the next village."

"What happened?"

"Tell you later. Just run."

***

When the village of Müllwalde was out of sight, they finally stopped. They rested for a minute in the shade of a beech tree.

"What on earth made you bolt like that?" Paul asked.

"When we entered the forest at Falkendorf, what did the innkeeper yell?"

"Something like, 'Dieter, Asmus, strangers in the forest. Catch them!' So?"

"And what were the names of the woman's two sons?"

"Erasmus and Dietrich. For no reason at all, you asked her if they're foresters. Apparently they are. So what?"

"Dieter is short for Dietrich, Asmus is short for Erasmus."

Paul's mouth fell open. "We walked right into their mother's house?"

"Yes. And perhaps it's not such a great coincidence. The local foresters presumably live in the villages on the edge of the forest. But isn't it a good thing I put two and two together in time?"

"Are they going to come after us?"

"I don't know. One possibility is that she won't say anything for a good while. The shock of our instantaneous departure may have been too much for her. Also, her sons presumably know that their mother isn't totally *compos mentis* so, even if she tells them that two strangers came to the door, it's possible that they'll take no notice of what she says. And they've been up all night searching for us in the forest, they're tired and they're hungry, and maybe they just want to eat and sleep."

"And another possibility," said Paul, somewhat bitterly, "is that she described us accurately to them, and the two of them are following our trail right now. Or worse, they've called out the rest of the searchers as well."

"If it's just them, we have three loaded pistols."

"Yes, and all three may misfire, just like yours did last night."

"Yes, that could be a problem. Let's walk on, and when we find a large enough clump of trees to hide in, we'll clean the touchholes and put fresh gunpowder in the flash pans of the pistols. I don't know for sure why mine misfired, but perhaps the powder got damp."

After attending to their pistols, they started walking once more, using the sun to ensure that they kept moving northward, in the general direction of Potsdam.

"After seeing that truly scrumptious breakfast," Paul said, "I'm really hungry."

"We're not stopping until we're well clear of Müllwalde."

"Yes, I agree. And there's another thing," Paul added. "We're in Prussia, not Saxony. Prussian foresters like Dieter and Asmus who work in Prussian forests live in Prussian villages like Müllwalde. That means that the police are probably after us. Yes, the report—supposedly written by Mössbauer—that Max had composed was a stroke of genius. But even if it was clever enough to convince the authorities in Berlin, news that the other two assassins are actually Saxons may not have permeated to the local constabulary or the soldiers in this rural corner of Prussia. So the fact that we're apparently Prussians in every respect won't necessarily keep us out of trouble. They may still be looking for the two *Junker* who collaborated with Hoffmann to kill von Hochenheimer. We could be stopped at any time at a roadblock or control point. What's our reason for being here?"

"Could we tell them that we were on a coach that needed a bearing repair, so we took a walk into the middle of the forest in the middle of the night, got hopelessly lost, and ended up in Müllwalde? I don't think so!"

"Well, what do we tell them?" Paul asked. "According to this map, we're actually quite close to the high road, the coach route to Berlin. We could tell them that the coach needed repairs, and we decided to walk ahead to get another coach at Pferdeschwemme. It's here on the map, not too far ahead."

"Yes, we'll tell them we walked along the coach route—not a word about forests, foresters, villages, or anything like that."

***

The two men immediately headed west. They scrambled through large stretches of heath before finally reaching the road. Once there, they turned right and started walking toward Pferdeschwemme.

As they reached the crest of a hill and started to descend the slope, they saw in front of them four men dressed in black—secret police. They thought of fleeing or of using their pistols. Then they looked behind them and saw three more men in black emerging from the trees. The Austrians kept walking slowly forward until they reached the control point.

"Papers, please!"

Paul and Franz produced their papers, which the secret police agents carefully inspected and retained.

"What is your business here?" asked one of the men. He oozed self-importance and officiousness in equal measures. Franz guessed he was the one in charge.

"We were on the coach from Dresden to Berlin," Franz explained. "One of the wheel bearings needed to be replaced at Falkendorf. It was going to take hours and hours, so we decided to walk from there to Pferdeschwemme to take another coach."

"What route did you follow?"

"The main road, naturally," Franz answered, "just in case the repair was completed sooner than the blacksmith had anticipated. We arranged with the coachman that, if the bad wheel was fixed earlier than expected, he'd stop and pick us up."

"What were you doing in the forest?"

"Which forest?" Franz asked.

"Don't get clever with me. The forest behind the inn at Falkendorf, of course."

"We stepped briefly into the forest to discuss what we should do. We're import/export merchants, and we're not in the habit of discussing our plans in public. The trees next to the inn offered a little privacy, so we stood there and considered what we should do next."

"And then?"

"And then we decided to walk to Pferdeschwemme. So we went to the coachman, told him of our plan, and we started walking."

"Along the main road?"

"Yes, along the main road. So that the coach could pick us up."

"We've received reports that soldiers were chasing two men in the forest. Why were they chasing you?"

"I've no idea who they were chasing or why, but it wasn't us. It couldn't have been us. We were on this road."

"Did you sleep on the way?"

"I napped for two or three hours under a tree while my friend watched in case the coach came. Then I watched while he napped."

The secret policeman counted on his fingers, trying to work out how long it should have taken them to walk from Falkendorf to Pferdeschwemme and then added on the time they said they had been napping. Franz had worked it out in his head earlier, just in case they were stopped, so he knew that his answers were consistent with his story. Eventually the man in black came to the end of what for him was an exceedingly complex computation, and which had taken him much longer than Franz had expected.

"Wouldn't it have made more sense for both of you to sleep comfortably at the inn at Falkendorf, and then start walking only if the bearing hadn't been fixed by the time you awoke?" the man asked.

"Undoubtedly you're quite right," said Franz, trying to inject a strong note of admiration in his voice, "but when we're suddenly marooned in a tiny village in the middle of the night, we don't think as clearly as you do."

Franz's flattery technique worked extremely well. The self-important mien of the secret policeman had virtually guaranteed that his ploy would succeed. The man in black smirked and all but purred. Then he changed topics again.

"So you weren't in the forest last night?"

"No."

"Do you have any idea who the men were who were being chased in the forest?"

Franz had found the man's weak spot, and decided to capitalize on it. "No, I've no idea at all. But the forest is on the border with Saxony, so my best guess is that the men in the woods were smugglers. But that's just speculation on my part. You would know much, much more about that sort thing than I could possibly know, of course."

The whole body of the leading secret policeman seemed to swell with arrogance and pride at being praised in this way, especially in front of his underlings. "Yes, yes, certainly. They must have been smugglers."

He returned their papers to the Austrians. "You may proceed."

And then, addressing the other six secret policemen, he declared pretentiously: "Always remember to keep an eye open for smugglers."

Paul and Franz thanked the man in charge, nodded politely to his colleagues, and proceeded toward Pferdeschwemme at their same walking pace as before. When they were well over the next rise, the two men glanced around carefully. They were alone. They looked at one another and just shook their heads.

"I cannot believe that the man in charge was so susceptible to your fawning," Paul said. "Yes, he was clearly brimming with pomposity, and his vanity flowed like the River Danube in flood, but to fall for such obvious sycophancy really surprised me."

"We were lucky, really lucky. If I'd made a mistake in the time calculations, we would've been in big trouble."

"Actually," Paul said, "it seemed to me—during that interminable computation—that he was going to get the answer wrong, and we'd have been arrested because of a numerically-challenged secret policeman."

"I wonder how many people are languishing in prison—or worse—because of the sheer incompetence of officious oafs like that one," Franz added.

"I don't know the answer to that, but I do know that we were extremely fortunate in that exchange. But I've just thought of something worrisome. When the wheel bearing of our coach is finally repaired and the coach is stopped at that control point, the man in charge is going to ask the coachman about us. The coachman will obviously deny that we told him that we were going to walk along the main road and that we'd asked him to pick us up if the repair was finished sooner than anticipated. What will happen then?"

"Nothing," Franz said, "because there's no way that opinionated fool is ever going to ask anyone about us. The fact of the matter is that he's decided that we're telling the truth. If he were to interrogate the coachman, he'd be admitting that there was a remote possibility that he'd made a mistake in letting us go. No, he's made up his mind that we're innocent import/export merchants, and that's the end of the matter. The incident is closed, like his mind."

"I hope you're right."

"I know I am—and I'm as certain about that as that puffed-up moron is about everything."

***

The next control point was surprisingly close. The two men hadn't walked for more than 10 minutes when they were stopped by three men in civilian clothing—Prussian spies. Just as Wilhelm Friedemann Bach had repeatedly explained to his father during their coach trip from Leipzig to Potsdam, the two Austrians realized that there just was not enough work for the vast number of Frederick's spies to do. In order to earn their pay, they set up control points and interrogated travelers.

"Papers, please!" Yet again, like a litany, the Austrian secret agents heard the insistent demand couched as a polite request.

They handed over their documents. All three Prussian spies made a show of examining their papers, but it was obvious that they had no idea what they were doing.

Next, one of the men asked Franz a series of questions. During the lengthy inquiry process, it seemed to the Austrian agents that the spy had been present when trained secret policemen had interrogated suspects, and he was simply repeating questions that he had heard. He did not seem to appreciate why those questions had been asked.

The second man, now seated on the ground, held a wooden board, along with paper, pen and ink. He laboriously wrote down each question and the answer that Franz provided. He wrote so slowly that he would not allow Franz to respond until he had recorded the question in full. As a result, Franz had plenty of time to think up the best possible answer under the circumstances. The problem was that written answers might be used against them at some future time. So Franz was torn between giving brief answers that would reveal the bare minimum of information, and long, involved answers that would overwhelm the capacity of the scribe.

"Your name?"

"Franz Braun."

"Your address?"

Franz gave an address at the southern end of Charlottenstrasse, Berlin, not far from Fritz Apfelkern's workshop.

"Profession?"

"Import/export merchant."

This answer bewildered both the inquisitor and his scrivener, neither of whom seemed to understand what Franz had just said. After repeated whispering to and fro, the third spy finally interjected, "Just write 'merchant.'"

"Purpose of journey?"

"To buy Prussian goods in Berlin to sell in France."

"Why would you want to do that?" asked the questioner, deviating from his script for the first time.

"To make money," Franz said.

This response totally perplexed his interrogator. The man then turned to Paul. Paul gave identical answers to the same set of questions, including the last one.

Then the questioner started a new line of examination with Paul.

"What are you doing on this road?"

"Our coach broke down, and we're walking to the next town to take the next coach."

"But why didn't you just wait until the coach was fixed?"

"We're in a hurry to get to Berlin."

"Why?"

"Because we can't make any money just sitting and waiting for the coach to be repaired."

Once more, the mention of making money threw both men off balance. The third man, realizing the problem, quickly said to his colleagues, "Don't worry; my father's the same. He's also a merchant, and all he thinks about is making money."

This stamp of approval from the third spy so impressed the questioner that he indicated to the two Austrians that they could leave. The recorder was still chronicling Paul's last answer as they resumed their walk toward Pferdeschwemme. This time, when they were out of earshot, they did not deign to discuss their encounter. Both implicitly agreed that the three bumbling spies were beneath contempt.

After walking for about half an hour, they reached Pferdeschwemme. At the first inn they encountered, they stopped for a meal and to ascertain when and where they could take a coach to Berlin.

"The post coach to Berlin stops here every morning at about 4 o'clock," the waitress informed them. "Come to think of it, today's coach hasn't come yet; it's about eight hours late."

"Could it have passed by without stopping?" asked Paul.

"Impossible. They change horses here."

"Well, we'll wait here for today's coach to arrive," he said. They placed orders for food and beer.

They were finishing their meal when the coach rolled in. They quickly paid their bill and went outside. The coachman was most surprised to see them.

"I thought you ran into the forest. I heard they sent foresters into the woods to catch you, and then soldiers, as well."

"That had nothing to do with us," Franz said. "We took a short walk in the forest, returned to the inn, and saw how much work had to be done to the bearing. So we decided to walk to Berlin. But we got tired when we reached Pferdeschwemme, and that's why we're waiting here for you."

The coachman just shook his head and said nothing.

The post coach was now several hours behind schedule, so the stop at Pferdeschwemme was reduced to only a few minutes. Passengers had no time to disembark and enjoy refreshments. Franz and Paul nonchalantly re-entered the coach, greeted their former fellow passengers, and resumed their old seats. Some of the passengers were too surprised to say a word; the others were too polite to ask questions, so no one offered anything other than muttered greetings in reply.

The journey to Berlin re-commenced. They'd traveled for no more than 20 minutes when the coach came to a halt at a roadblock, manned by three soldiers in the middle of nowhere. The coachman got off, and the passengers followed. They all formed an orderly line in front of the authorities.

"Papers, please!"

The coachman handed over his papers and whispered something in the ear of the sergeant in charge. The conversation seemed to go on for a long time. Then the three soldiers marched over to Paul and Franz.

"You two stand there. The rest of you, get back on the coach."

"What's all this about?" Paul asked the sergeant. "We're in a hurry to get to Berlin."

"You'll go to Berlin when I say you can go to Berlin. In the meantime, shut up!" He turned to speak to his subordinate soldiers.

Franz took the opportunity to whisper to Paul. "We'll have to shoot."

"Sergeant," Paul said, waiting for the man to turn and face them, "we are traveling to Potsdam by way of Berlin to deliver a very special flute to our good King Frederick, God bless him!"

The sergeant stood transfixed. The coachman's mouth dropped open. The other passengers stared.

"Sergeant," Paul continued, "we've already been delayed for eight hours due to that wheel bearing. Do you want me to tell His Majesty that a disloyal soldier further delayed us here? Do you know what His Majesty does to disloyal soldiers?"

The sergeant pointed to the coachman. "But he says that you left the coach at Falkendorf and ran into the forest, and that you were chased by foresters and soldiers."

"We're in such a hurry to get to His Majesty that we started walking when our coach broke down. That's why we're here in Pferdeschwemme ahead of the coach."

"But why were the foresters and soldiers chasing you?"

"They weren't chasing us. We took a few steps into the forest to talk privately. Naturally, we didn't want to discuss His Majesty's business in public. We decided that His Majesty's flute is so important to him that, if necessary, we'd walk the whole way to deliver it to him. Then we returned to the inn. We saw how much work the blacksmith had to do to repair the wheel bearing, so we began walking along the high road to Berlin. We got as far as here in Pferdeschwemme when the coach finally caught up with us."

"I understand. But why did the foresters and soldiers search the forest?"

"Sergeant, the answer to that question is for your ears only," said Paul. He leaned forward. "There are two Austrian secret agents following us, trying to steal His Majesty's flute. The foresters and the soldiers were trying to catch the Austrians. I believe that they are only half an hour behind us. If you catch them at your roadblock, I can assure you that His Majesty will be more than grateful."

The sergeant jumped to attention, saluted Paul, then turned and saluted Franz. He then walked to where the coachman was standing. The sergeant clouted him hard across his face. "The next time you spread false reports," he said, I'll have you shot, you insolent *Schweinehund.* Now all of you get back on that coach. Coachman, get to Berlin as fast as you can. Ride as if your life depends on it. Actually, it does."

The passengers scrambled back into the coach. Franz and Paul followed. The two secret agents were careful not to smile at the way that Paul had fooled the soldier, who did not have the sense to ask to see the flute. Paul sweated at the very thought of what would have happened if the sergeant had ordered him to produce the precious instrument.

The coach eventually reached Verasdorf for another change of horses. The passengers got out to stretch their legs. Paul and Franz approached the coachman. "It's a four-hour walk from here to Potsdam," Franz said. "It'll be quicker than taking this coach to Berlin and another coach to Potsdam. I'm sure you agree that, with the eight-hour delay, we have no choice."

The bruised coachman nodded carefully.

Paul and Franz walked toward Potsdam, and when the coach was finally out of sight, they laughed.

"Paul, what made you pull that flute trick?"

"I didn't want to kill any more innocent people. Enough blood has been spilled on this mission. I don't feel the least bit bad about the Prussian spies in Vienna. They knew exactly what they were doing when they came to Austria as secret agents, and now they must pay the price—just as we'll have to pay the price if we're caught here in Prussia. But I'm not happy that we had to kill the poacher in his hut or the two soldiers outside Potsdam. Yes, we had no choice in both cases, but I still feel guilty about it. As for Hoffmann, he was tortured because of our actions, and eventually we had to kill him to save ourselves. I feel bad about poor Hoffmann."

Franz said nothing.

"However, I have no problem with killing Frederick. He captured Silesia. Now, two Silesian Wars and eight years later, he has peace with Austria and he has all of Silesia. And it looks like he's going to be able to keep all of Silesia. But I wasn't in any way happy with the idea of shooting three more soldiers."

As before, Franz made no response.

"And I can't blame the coachman, either. He's obviously a loyal Prussian citizen, and it's been drummed into their heads to report the slightest suspicion to the authorities. He did what he'd been taught was the right thing to do, and he was beaten by that sergeant for his trouble. But at least he's alive."

Franz couldn't control his tongue any longer.

"Paul, what would you have done if the sergeant had absolutely insisted on seeing the flute, and just wouldn't take no for an answer?"

"I don't know. You're right, of course. My approach was risky, and it just happened to come off. If he'd insisted on seeing that flute, we'd have been finished. Your approach was certain to succeed, provided the pistols worked. And even if our pistols had failed again, we probably could've used their own muskets to kill them. But I've seen too much innocent bloodshed."

All this talk worried Franz. Paul's loyalty wasn't in question in any way, but now Franz questioned whether or not he could completely rely on his colleague. He resolved to try to modify the plan that Max had given him in order to minimize Paul's role.

CHAPTER TWENTY-FOUR

They were stopped only once, and that was just before they crossed the Havel River to enter Potsdam. In order to bypass any other control points, the moment they entered Potsdam they turned left into the first lane they encountered, and stuck to back streets until they reached Paul's room.

They were as tired as they had been when they had walked to Potsdam from Brandenburg an der Havel about two months before, but for a different reason. This time, their exhaustion was mental as well as physical. They had been forced to keep their wits about them from the time their coach from Dresden had crossed into Prussia.

Being young and fit, and fanatical in their hatred of Frederick, it did not take them too long to recover from the rigors of their journey by coach and on foot. The most important order of business was a meeting two days later with Kurt in his comfortable lodgings. He was delighted to see them. Franz told Kurt that he'd been right all along about Gerhard Schuster. He congratulated Kurt on his intuition.

During the three weeks that Franz and Paul had been away, Kurt's primary objective had been to wait for them to return so that he would be able to assist them in carrying out the latest instructions they had received from Max in Vienna. But Kurt had used the time productively by surreptitiously observing the level of security surrounding Frederick.

Within hours of the assassination of von Hochenheimer, Sanssouci had been turned into an armed camp. Instead of just the two security cordons—namely, the outer cordon, protecting the perimeter of the estate, and the inner cordon, guarding the building itself—an overwhelming military presence swarmed the domain. Entering the grounds had become a nightmare. Teams of soldiers, led by senior officers, repeatedly searched everyone, even ministers.

However, once it had been established that an Austrian invasion was not in progress, the intensity of surveillance had begun to drop. More precisely, when the authorities in Potsdam became convinced that the killing of Baron Manfred von Hochenheimer was an isolated incident, even the most cautious of King Frederick's advisors had realized that the high level of security in Sanssouci was now unnecessary. Accordingly, the King and his advisors had decided to assign the troops to other locations in Prussia. As incident-free day followed incident-free day, the steady demilitarization of Sanssouci proceeded. Finally, after the King had informed von Kunersdorf that the murder had been solved and the files were to be sealed, he instructed his aides that the level of security was to revert to where it had been before the assassination. Consequently, at his meeting with Paul and Franz, Kurt was able to confidently inform his colleagues that entering Sanssouci would be as difficult as it had been before they had left, but no harder.

"Before Max sent me to Prussia the first time," Franz said, "he devised a number of different plans for killing Frederick. I tried them one after the other but, in turn, each one failed dismally. I was extremely fortunate not be arrested, and each month I was grateful when all the members of the group trooped into the back room of the Taverne zum Schwarzen Adler."

Franz then continued, "Paul, do you remember what I was saying to you in the back room just as the police had arrived?"

"Quite frankly, no."

"Well, I was going to tell you about a desperate move on my part, my last plan, a plot with a low probability of success, but it was the only plan I had left. I quickly realized that telling you anything at all about it would've been a severe breach of confidentiality. The police raid brought me to my senses. For the sake of security, I'm going to have to keep the two of you in the dark as much as possible.

"Before we left Vienna," Franz continued, "I discussed many possible plans with Max. We concluded that we'd come to the end of the road. That last plan is the only remaining arrow that Max and I have in our combined quivers. Irrespective of whether that final plan succeeds or fails, when it's all over, we three return to Vienna. And on the subject of returning to Vienna: I may or may not need your help as I bring the plan to its successful fruition. But neither of you will be involved in carrying out the plan itself. On the contrary, once the plan reaches a certain point, I'll send you a message ordering the two of you to race back to Vienna. When you receive a message saying, "Frau Steiger is ill," head back to Austria as fast as you possibly can."

"Why do we have to leave?" Paul asked.

"I devoutly hope that the plan succeeds. But whether it succeeds or fails, the plan will be traced back to me. And once I've been arrested, neither of you will be safe. So, as I explained, at a certain point in the execution of the plan I will instruct you to leave, and you will do so immediately and without asking any questions. In the meantime, burn any incriminating documents. In fact, destroy all documents right now. You're not going to need them. The only reason you're still in Potsdam is just in case I need your help for this final plan. Pack your things now. You need to be ready to leave at literally a moment's notice. And one other thing: From now on, if you see me, pretend you don't know me and that you've never seen me before.

"As I said," Franz continued, "I'm going to try to carry out the plan all by myself. I'm unsure at this point if I'm going to need any assistance. If I do, I'll certainly call on one or both of you. But for now, I'm going to work on this alone."

"What if something goes wrong during the execution of your final plan?" Paul asked. "Shouldn't one of us know what you're doing so that we can take over?"

"If something goes wrong," Franz said, "then the plan will have failed. If I cannot make this plan work, then there's no point in anyone else taking over. It's not that I'm so marvelous that no one else could take my place—on the contrary. But once the authorities learn any details, the plan becomes completely unworkable. Furthermore, Paul, dear friend, please don't be offended, but I need my own room now. I cannot let you see what I'm doing. By the time you get back to your room I'll have moved out."

Franz shook hands warmly with Paul and Kurt, and then embraced them both. As he left the meeting, he wondered whether they would ever see one another again.

CHAPTER TWENTY-FIVE

Walking fast, Franz headed toward the musical instrument shop on Burgstrasse. "Do you sell second-hand flutes?" he asked.

"Certainly, sir. I have a large selection," said a chubby, fair-headed man with a squint in his left eye and a large, unruly moustache. "Parents here in Potsdam are forcing their children to learn to play the flute, for obvious reasons, and after a few months we get almost all of them back, for equally obvious reasons. Thanks to King Frederick—may God bless him—I have a flourishing trade in flutes, both new and second-hand." The owner went to the back of his shop, and returned with seven flute cases. He laid them on the wooden counter and opened them one by one.

"How much is that one?" asked Franz, pointing to a transverse flute in a large case.

"I can let you have it for 15 reichsthaler. That's half the price that it cost new. By the way, the carrying case is somewhat large. Would you like me to put the flute in one of the smaller ones I have? That case is actually for carrying three flutes at the same time: a transverse flute, a recorder, and a piccolo.

"No, I'll take it as it is. And there's no need to wrap it up. Everyone else in Potsdam today seems to be walking around with an instrument case. In addition to having an instrument on hand, they're probably also using their cases to carry their lunches to work."

As he made the witticism, Franz bit his tongue because he, too, was going to use the case to carry something else, as well. But it was too late; the words could not be unsaid.

Suddenly, he remembered something else. "Do you have an empty carrying case for a horn?"

Once more, the shopkeeper was able to oblige. Franz paid for the flute and the horn case. He left—and with a musical instrument case in each hand—he walked back to Paul's lodgings.

When he reached the room, he opened the horn case and threw in his few possessions and one of the boxes of dueling pistols. He left as quickly as he had come. He did not want to bump into Paul while he was carrying his two cases.

The day before, Franz had seen a sign in a window, advertising a room for lease. When he arrived at the building, three blocks away on the same street, the room was still available. He paid his new landlady for two weeks in advance.

Locking the door of his room, he opened his flute case. Removing the flute, he carefully manipulated the padding to create two cavities between the back of the case and the padding. Each space was sufficiently large enough to hold a pistol.

Franz next wrote a letter to a member of Frederick's Royal Orchestra, inviting him to visit him the next day. He then went to the nearby office of uniformed couriers and paid the clerk to have the letter taken to the palace.

***

The next morning, Franz had a visitor. "I understand that you were present at the massacre at Grossbrock," he said.

"Yes, my wife comes from there," the visitor said. "We were in Grossbrock visiting her family when the Prussians did…what they did."

Franz waited until his guest had collected himself. Then he explained to the musician what had to be done, and gave him the case containing the flute and the hidden pistols. The man was most enthusiastic to carry out the plan to the letter.

***

Franz's guest walked back to the palace, where the guards stopped him at the entrance to the park and again at the back entrance to Sanssouci. Despite the fact that he was wearing the uniform of a member of the Royal Orchestra, and even though at least one guard at each of the two control points knew him personally, he was told to open the flute case for inspection. They let him pass.

***

Once the musician had left his room, Franz grabbed his valise and rushed back to the office of uniformed couriers, where he sent "Frau Steiger" messages to his two colleagues. From there, he walked to the inn from where the Leipzig coach departed.

As the departure time neared, a small crowd of people joined Franz to board the coach. After everyone had been seated, there were still three places left. The coachman was about to crack his whip when two men came running toward the coach. The passengers quickly opened the curbside door to allow Kurt and Paul to climb in. As previously instructed, they ignored Franz. Long before nightfall, the post coach had crossed the border into Saxony. Even though the three Austrian secret agents were now safe, discipline prevailed and Kurt and Paul continued to ignore Franz.

CHAPTER TWENTY-SIX

The concert at Sanssouci that evening consisted, yet again, exclusively of Old Bach's music. The first item on the program was his Brandenburg Concerto No. 2 in F major. Bach wrote the piece for four solo instruments: trumpet, recorder, oboe, and violin, plus strings and harpsichord. Naturally, Bach himself sat at the harpsichord, and King Frederick played the solo recorder.

Bach had two roles: he conducted the orchestra, and he played the *basso continuo* (bass harmony) part on the harpsichord. Undoubtedly, doing only those two things at the same time was hardly a challenge for the great Bach. While conducting and playing the concerto, he almost certainly could have simultaneously performed brain surgery, composed a six-part fugue, and written a romance novel without batting an eyelid.

However, halfway through the first movement, something happened that even Old Bach could not understand. He turned over the page of the score in front of him to find a message written at the top of the next page that appeared to be in his own handwriting: "Play the concerto EXACTLY as written in the score."

Given that Johan Sebastian Bach had composed the concerto, this made no sense. He always played his music exactly as he had written it. If there had been a better way to play it, he would have written it that way. Also, he knew that he had not written the message, even though it seemed to be in his handwriting. And it certainly had not been there that morning when, under his direction, the orchestra and soloists had meticulously rehearsed the piece.

Four pages later, he found another message written on the top of the page that also seemed to be in his own handwriting: "Do not deviate from the score by even one note."

Old Bach looked around. As the conductor, he was seated at the harpsichord keyboard near the front of the stage, with his back to the audience so that he faced the other musicians. The four soloists faced the audience, standing in a row in line with the harpsichord keyboard, two on each side of the instrument. The trumpet soloist was on Old Bach's far left; next to him stood Bach's son, Wolfgang Gottlieb Bach, the solo oboe player. King Frederick, playing the solo recorder, stood on the other side of the harpsichord. The violin soloist was on Old Bach's far right. The strings players stood in an arc behind the harpsichord. Looking up from the score as often as he could, Bach carefully scanned each musician in turn, soloists and strings players alike, but everything appeared normal.

All went well until about halfway into the second movement. Johan Sebastian Bach turned over the page and found that, since the rehearsal that morning, someone had changed his score. Staves containing nothing but rests had been pasted over the *basso continuo* part, indicating that Bach was now to play nothing at all for several bars.

The composer was stunned. The changes to the score made no sense. Without the *basso continuo* on the harpsichord, that part of the piece was greatly weakened. But he remembered the messages that he had apparently written on the score and stopped playing.

King Frederick immediately realized that something was wrong. Fearing that the elderly Bach was no longer participating in the playing of the concerto because he had suddenly been taken ill, he turned to his right to rush over to Old Bach. At that instant, Wolfgang Gottlieb Bach turned to his left to face Frederick, drew a pistol, pointed it at the King's heart, and fired.

Wolfgang Gottlieb Bach had known in advance the precise instant when the King would turn his body toward Old Bach, thereby making himself vulnerable to the shot, because Wolfgang Gottlieb had doctored the score that afternoon, imitating his father's handwriting.

The bullet hit Frederick's recorder, which shattered into fragments. Pieces of wood flew into the air—some slammed into King Frederick. His clothing stopped most of the splinters, but a few sharp shards scratched his skin. Wolfgang Gottlieb Bach quickly drew the second pistol. But before he could aim it, the trumpet soloist, who stood next to him, bludgeoned him on the head with his brass instrument.

Johan Sebastian Bach fainted.

AFTERWORD

Johan Sebastian Bach had a total of 20 children by his two wives: seven by his first wife (and second cousin) Maria Barbara Bach, and 13 by Anna Magdalena Wilcke, his second wife. Sadly, 10 of his children died in early childhood.

An astute reader of an early draft of this book noticed that the list of Old Bach's progeny does not seem to include a Wolfgang Gottlieb Bach. My response was to point out that the German name *Gottlieb* means "lover of God"—the equivalent Latin name is *Amadeus*. After all, as I stated at the beginning of the book, this story is a work of fiction.

ACKNOWLEDGMENTS

I warmly thank my publisher, Jennifer Chesak of Wandering in the Words Press, for her meticulous and constructive editing of my manuscript. It was a pleasure to work with a consummate professional like Jennifer. In particular, I am most appreciative of her striking cover design. Thanks, too, to assistant editor Victoria Shockley for her help and suggestions.

I am extremely grateful to my first publisher, Howard Aksen of Aksen Associates. In 1987 Howard came to my office and persuaded me to write my first book, *Software Engineering*. That cold call led to a warm friendship that has lasted to this day. Had it not been for Howard, I would have missed out on 25 wonderful years of writing books.

Finally, as always, I thank my wife, Sharon, for her continual support and encouragement. As with all my previous books, I did my utmost to ensure that family commitments took precedence over writing. However, when deadlines loomed, this was not always possible. At such times, Sharon always understood, and for this I am most grateful.

ABOUT THE AUTHOR

After 26 years as a professor at Vanderbilt University in Nashville, Tennessee, Steve Schach, a Cape Town, South Africa native, recently moved to Sydney, Australia. Before he began writing thrillers, Steve wrote 13 best-selling software engineering textbooks, which are used in universities all over the world. Down Under, Steve intended to become a full-time grandfather, and limit his intellectual activities to solving cryptic crossword puzzles and avidly watching *Sesame Street* with his grandchildren. However, the urge to write proved to be far too strong to overcome, hence *Old Bach Is Come*.

Made in the USA
Lexington, KY
18 March 2013